NOW HE FROZE IN PLACE. IT WAS UNMISTAKABLE: HE COULD EVEN SEE the fuel shaking a little inside the bottles.

Something was approaching, fast. Some of what Eli heard wasn't human, just the faraway thump of tire threads. But he could also detect faint whooping and whistling, a scary celebration.

Eli's eyes flickered around as he braced himself. Alone on the side of the highway, they were brutally, nakedly exposed. It was too late for them to do anything—to run away, to hide, to even scream for help.

"Aww, no—" Till murmured, under his breath. It was almost a prayer.

And at that moment, it began.

SUSAN KIM & LAURENCE KLAVAN

WASTELAND

HARPER TEEN
An Imprint of HarperCollinsPublishers

HarperTeen is an imprint of HarperCollins Publishers.

Wasteland
Copyright © 2013 by Susan Kim and Laurence Klavan
All rights reserved. Printed in the United States of America.
www.epicreads.com

Library of Congress Cataloging-in-Publication Data
Kim, Susan.
    Wasteland / by Susan Kim and Laurence Klavan. — 1st ed.
        p.   cm.
    Summary: In a postapocalyptic world where everyone dies at age nineteen and rainwater
contains a killer virus, loners Esther and Caleb band together with a group of mutant,
hermaphroditic outsiders to fight a corrupt ruler and save the town of Prin.
    ISBN 978-0-06-211852-3
    [1. Interpersonal relations—Fiction.   2. Virus diseases—Fiction.   3. Mutation (Biology)—
Fiction.   4. Science Fiction.]   I. Klavan, Laurence.   II. Title.
PZ7.K55992Was 2013   2012026744
[Fic]—dc23

Typography by Michelle Gengaro-Kokmen
14 15 16 17 18   LP/RRDH   10 9 8 7 6 5 4 3 2 1
❖
First paperback edition, 2014

For nieces and a nephew (in order of appearance)
Jackson
Evelyn
Melody
Kathryn
Maple

You still have time.

PART ONE

ONE

ESTHER RAN ACROSS THE BROKEN ASPHALT.

Her destination loomed in front of her: an odd concrete structure, standing alone in the trash-filled lot. At a glance, it seemed unoccupied. As she neared it, Esther gave a final look in all directions; then she grabbed the low brick wall and vaulted over. Despite the searing heat of the early November morning, it was cool and dim inside. Esther blinked to get her bearings, then took off again.

The sound of her breathing, harsh and ragged, was the only noise; it seemed to echo in the vast space. She sensed this and cursed herself. Clamping her lips together, she tried to hold back the sound, to breathe so as to not to draw attention to herself. But it was impossible to do this without slowing down. She gave up and put on extra speed instead. She had been running a long time and as she gulped air, her lungs burned and a sharp pain gripped her side. But she was almost at the safe place and then she would have time to rest.

Esther was on the second floor and there were four more to go. She ran low, crouching down and sticking close to the center of the structure. It was a strange building, one that offered neither protection nor privacy. There were no walls; the sides were too exposed, open to the world outside, with the rooftops of Prin visible in the distance beneath a dirty yellow sky.

Esther was aware that she was wearing a red hoodie and jeans. With sharp eyes, somebody could spot her from half a mile off, even though she was a skinny fifteen-year-old with a real talent for not attracting attention, a girl who'd spent a lifetime learning how to slip in and out of shadows without being seen.

Right now, not being seen was all she cared about. After all, those were the rules of the game, the game they called Shelter.

Shelter was simple. You and your opponent started in one place. Then you both raced to the safe place and whoever got there first won.

Easy.

But the safe place was always three or four miles away from the starting point. You had to run as quickly as you could in the searing heat (for it was always hot in Prin, even in November).

If you were detected and called out by your opponent, you lost. And lastly, in order to win, you had to navigate your way through the ruins of old buildings, cracked pavement, and a jagged landscape of twisted metal and shattered glass. A single misstep could break a bone or slice your skin. If you were especially unlucky, one false move could send you crashing down through a rotting surface into some forgotten basement, where chances were your cries for help would go undetected for hours, maybe even days. If anyone heard you at all.

But to Esther, that was part of the fun. Right now, she had been running for nearly two hours, but nothing mattered: not the pain, the exhaustion, or the suffocating heat.

She was about to win.

Esther rounded a corner of the place she knew well. She ignored the cars, each in its own space, separated neatly by faded yellow lines painted on the cracked cement. They were like ghosts, silent hulks so covered with gritty white dust you could hardly tell what color they had once been. They had long since been drained of their precious fuel and were now still and lifeless, just part of the landscape, like boulders or buildings or stunted trees.

Esther's sneakers skidded as she sprinted up the second and then the third concrete ramp. The ground underfoot was broken and uneven, but she didn't notice. She was too busy searching the landscape for any flicker of movement, her eyes darting from car to pillar to car. There was trash everywhere, which she skirted effortlessly: shards of glass, crushed beer cans, a sodden cardboard box, a shoe.

As she made it to the roof, the heat and glare of the sun hit her hard. Sweat was stinging her eyes and running down her neck. When she yanked down her hood and ran her hand across her head, her dark hair was wet, with some parts sticking up in spikes. Here, there was no breeze, nothing but yellow sky. Surrounded by concrete and dead grass that shimmered with heat, she could see for miles past Prin to the empty roads leading off to wherever they went.

Esther didn't turn to look. Exhilarated, all she knew was that she'd made it. She was the first.

For standing in the far corner of the roof was the safe place. It was a brown box, taller than Esther and wide enough to hold at least four of her. Although it had only been there a few days, it was already fading and starting to soften from the sun and rain; soon, it would be worthless. There was a simple picture and black arrows on the side, as well as meaningless words written in large, block letters.

THIS END UP. KENMORE. 24 CU. FT. REFRIGERATOR.

Esther hadn't taken the time to decipher the words. If her older sister, Sarah, knew this, she would pinch her lips with disapproval, the way she did at practically everything Esther said or did. Sarah was one of the few who could read, one of the last in Prin, and she was forever nagging others to learn how to do it too. When she was little, Esther had memorized the alphabet and could sound out simple words, but that was as far as she got.

All she had to do was touch it.

Jubilant, Esther approached the box, extending her hand.

But at the last second, someone emerged from behind it.

Esther froze.

The creature was small, with dark, hairless arms and legs, and a bald skull. It appeared to be neither male nor female and wore a brief tunic that was little more than a sack, with a cloth pouch slung across. Its face and body were covered with a dense network of intricate designs, swirling patterns, dots and slashes, strange curls that snaked like vines across the skin in various shades of black, brown, and pink. On close examination, you could see the designs were not painted on but were a complex network of crude tattoos and hundreds, maybe thousands, of scars. Some of the marks were so tiny, they seemed like mere threads against the skin; others were vivid, pink gouges of raised flesh. It had bulging lavender eyes and a flattened nose, which crinkled as its mouth, with its tiny, sharp teeth, twisted upward.

Esther recoiled, with a gasp.

"No!" she screamed.

"Got here first," the variant said. "I win!"

Half laughing, half groaning, Esther tried to catch her breath. She bent over to relieve the pain in her side.

"Skar!" she exclaimed. "How did you got here before me?"

Skar shrugged, smiling. She was so pleased with herself, she couldn't resist dancing a little, bouncing up and down on thickly calloused feet.

Skar was the same age as Esther. Yet unlike her friend, she had been female for only five years, having selected her gender on her tenth birthday, the way all variants did. At the time,

Esther was delighted when her friend chose to be a female because it was one more thing they had in common. Skar had a circle, the mark of being female, tattooed on her upper arm.

No one understood where the variants came from, why they were hermaphroditic, hairless, disfigured. Most in town seemed to believe that the variants were once animals, living off contaminated goods and drinking groundwater. The accumulated poisons had permanently affected them and their unfortunate offspring, creating a new race of freaks. Certainly Esther's older sister, Sarah, had mentioned this theory more than once, much to Esther's annoyance.

The variants had always lived far from town, shunning the ways of Prin and its people. They dressed oddly, not bothering to shield themselves from the dangerous rays of the sun. Rather than work, they eked out a meager living from hunting with feral dogs. Occasionally, they foraged for food and bottled water amid the wreckage of the outlying buildings and homes of Prin. The variants' way of existence was a harsh and dangerous one, where one's next meal or drink of water could result in sudden sickness, pain, and death. Their life expectancy was even shorter than that of the people in town.

In the best of times, the townspeople looked down on the variants as shiftless and dirty and called them the ugly word "mutant." Lately, after the rash of strange, isolated variant attacks, the feeling had grown from one of contempt to that of terror and even hatred. No one knew this better than Esther and Skar, who chose to spend their time together far away from the judgmental and fearful minds of Prin. Esther believed the variants weren't a separate species like damaged snakes or wild boars; she believed they were human somehow, yet spurned for their differences. But she had never dared mention this to anyone.

The life of the average townsperson was one of mindless labor rewarded by the occasional treat of something new: a piece of clothing that wasn't filthy, a wristwatch with a shattered face, a pair of sunglasses. Rather than stoop to such a level, the variants had created their own society high in the mountains, with its own rules, customs, and rituals. There they lived freely, without the need for labor or commerce. They existed without apologies, and with pride. And for that, Esther secretly loved them.

"That's three times in a row," Skar now said. "Do you want to try again?"

"Sure," said Esther. "Only let me catch my breath first. And this time, give me a head start or something."

Skar's smile broadened. "What fun is that?"

Laughing and chatting, the two headed back down into the relative coolness of the building. They argued over what should be the new starting point: the abandoned steel tracks several miles down the road, or the dried-up lake on the far side of town? But as they approached the ground level, Esther's face froze and she made an abrupt gesture at her friend, who stopped in midsentence.

Skar heard it, too: a faint thread of faraway voices.

In the distance, heading off the main road and turning

into the asphalt lot, were three figures on bicycles. One was pulling a red wagon; from where she stood, Esther could even hear the faint clank of its metal handle. They had clearly seen Esther; had they seen Skar? The trio was headed to the parking garage, straight toward them.

Esther and the variant shared a quick glance, and Esther gave a nod. Without speaking, Skar crouched low and slipped away, disappearing behind a row of parked cars.

Esther waited a few moments. Then with fake casualness, she sauntered to the edge of the wall and looked down. She was trembling and her heart was pounding, but her actions revealed nothing.

Within seconds, the three were clustered below, gazing upward at her. From their expressions, Esther could tell they didn't notice Skar and she felt some of her tension ease.

Yet she had to make certain they didn't come up to where she was, where they might see her friend. No variant was safe since the attacks. She rested one hand in front of her on the low wall and gazed down at them.

It was impossible for Esther to tell who they were. Indoors and away from the burning rays of the endless summer, the three wouldn't resemble each other at all. Yet at that moment, they were nearly identical, dressed the same as everyone in Prin except Esther: swathed in filthy sheets, with towel headdresses hanging down their necks, scarves masking their lower mouths, and thick cotton gloves protecting their hands. The billowing folds were belted close to their legs, in order not to get caught in the spinning gears. All three wore dark sunglasses. In the wagon, Esther could see two empty plastic bottles, coiled rubber tubing, and a crowbar.

The three were on their way to a Harvesting.

There were three jobs in Prin—Harvesting, Gleaning, and Excavation—and they were assigned by a lottery held every two weeks in the center of town. Everyone over the age of five was required to attend and, once given a job, expected to work every day from sunrise to sundown. The rules had always been strict but they had become much tougher of late: Not to show up resulted in a Warning filed by the team Supervisor, which Esther had incurred at least four times in the past year.

One more and she risked Shunning. And Shunning from town meant certain death.

Two of the three jobs were grueling but mindless: the Excavation and the Gleaning. The few times she had deigned to show up for an assignment in recent months, in order to placate Sarah, Esther had opted for one of those two. But the Harvesting—a search through the outlying areas to find the most tradable commodity, gasoline—called for real concentration. It was by far the single most important job in town and one that had grown only more difficult and time consuming as the years went by.

When Esther had drawn the Harvesting as her assignment at the last lottery, she'd cursed her luck. Then she ignored the task and instead headed to the overgrown fields and vacant lots to play with Skar.

It had taken the rest of her team this long to find her, and their fatigue and frustration were obvious. She had to be careful not to provoke them: There was too much at stake, for both her and Skar.

The biggest figure called up to her. "Look who's here," it said. Although they were cloaked, Esther had no trouble recognizing who was speaking by their voices. This one was Eli. At fifteen, he was the oldest and was therefore Supervisor of today's expedition.

"Where you been?" shouted another, revealing herself to be a girl called Bekkah. Shorter and younger at eleven, she acted as second in command. "We been looking for you!"

"I showed up the first day, and you guys had already left," Esther said from her perch, trying to sound sincere. She knew that from a hiding place behind her, Skar was listening too.

"Right," said the smallest and youngest. This was Till, and his tone was sarcastic.

Esther knew this boy the least and, as a result, feared him the most. She turned beseechingly to Eli.

Her appeal was not lost on him. Eli was well aware that after two weeks, their work detail was almost over and had been unsuccessful. The two others in his team were on the edge, ready to vent their fury on any target. He had to keep them at bay.

"Let's go up there and get her," Till said.

Eli held up his hand. He exchanged a look with Esther.

In spite of himself, Eli smiled; he couldn't help it. For some reason, he had always been attracted to Esther, despite her utter irresponsibility and almost total lack of female affect. He couldn't explain why, even to himself. His eyes still holding hers, he gave a dismissive wave to the others. He tried to sound cold and unfeeling.

"Let's go," he said. "She ain't worth the trouble."

He remounted his bike, looping around to head back out to the main road. For a moment, the other two were angry and confused; then, resigned, they got on their bikes. Bekkah made the turn with difficulty because of the wagon. Only Till couldn't resist a parting shot.

"Looks like you got off this time!" he yelled back over his shoulder.

Eli stopped at the edge of the parking lot.

"Better get back to town," he called to Esther, meaningfully. "You ain't safe alone out here."

"I'm not afraid of wild dogs," she said.

"I don't mean dogs." He spat before he took the turn.

Once they were gone, Esther expelled a long breath. She was surprised to find that she was trembling and even a little sick. Why?

Was it because Eli had done her a favor, meaning she was now indebted to him? True, he had often seemed sympathetic to her in the past, and she had never minded. He had always been kinder than the others, and not as close-minded. Yet now that she had asked for his help, and he had given it, they were linked, somehow, in a way they hadn't been before . . . and Esther was not at all sure how she felt about that.

In Prin, Esther and Eli, not to mention Sarah, stuck out for being single. Nearly everyone got partnered when they reached fourteen. By seventeen, they were considered town elders, and by nineteen, they were dead. That was the longest anyone managed to escape the disease; it was everywhere there was water, carried in the rain, lakes, streams. Couples spent their short lives together at meaningless and backbreaking jobs, often toiling side by side, and all for just enough food and clean water to survive. Esther was already fifteen, a year past the age of partnering. Was this really all she had to look forward to?

When she was old enough to rebel, Esther began breaking curfew and spending more time with Skar. At first, people in town treated her with condescension, as an oddball. Now, they viewed her as a pariah, a freak. And Esther had been fine with that. Being an outsider made her feel strong, even invincible. But lately, she found she was often beset by a strange sadness.

She would always love Skar. But despite Esther's efforts to embrace their culture and learn their ways, the variants themselves still refused to accept her as one of their own. Her one trip to the variant camp had been a disaster: She was treated coldly, with suspicion and hostility, by the rest of Skar's tribe. Esther hoped that one day she would be welcomed as the ally she was; but after so many years, she had yet to even meet her best friend's brother.

The town of Prin wasn't home, either. She fit in nowhere.

Esther knew how she really felt.

She felt alone.

Maybe there could be someone else to be truly *close to,* she thought. Or maybe there could be something bigger to be a part of—what, she wasn't really sure. A little while ago, Esther would have laughed at the idea. But she wasn't laughing now.

"Are they gone?"

Hearing her friend's voice, Esther snapped to attention.

The variant girl now crept from behind a row of parked cars and stood by Esther with fists clenched, tense and ready to run.

Esther brushed aside her own concerns, to put her friend at ease.

"We're fine," she said, nudging Skar in the side. "Now let's see who makes it to the tracks first."

Eli and the others rode their bikes single file down the main road heading away from Prin. He led them past the hulking, plundered ruins of buildings on the edge of town, places that still had names, meaningless words they didn't know how to read: STAPLES, HOME DEPOT, THE ARBORS NURSING HOME, STOP & SHOP.

Eli pedaled slowly, so Bekkah could keep up. He was careful to steer around the broken glass, discarded bits of machinery, and chunks of dirty plastic that littered the pavement beneath their tires.

They avoided detritus left by the periodic rising and retreating of floodwaters: bleached-white shells and stones, the rotting remains of a rowboat. There were other things that must have been swept away by the dank waters: a rusted hunting rifle; a blond wig that had become a filthy, tangled mop; a safe deposit box with the top torn off and the dust of long-dead crabs inside.

Ahead, the road became a bridge, passing over a much larger avenue underneath.

Eli stopped as he considered where to go.

"We already checked over the bridge," commented Bekkah, as she pulled up alongside him.

"Yeah," said Eli. "But we didn't go down *there*."

He pointed, and Till swallowed hard.

"Are you sure," he muttered, "we have to?"

Eli shrugged. "We been out here two weeks and ain't got a drop. There's no place else to check. Come on—it'll be fine, and maybe we'll even be done today."

The others seemed reassured. Eli pretended to look at ease as they glided down what had once been the on-ramp to the northbound lane of the interstate.

At times, the deserted road was almost impassable with fallen trees, downed streetlights, dead power lines; but the three managed to find a way through. Both sides of the highway were overgrown with heavy, tangled undergrowth that in some areas spilled past the shoulder and onto the road itself, and in some places obscured the aluminum barriers once built to muffle the sounds of traffic.

"Nothing so far," Eli called over his shoulder. He was talking too loudly, he realized, from nervousness.

He was on edge in case they saw a body.

Although none of them talked about it, they all knew that people with the disease were Shunned, sent from town on this highway to die; that way, it was said, they wouldn't contaminate the others. No one knew exactly where they ended up. There were rumors in town of a Valley of the Dead, a mass grave filled with the remains of innumerable children, although such a place had never been seen. Some thought it was no more than a bedtime tale told to frighten the little ones.

Eli was not sure he believed the story, but he worried they would see or smell remains on the road or off to the side. *Which would be worse,* he wondered: *if the body was fresh enough to be recognized or too rotted to identify?* The smallest ones would be the worst, he decided, and skeletons of any size.

"Hold on! Back up!" Till yelled.

They slowed down. Sure enough, they could see something peeking out from a dense tangle of vines, brush, and litter, close to the highway wall, where no one would have searched.

"Yeah," Bekkah said. "Looks good."

It was a dark green car, compact yet roomy, with an incomprehensible word framed by a steel circle on the front grill: VOLVO. The three pedaled onto the curb, then got off and walked their bikes through the clotted grass of the shoulder to reach it. With difficulty, Till pulled the wagon as well.

Bekkah fished out a steak knife hanging from her belt on a nylon cord and sliced away the vines and branches that strangled the car. Working methodically, she cleared away a space on the left side of the vehicle, above the back tire.

Eli took the crowbar from the wagon and flipped open the small metal panel in the side of the car. Then, with a few yanks, he pried off the cap to the gas tank. Till handed him the tube, and Eli snaked it down into the tank, feeding it inch by inch.

In the hot sun, the others watched his expression. Moments later, Eli smiled as he felt the end of the line hit gas.

"A decent amount," he said, relieved.

"Good," Bekkah said. "He was mighty mad last time. Wouldn't hardly give us nothing."

"He's been like that for a while now," Eli said.

They were talking about the one they worked for, the one who lived on the outskirts of town. The boy called Levi.

Levi lived in a kingdom of sorts, in that he saw himself as a kind of king. Yet his home was more of a fortress, as the windowless building was massive, guarded, and impenetrable. It was nicknamed the Source because while no one in Prin had ever ventured inside, it was quite literally the center of life; the townspeople would soon die without it. It was powered by the only electricity any of them had ever seen, electricity generated by the countless bottles upon bottles of gasoline everyone in town spent so much of their lives searching for.

The gasoline was exchanged each month for food and water from Levi's endless supplies. This didn't include his tuna, soup, meat, jelly, cereal, tomato sauce, peanut butter, stew, pickles, or vegetables; they had long since rotted to blackened tar, exploding their containers. His dry grains and beans were edible, barely, but had to be pounded into flour and boiled for hours before they could be digested. Salt, sugar, spaghetti, honey, and hard candy were available, packaged and sealed in plastic bags, cloth sacks, and cardboard containers; there were also countless gallon jugs of water. Everything was brought outside by Levi's boys.

There were eighteen of these guards, hulking and hooded

brutes armed with small, harmless-looking contraptions that made a terrible hissing sound and, upon contact with skin, could cause a teenager to drop to his knees in agony. (The word "Taser" was printed on the rubberized grips; a dozen had been found in a building on the outskirts of town, one with cobwebbed desks in the front room and barred cells in the back.) Levi's boys measured the gasoline and doled out the provisions, watching over the transactions with a hawk-like attention that had only grown worse since the supply of untapped cars in Prin began dwindling.

For Eli and his fellow Harvesters, the "Volvo" guaranteed that the exchange would continue for at least a few more weeks. And so by extension would their lives.

"Lucky we found this," Eli said. "Should last us a long while."

With that, he bent down and sucked the tube until he sensed the fuel was about a foot from his mouth. Then he yanked out the tube and stuck the end into the neck of an empty plastic bottle, which Till was holding steady for him. A second later, the air was filled with the pungent smell of gasoline as it gushed forth into the container.

Without looking, he addressed Till. "Good eye," he said.

Till smiled, abashed. "It was your idea to come down here."

Eli filled one bottle; then, taking care not to spill a drop, he transferred the tube to the next bottle.

Yet something wasn't right.

Eli looked up. Then he stood. As he did, the tube fell from the bottle neck, sloshing gasoline onto the ground.

"Hey!" Bekkah said. "Watch out!"

"Sorry." Eli bent to put the tube back into the bottle, which by now was almost full. "I just thought I heard—"

Now he froze in place. It was unmistakable: He could even see the fuel shaking a little inside the bottles.

Something was approaching, fast. Some of what Eli heard wasn't human, just the faraway thump of tire threads. But he could also detect faint whooping and whistling, a scary celebration.

Eli's eyes flickered around as he braced himself. Alone on the side of the highway, they were brutally, nakedly exposed. It was too late for them to do anything—to run away, to hide, to even scream for help.

"Aww, no—" Till murmured, under his breath. It was almost a prayer.

And at that moment, it began.

The air was split by noise, a blood-curdling shrieking that seemed to come from no one direction but from everywhere at once, pulsating and echoing. It was an uncanny noise that seemed neither human nor animal.

Bekkah stood still with her mouth half open, a hypnotized mouse in the sights of an owl, the now-forgotten plastic container at her feet overflowing. Gasoline splashed over her sneakers and filled the air with its fumes.

From nowhere, an object whistled at her through the air; it was a fist-size rock, ugly and jagged. There was a sharp cracking sound; it knocked Bekkah from her trance and she emitted a scream, high and thin and terrified. She reeled backward. Clutching her forehead with both hands, she knocked the rubber tubing from Eli's hands and sent a stream of gasoline flying in a clear arc through the air. Blood spurted from between her fingers and ran down into her eyes. It dripped onto and splattered her filthy white robes. Her knees buckled and she sank to the ground.

Eli was backing up, his eyes darting as he looked in vain for their assailants. His forgotten bike lay on its side only a few feet away. Several rocks flew at him, too, and he ducked them, one arm held up in front of his face, as too late, he remembered the single weapon they had thought to bring with them, an aluminum baseball bat tossed in the back of the wagon.

Behind him, Till was scrambling for the vehicle closest to him, Bekkah's bike, trying to detach it from the wagon, which he knew would slow him down.

"C'mon, c'mon," he whispered.

But as his useless fingers picked at the knotted ropes, a fresh barrage of rocks was unleashed on him from all directions. Panicked, he gave up and made a dash for the side of the road, crawling into the underbrush to the sounds of jeering and mocking laughter.

And with that, the mutants, shrieking, descended from all directions.

It was impossible for Eli to tell how many there were—ten? Twenty-five? They attacked in a swarm, and at that moment looked exactly alike—all slight of build, androgynous and covered with road dust, with the same bulging lavender eyes and ornate labyrinths of scars and tattoos covering their faces and bald heads. Each wore a meager tunic, with a canvas bag loaded with rocks slung across his or her body.

The bikes themselves were strange-looking and menacing: black and low to the ground, festooned with strips of leather, with weird metal pegs and handles attached to the frames and axles. The mutants rode two to a bike, one pedaling and the other standing behind, straddling the rear tire and balancing barefoot on the foot pegs while wielding their slings, metal clubs, and chains.

Eli had heard tales of these recent and confusing attacks by the mutants, of ambushes sprung from nowhere and for no reason. He had taken comfort in the fact that the mutants had chosen not to kill but saved the worst of their savagery for buildings and objects. Still, hearing of such things was far different from experiencing them firsthand. He was choked with panic.

Covering his face with his arms, Eli ran forward, bent over to make himself as small a target as possible. He was able to reach Bekkah's side unscathed. Grabbing her under the arms, Eli dragged his unconscious friend to the underbrush, near Till.

From there, Eli watched as the mutants dismounted from their bikes and turned their attention to the car. Soon glass was shattering, heavy chains smashing against metal, and bodies were jumping up and down on the roof. *Better the car than them*, he thought. He turned to the side and, when he did, his heart skipped a beat.

The two plastic bottles, still brimming over with gasoline, were where he and the others had left them, miraculously untouched by the side of the road. To Eli's horror, one of the mutants backed into one as she whirled her chain overhead and knocked it over. Shocked, the boy watched as the precious contents glugged out, spreading across the pavement and spilling into the dust by the side of the road.

He was not the only one who noticed.

The biggest mutant, wiry and with a distinct network of swirling scars forming a rising sun across its face, had been standing to one side, arms crossed. Eli noticed the triangular tattoo on its bicep; clearly, it was a male. This mutant had been watching the others attack the car with an unreadable expression. Now, he cocked his head. With one swift movement, he crossed over to the second bottle, which was still full of gasoline. Then, he lifted it by its neck with two fingers in a gesture that seemed almost dainty and carried it back to the others.

Eli knew the mutants traded for nothing. They had no use for Levi's supplies; mostly, they scavenged and killed wild animals. They didn't need gas.

The big mutant said something, a few words the boy couldn't hear on account of the noise; but whatever it was, everyone stopped what he was doing and backed away from the car. In the silence, Eli could hear their bare feet crunching on the pebbled green glass sprayed across the shoulder and road. Once everyone had cleared, the mutant took the bottle and started splashing its contents over the remains of the mutilated Volvo.

Eli realized what the big mutant had pulled from his shoulder pouch, what he now held aloft in one hand and was tossing in the air like a toy.

It was a small plastic object, bright pink, the size of a thumb. A firestarter.

"Oh no," said Till next to him, involuntarily. "Please . . . don't!"

As if he had heard, the mutant gave a faint smile. He pressed a button on the side of the object once, twice; on the third time, and with a distinct *click*, a small orange flame blossomed out of the top. Then he bent down and touched the flame to the wet, glistening asphalt.

The mutants scattered as fire licked and spread across the pavement and trampled grass, racing with unbelievable speed in rippling blue and yellow waves toward the car, the car that still had gas in it, at least half a tank of the precious stuff, maybe closer to a full tank. Leaping onto their bikes, the mutants took off and within seconds, they disappeared.

From their hiding place, Eli covered his head with one arm, the other around the unconscious Bekkah, his face pressed hard into the dusty ground. He braced himself and prayed that Till, next to him, would do the same.

Then the car exploded.

By the old railroad tracks, rusty and nearly obscured by weeds and trash, Esther heard the faraway blast. She froze; then she pulled Skar down so they were nearly hidden by the tall grass.

"What's going on?" Skar asked, although she already knew.

"Nothing," Esther lied.

* * *

Whooping and shrieking, the variants rode single file into town, rattling the broken, faded WELCOME TO PRIN sign as they thundered past. They spread into a V formation as they headed down the central street, flanked on both sides by sidewalks and two- and three-story buildings, with empty storefronts on the ground floors. While a few structures showed the effects of earlier recent attacks, most were unscathed.

The variants did not spare the first buildings they encountered. One stood on the foot pegs of a bicycle and whirled a sling around his head. He let fly with deadly accuracy, and the window of what had once been a clothing store shattered, collapsing in an explosion of broken glass.

Most of the variants rode ahead, while several dismounted, wielding chains and clubs. Using a broken windowsill as a foothold, one reached for the neon sign above the remains of a pharmacy; with one blow of her cudgel, she smashed it partway off the building, so it dangled at a crazy angle. She swung at it again, this time bringing it crashing down in pieces; then she proceeded to beat it into fragments on the street. Another whirled his sling above his head, launching rocks to smash one window after another.

Residents scattered for cover, taking refuge wherever they could find it. They had no time to consider the senselessness of the event; they had witnessed it in the weeks before, but this ambush was far worse, more savage and out of control.

A girl, age eleven or twelve, ran to a rusted car in the street and managed to roll underneath before being seen. As she lay there, she saw bare feet stop in front of her. Holding her breath, she watched as the feet paced back and forth. After what seemed an eternity, they walked away and she heard a bike take off.

Elsewhere, faces appeared in second-floor windows, looking at the mayhem.

One boy, Jonah, decided he would try to save the town single-handedly.

When the variants blasted down the main street, the ten-year-old had managed to scale the fire escape of a battered building without drawing attention. He had made his way to the roof, and now, lying on his belly on the hot tar, he gazed down at the destruction. In one hand, he gripped a lead pipe, which he had kept in his back pocket for weeks for exactly a moment such as this.

He watched as variants kicked in the front door of what had once been a bar. He watched as they caught a boy trying to escape, ripped his headdress off him, set it on fire, then tossed it through the broken door of an old hair salon. He watched until they seemed to tire of causing chaos, until they were ready to move on, and gathered to huddle their bikes to make a plan, waiting for someone to tell them what to do.

They waited for the one they called Slayd.

The variant leader approached, skidding his bike to a halt. Leaning over the handlebars, he addressed the others with emphatic gestures. His back turned to the stores, Slayd didn't see the iron pipe, flung like a boomerang, winging toward his head.

Another variant saw it. He leaped forward, pushing Slayd

out of the way and Slayd's protector was clipped on the side of the head by the pipe and was knocked cold, feet jerking up and down on the pavement.

The boy on the roof became an easy target. As Slayd got to his feet, the others let loose a volley of rocks toward the boy, who was scrambling down the fire escape. They nailed him at once—on the back, the legs, the head. He rolled down the final steps and dropped to the pavement with a sickening thud.

In the silence that followed, Slayd brushed off his tunic, dignity intact. He didn't acknowledge the protector any more than the assailant; both still lay, unconscious, on the ground. Instead, Slayd got back on his bike and led the rest of his band away, with a final, piercing shout. The last to leave grabbed the fallen variant and slung him over his shoulder. Then he too remounted his bicycle and was gone.

One by one, the townspeople straggled out of their hiding places. They stood in a state of shock on the street, breathing in the dust stirred up by the variants that still hung in the air.

There had been little left of their town in the first place. Now, there was even less.

TWO

HOURS LATER, THE STREET WAS STILL EMPTY AND SILENT, LITTERED WITH shards of broken glass, rocks, and splintered wood. The dusty asphalt showed the scuffed marks of bike treads and bare footprints that the wind would soon erase. On the ground beneath the fire escape, a few red splatters had dried and were blackening in the afternoon heat.

Far in the distance, a thin plume of gray smoke spiraled upward before disappearing in the darkening sky.

At the edge of the main street stood a one-story brick building surrounded by a cement field marked with fading white lines. Two battered yellow arches loomed overhead atop a high metal pole. By some miracle, the large windows that dominated three of the walls had been spared in the recent attack.

Now a small, anxious face peered out from a clear spot rubbed on the grimy glass.

It belonged to a sentry, a dark-eyed boy perched on a molded table attached to the floor and focused on the empty street, keeping watch in case of another attack. He was perhaps six or seven years old and he fought to stay awake. Behind him, the crowded room was restless and noisy, with a shrill clamor of voices raised in anger, fear, and confusion.

Everyone from town, more or less, was present; and it seemed everyone had something to say. More than a hundred children and teens huddled on top of tables and chairs, along the grimy tile floor and the stainless-steel counter. A lone child sat in the corner, soothing a younger girl who lay cradled in her lap, sucking from a dirty soda bottle. A few others retreated deep into their thoughts, staring upward at the ceiling.

One boy banged his fist on the metal counter until the others stopped talking.

"We got to go after them," he shouted, his voice hoarse. He was nine, with a baseball cap pulled backward over his shaggy brown hair. "Before they attack us again."

An older girl sitting on a table across the room shook her head. She was dark skinned and had several colorful belts cinched around her grimy robes.

"You mean go into mutant territory?" she shouted. "That's crazy . . . they got more people. Or whatever they are."

At that, the room erupted as everyone started talking once

more. Another boy, pale and freckled, spoke up from where he sat on the floor.

"Maybe they *are* people," he said. He looked to be about eleven. "Like us, only different. They're boys and girls in one body. Maybe—"

The older girl sitting next to him, also freckled, smacked him hard across the ear. "Shut up!" she hissed; but no one had even heard. Another boy, so small his feet dangled a good two feet off the floor as he rested on the edge of the counter, piped up.

"And they got weapons. How can we fight if they got weapons and we don't?"

Others chimed in.

"He's right. We don't got a chance."

"But if we do nothing, they're gonna come back. Maybe next time, they'll kill us all."

"They almost killed Jonah. When we brought him inside, he was bleeding pretty bad."

People glanced at the would-be hero from the roof, who leaned against the counter; the side of his face was badly scraped and his left arm hung at a useless angle.

Nearby, Bekkah stood close to Eli, the blood-soaked T-shirt tied around her head not quite hiding the ugly purple and yellow bruise spreading down her cheek. Her left eye was swollen nearly shut and when she spoke, she sounded exhausted.

"They always been peaceful," she said. "Now they've attacked us four times. What do they want? It don't make sense."

As the arguments raged, one person was watching the proceedings with a shrewd eye.

It was the leader of the town, who leaned against the far wall, with his arms folded. Short, with wide hips and stringy hair, eighteen-year-old Rafe had been elected to his one-year term the previous winter by the usual show of hands. It hadn't taken him long to realize how much he enjoyed not only the prestige of his position but the perks as well. He was spared work assignments and was also given an extra weekly allotment of food and water. And so despite his advanced age, he was planning how he could be reelected for another term.

The recent variant attacks, he figured, gave him as good an issue to run on as any.

Rafe held up his hands for calm. As usual, he remained silent while the others exhausted themselves with bickering and suggestions. When he did speak, this gave him the impression of both thoughtfulness and authority.

"There ain't never been sense to mutants," he said. He also knew enough to speak softly; this forced everyone in the room to lean forward to hear him. "They're like wild dogs. And I say we wipe 'em out."

The girl next to him was shaking her head, arms folded over her thin chest. "That's always your answer, Rafe," she said. Against the relative whiteness of her robes, her skin looked dark and withered; she appeared at least two decades older than her sixteen years. "It ain't so easy."

"Let him speak," shouted the boy with baseball cap.

"Yeah," chimed in another voice. "How do you say we do it?"

Again, Rafe waited until the room grew quiet.

"We go to Levi," he said. "We go there and we ask for weapons. *Real* weapons, I mean. Knives. Arrows. That way, at least we got a chance—"

The dark-skinned girl sitting on the table cut him off.

"But there ain't no gas left to trade for the things we really need—like to eat and drink," she said, her voice shrill. "And Levi's been cutting back on what he pays us."

Most were nodding their heads in agreement. The dark girl continued. "We got nothing else to give him. Without gas, why would he even talk to us?"

Rafe smiled. He had anticipated this question.

"Maybe not to you or me, unless we got something to trade," he said. "That's all he cares about. But there's *one* of us I bet he'd talk to."

Then he turned to look at a girl sitting alone by the window.

It was dusk; the meeting had been going on for nearly two hours. The small sentry at the window had relaxed his vigilance and dozed at his post. Behind him, several of the townspeople had lit candles, which they set on the tables and counters. As the nighttime darkened around them, the gritty windows reflected what was going on inside the room. From outside, the townspeople were all too visible, and with no view of what might be approaching.

If attackers were to come, they would arrive unseen.

And in fact, two people were now scuttling toward the lit building. Yet they were not there to do harm.

Esther bent low and ran from one shadow to the next,

zigzagging down the sidewalk. She had been gone since before dawn. Although Esther chose to ignore the far-off explosion, she knew that it had to do with the variants. Now, uneasy, she could not help but notice the freshly smashed windows and broken storefronts that lined the main street of Prin.

Behind her was a reluctant and increasingly panicked Skar. With the stink of burning gasoline still lingering in the night air, the last thing she wanted was to be confronted by the town.

"Esther," Skar whispered, pulling at her friend's arm for what must have been the hundredth time, "please. Let's not do this!"

"Don't worry," said Esther. "They can't see us."

And Skar had to admit: This part was true.

It wasn't just that the darkness gave them ample cover. Over the years, Esther had worked hard to become adept at variant ways—the peculiar stalking, hunting, and trapping methods that Skar had taught her, skills that had been second nature to the variant girl since early childhood. Skills that let you become almost invisible.

Esther ran on the balls of her feet, using cover and shadow to hide her progress, avoiding the straight line of approach, doubling back, leaping up to edge a few steps along railings and windowsills, seizing every possible handhold and foothold available to her: all the tricks a variant did to confound expectation and confuse the eye. If she were to be honest, Skar could fault Esther on a half dozen mistakes: Her tread was too heavy, her breathing too loud. The worst was that the girl still couldn't interpret the terrain as having many possible pathways, not just the obvious one; she didn't know how to strategize on her feet. Even so, although she would never say so out loud, Skar had to admit:

Not bad for a norm.

The two reached the building where the meeting was taking place and slipped into the adjoining alley. Esther took a swift, birdlike peek into a window, as Skar cringed in the shadows beside her, trembling with anxiety.

"Big group in there," Esther said; "looks like everybody in town."

Skar's expression grew even more tense. "Can we go now?" she begged.

"Not yet," replied Esther. "We've got to hear what they're planning. It could be important."

"What are you going to do?"

Esther didn't answer. Skar was about to repeat her question when she saw what Esther was doing.

She was trying to climb the bare brick wall.

Despite her mounting anxiety, Skar couldn't help smiling. Esther was attempting something she had learned only that week: using the tips of her fingers and toes to gain a hold on even the shallowest dents and faintest bumps in a surface. In this way, a variant could—with practice and the right combination of strength, balance, and weight distribution— scale even the smoothest-seeming wall, like a fly. Esther was able to grip the bricks with both her fingers and the tips of her sneakers, and she moved upward clumsily, yet with surprising speed.

By now, Esther was too far up the wall for Skar to call her back. Feeling resigned, the variant made a quick decision and followed.

Moving at twice the speed of her friend and with enviable grace, Skar clambered up the brick wall and caught up with Esther within moments. At the last second, she was polite enough not to overtake her. Instead, they reached the roof together and Skar even allowed Esther the illusion of pulling her up once she had reached the top.

"Don't worry," Esther whispered, clearly proud of herself; "I got you. And I got here first!"

But her jubilation made her forget herself and she stood upright, something a variant would never do, especially not in a moment of triumph, the one moment your guard was down.

Skar hissed a warning at her, but it was too late.

Esther wavered and then lost her balance, falling forward onto the roof and landing hard. The top of the building was steeply tilted on both sides like an old-fashioned cottage from a picture book, covered with overlapping reddish-brown tiles. Esther started to slide, her fingers scrabbling in vain to get a grasp of the tattered clay rows.

Skar reached out a hand, but it was no good. Esther kept sliding, rapidly approaching the edge.

At the last possible second, she was able to wedge one foot into the shaky rain gutter while grabbing onto a few secure tiles. One broke off under her hand; it skittered down the roof and disappeared in the darkness beneath them with a faint crash.

With surprising speed, Esther crawled her way back up to her friend, who was huddled miserably, waiting for her.

"I knew this was a bad idea," Skar said.

The variant was astounded that inside, no one had heard the incredible noise Esther had just made. Any one of her people would have been outside investigating the suspicious sounds within seconds. She wished (and not for the first time) that Esther wasn't so stubborn.

"But we just got here," Esther whispered. She flattened down onto her stomach and crawled toward one of the many gaps in the tiles. "And I want to hear what they're talking about."

Skar had no choice but to follow her. She sat next to her friend, knees huddled close and bulging eyes shut tight.

One gap afforded a limited view of the room below. Esther glanced down, then placed her ear over the hole and concentrated. There were many people speaking at once, but she was able to detect a female voice. She had to strain to hear what she was saying.

"We got nothing else to give him. Without gas, why would Levi even talk to us?"

She peered through the hole. Esther could see the tops of heads, a few familiar faces. She recognized Rafe, the current leader of the town elders, a boy she hated because beneath his superior airs, he was both a coward and blowhard. As usual, he was doing his trick of talking softly. Esther had to put her ear close to the hole and focus hard in order to discern his words.

"Maybe not to you or me, unless we got something to trade," he was saying. "That's all he cares about. But there's *one* of us I bet he'd talk to."

Who were they talking about?

There was a brief silence, followed by a faint murmuring as people stood and craned their necks, looking to see who he was discussing. Esther followed their gaze and was startled.

It was a girl, seventeen, with dark, straight hair held back in a ponytail. Unlike everyone else in town, her robes were relatively clean and gathered neatly at her waist with a dark cord. She seemed embarrassed by all the attention, yet flattered as well.

"I . . . I don't know," she was saying. "For one thing, I don't know what good it would do. I've never been to the Source. I can't even remember the last time I spoke to Levi . . ."

Esther pulled back, as if struck. "Hey."

"What is it?" Skar asked, opening her eyes.

"It's my sister. Sarah."

Frowning, Esther sat back on her heels. In that position, she could see the place they were talking about, where Levi lived. The Source lay to the northeast of town and was something she saw every day, as much a part of her landscape as the sun. Although it was nearly a mile away, it was hard to miss from anywhere in town.

The gigantic white building was like a beacon, huge and blindingly lit with electrical lights. They threw deep shadows across the trenches that lay next to it, black gashes in an overgrown field. The holes were just three of the dozens of pits scattered across town that the people dug day after day when they were unlucky enough to be assigned to the Excavation. The front and side of the Source faced a monstrous asphalt field marked with fading white lines and still crowded with the dusty remains of cars.

Now, it seemed Rafe and his followers wanted something from Levi, something new. And they apparently needed Sarah, the childhood friend who once knew him best of all, to be the intermediary.

Esther didn't like it.

She glanced at Skar, who was amusing herself by tossing a small knife up in the air and catching it. She wasn't even paying attention, and for that, Esther felt a stab of exasperation. Skar was, after all, only who she was—a great friend, but one who was easily bored, like a little child.

And little children needed to be protected.

Esther knew it would be up to her. She was not sure how she would do it, but at least she knew where to start.

It was evening. Shadows cowered low to the ground and scurried through the streets and alleys of Prin.

They were feral dogs, rooting through piles of garbage for something to eat. They snapped and fought over whatever they could sniff out, anything that was remotely edible: the stale and salty ends of flatbread, rabbit bones that had been sucked of their marrow, the burned crust of rice porridge. The dogs of Prin were dingy and skeletal, cringing yet vicious beasts accustomed to skulking in the shadows and traveling by night in packs.

There was, however, one stretch of sidewalk that had been swept clean. The storefront window behind it had not only been patched over with flattened cardboard and gaffer's tape; it looked like someone had actually taken the trouble to measure it so it fit properly. A cracked and battered sign above what was once the window read STARBUCKS COFFEE in block white letters on a green background. And above the sign, a light was visible in the second-floor window.

Agitated shadows moved across the curtain. Behind the thin fabric, Esther was getting in her sister's face.

"But you can't go," she was saying.

Esther was trying hard not to raise her voice, because she knew losing her temper would only cost her the argument the way it always did. Instead, she tried to sound reasonable, clasping her hands tightly behind her back.

"You can't ask Levi for weapons," she said. "This whole thing is starting to get crazy."

Sarah stood at the kitchen counter, cleaning out the firebowl with a rag. The older girl acted as if getting rid of every last trace of soot and ash was the most important thing in the world. She was doing what annoyed Esther the most: ignoring her because she was focused on something more meaningful, something *adult*.

"Pass me those," was all Sarah said, nodding at the forks and spoons.

Frustrated, Esther picked up the handful of dirty silverware. She couldn't help herself; as she handed them over, she slammed them down on the counter harder than she intended to. At the noise, her sister jumped, to Esther's private satisfaction. Then Sarah turned all her attention back to cleaning up.

"How could you listen to those people?" continued Esther, still trying to sound calm. "Rafe? He's a big mouth, that's all. And the others—they're just thugs who want an excuse to hurt people."

"I didn't say I was definitely going to see Levi," Sarah replied. Unlike everyone else in town, she spoke in a fussy, formal manner she had probably picked up from all her reading. It was yet another thing that irritated Esther about her sister. Sarah pushed a few grains of uneaten rice into a plastic container, which she sealed and put away. Then she finished wiping the silverware.

The plates, bowls, and cups were chipped and cracked, yet they were mostly a matched set, what had once been a pretty green and purple. Thanks to Sarah, the entire apartment was tidy and clean. Unlike the other homes in Prin, filled with piles of filthy blankets and clothing and utensils, their place was almost stylish, and the curtains in the windows were white.

The walls were decorated with tattered ads Sarah had found in town—mysterious posters for Absolut vodka, Continental Airlines, New York Yankees. There were even several shelves of books, which Esther had barely glanced at. "Besides," continued Esther, "why do you think Levi will even talk to you? You haven't seen him in years. And all he cares about is how much gas people bring him. He don't care about anything else."

"*Doesn't*, not *don't*," said Sarah, her face flushing. "And he's not like that. He's a good person."

Esther shot her sister a look, sensing something in her she hadn't seen before. She knew that when they were much younger, Sarah and Levi had been close friends and that she had taught him how to read. But that was about all she knew. Esther had a hunch she might be able to find a new point of vulnerability. "Well, if he's so good, how come we never see him?"

Sarah shrugged, seemingly unaffected, as she stacked the plates, her back to her sister. "Levi's a busy man," she said.

Esther scowled, looking down. There was a design on the countertop that she jabbed at with her finger. "Busy bossing everyone around."

Sarah's voice hardened.

"If he didn't run things," she said, "we all would have died a long time ago. And I don't see you turning down food you don't work for."

Esther's hunch was right; she had touched a nerve. Still, she flinched from the uncomfortable truth.

She could not deny that she lived off the food that Levi provided and that Sarah not only earned, but prepared as well. Esther didn't know the first thing about how to pound the otherwise inedible rice and beans into flour, or how to mix it with water and pat it into flatbread. She had never once stoked the firebowl with charcoal or cooked watery porridge on its blackened grill. These were all Sarah's jobs, and while Esther had always taken that for granted, she realized that it did not strengthen her position. If anything, it made her even more of a child, someone not to be taken seriously.

"Besides, who's better?" Sarah said. "The mutants?"

"Don't call them that," Esther said under her breath.

Her sister didn't stop. "At least we didn't go around attacking people, like the *mutants*." She emphasized the hateful word. "We're better than that."

"Whatever's happening now, it's not their fault," said Esther. Sarah rolled her eyes, but her sister continued. "Maybe they're just hungry. Besides, they mostly don't hurt people . . . only buildings and things." And despite herself, she opened up. "They're nice, Sarah, they really are. Maybe one or two of them are bad, but—"

Sarah snorted. "Oh, please," she said as she started putting the dishes away. "I wish to God you'd stop socializing with them. You and your little friend Star—"

"Skar."

"And that lunatic in that building, with all the cats. What's his name? Joseph? You're not a baby anymore, Esther. It's about time you weaned yourself away from all of them."

Esther tried to rein in her emotions, but she could feel her control slipping as tears sprung to her eyes. "Why do you hate my friends?" she asked.

"I don't hate anybody," said Sarah. Her voice sounded frozen. "I'm only looking out for you, since apparently you can't do that yourself."

A sob escaped. Furious and ashamed, Esther pushed her fists into her eyes to keep tears from falling.

Sarah sighed, and her tone softened. "I just wish you weren't so . . . naive, Esther."

Esther felt a new stab of annoyance. "You know I don't know what that word is," she muttered.

"Do you really think they want to be your friends?" Sarah said. She spoke softly, almost gently. "They're all probably waiting to break in here so they can rob us blind."

"Rob us? Of what? Our matching coffee cups?" Esther managed to say. Tears were running down her face and she wiped her nose with her sleeve.

Sarah gazed at her; you could almost see something settle in her mind. It was what Esther feared all along and she cursed herself. She had once again driven her sister in the opposite direction.

"Thank you," Sarah said. "If I wasn't sure about whether or not to see Levi, I am now. Why all this trouble is going on, I honestly don't know. But I'm sure he'll put an end to it."

Esther was overwhelmed with bitterness—at her failure to keep her sister from going to the Source, and her inability to control her emotions, to play it cool. To strategize, as Skar would say.

"Fine," Esther yelled. "Fine!"

She pushed past her sister.

Sarah's voice betrayed mild panic. "Where are you going?" she called after her. The only response was the slam of the front door. Inside one of the many cupboards, something fell off a shelf and broke with a small crash.

* * *

Once outside, Esther walked blindly through the darkness for several blocks before she calmed down enough to think. She could sense rather than hear a pack of feral dogs rummaging nearby. The animals were cowardly yet, when desperate, had been known to attack anybody unwise enough to be outside at night, alone, without a weapon.

Esther sat on a street corner, her ears keyed to a possible attack, adrenaline coursing through her body. She knew it was stupid to be outside, yet she needed to make a physical statement, to create some distance.

After an hour, she went back.

She suspected her sister would sit up waiting for her, as she had so many times in the past; in fact, she secretly wanted it to be true. Yet when Esther returned, she found Sarah in her room, asleep. As she stood over her, Esther experienced a strange, twisting sensation in her stomach. She had an impulse to touch her sister's long, black hair, fanned out on the white pillowcase and framing her face, but at the last second, she changed her mind.

Instead, she went back to the main room and sat alone in the dark. Stubbornly, she decided she would wait to watch the sun come up.

Hours later the first rays of light found her sound asleep, fully dressed, curled like a cat on the far end of the couch.

Miles away, someone else was watching the sun rise.

It was a solitary boy on a bike, on the major roadway that

passed by the outskirts of Prin. At sixteen, Caleb was lean and deeply sunburned, with a strong jaw and hazel eyes that, despite his distrustful gaze, had once been gentle.

Like Esther, Caleb chose to protect himself from the sun in his own way. He wore a long-sleeved denim shirt, jeans, canvas gloves, and a battered Outback hat. In his backpack, he carried a few belongings. His vehicle was a scuffed black mountain bike with patched tires that had seen many miles.

He had been on the road for months and could finally see his destination on the horizon: a glimpse of the lone church spire that marked the town of Prin.

And still, he hesitated.

He unzipped his backpack, took out a green steel bottle, and swished it around. As he feared, it was nearly empty. The sun had only just risen and the morning was still cool. Yet the sky was cloudless and he knew it would be another day of blazing heat.

By the side of the road was an old gas station, abandoned and in ruins. In front, Caleb noticed several rusty old oil barrels. One of them was uncovered and now brimmed over with rainwater from a recent storm.

Caleb walked his bike to the edge of where the grass used to be and released the rickety kickstand. Then he crossed to the barrels and looked down. The water was so clear, you could see all the way to the bottom, where a pink pebble lay. He couldn't help himself; he stooped to smell it, and at its irresistibly cold scent, he imagined plunging his head into it, opening his parched mouth and swallowing, gulping, drinking as much as he could without coming up for air.

His eyes were closed and his lips were at the surface of the water; at the last second, he gave a shudder and forced himself to pull back.

That would have been suicide.

The trembling surface reflected the cloudless sky above him. It also reflected his face, which shocked him with its gauntness and its look of need.

Making up his mind, he uncapped his green bottle, lifted it to his lips, and emptied it within seconds. It was only a few mouthfuls of hot and metallic water, but he savored every drop.

Then Caleb got back on his bike and headed for town.

THREE

As moths danced around the bright spotlights overhead, Sarah waited outside the Source, nervously brushing back her hair.

Before she left, she had primped in front of her cracked mirror, combing her long hair so that it lay across her shoulders in a style she thought was pretty. Now she tried to make it stay that way.

She had never been this close to the enormous building; few in Prin had. She stood in front of the giant steel front door that rose and lowered, powered by electricity. Posted at a discreet distance on all sides were armed guards, silent and hooded. Sarah had approached one with trepidation earlier that day.

She had passed along a note, requesting to speak with Levi, not knowing if she'd ever get a response. To her surprise, within a few hours, she received a note back, inviting her for dinner that night, alone.

Now the guards urged her forward and ushered her inside.

Sarah entered, nervous and excited. She adjusted her eyes to a dark and cavernous interior, lit by electric lights kept low.

Towering shapes hulked on all sides. They were giant shelves that rose to the ceiling, all of them fully stocked with oversize cartons. Sarah made out some of the words printed on them: THIS END UP. POWDERED MILK. DEHYDRATED CARROTS. WHEAT GRAIN. 200 GALLONS. POLAND SPRING WATER. HANDLE WITH CARE.

Then, emerging from the shadows was Levi.

Like everyone else in Prin, Sarah had not laid eyes on him in years. Levi was now a tall seventeen-year-old, with dark eyes and a mouth set in a hard line. He wore only black: jeans, button-down shirt, leather boots, all of which set off the extreme pallor of his skin. Yet when he recognized her, he smiled; and in that instant, he became the old Levi again, the boy with the watchful eyes she'd once known so well. The boy she had taught to read and who she thought might one day propose to her.

"Sarah," was all he said.

Levi escorted her through the dimly lit Source. When they rounded a corner, she almost cried out in shock. A single electric light overhead threw deep shadows into the surrounding cavernous space. It illuminated a large table, laid with a rich cloth and piled high with plates of roast rabbit and salted flatbread, enough to feed at least a dozen for days. There were also strange foods she had never seen before: bowls of steaming, fragrant liquids and soft, glossy breads that were still hot.

As they started to eat, Sarah told herself to focus. She knew that she was there on serious business. Yet for the longest time, she couldn't speak. She could only eat, ravenously. On the table was something new to her, a bottle of dark purplish-red liquid.

"Have some," Levi said, hoisting it.

Before she had a chance to answer, Levi was filling her glass. At first, Sarah winced at its sharp taste, but with each sip, she found she liked it more and more. By her second glass, she was simply listening as Levi spoke of small things: her health; Sarah's sister, Esther; the people in town. Sarah was thrilled by the thought that despite all of his power, her old friend evidently still cared about her and remembered names and details from a long-ago time, their shared youth.

Esther was wrong about him, she thought.

She was only vaguely aware that, unlike her, Levi had eaten very little. He grew silent, watching her from across the table with an unreadable expression as he toyed with a glass of the purple liquid he had barely touched. He seemed to be waiting for her to say something; and she remembered that, of course, that was why she was here.

Sarah guiltily wiped her mouth with a cloth napkin and cleared her throat.

"Levi," she said, "as you probably know, the mutants have been attacking, and it's getting worse. There's no one in town strong enough to do anything." She heard the contempt that had crept into her voice, but she didn't care. "They need your help."

She thought of the twelve-year-old who had arrived in town five years ago and broken into the shuttered and locked Source when no one else could. Before then, Prin was a ghost town inhabited by a few dozen, a wasteland on the verge of extinction. Through sheer intelligence and willpower, Sarah thought fuzzily, Levi had single-handedly transformed it. Sequestered in the white building, he became the hidden engine that kept the town running.

Now he would save it again.

"They need weapons," she said, in a rush. "Real weapons, not just sticks or rocks. They need knives, arrows, clubs . . . whatever you can spare."

Levi inclined his head in a slight nod but said nothing. The purple liquid had made Sarah expansive and uninhibited. She spread her hands out in a naked appeal.

"You've been so generous already," she said. "If you could supply them with arms, they would forever be in your debt."

There was a long pause before Levi answered.

"I see," he said.

He picked up his glass but only studied the liquid inside. An idea seemed to come to him and he looked up.

"To be honest," he said, "I'm not even sure if we have what you want in stock. Weapons, knives, clubs . . . I don't know if we've seen much of that kind of thing around here. Have we?" He addressed this last part to his guards, who murmured negatively.

Levi's guards were all clearly armed. Sarah was confused. "Are you sure you—"

Levi set down his drink and stood.

"May I show you something?"

The way he asked it wasn't a question. Unsteadily, Sarah got to her feet. Swaying from the drink, she took a final, surreptitious bite of rabbit before following Levi out.

The guards kept their distance as Sarah trailed Levi through the endless, murky recesses of the building. She struggled to keep pace with her host. It was not easy, for he walked swiftly, sure of the path. Silver things flashed on his wrists and fingers—rings, watches, bracelets—and Sarah focused on them, as if they were stars in the night sky, to keep from getting left behind.

The crowded shelves towered above her.

In her inebriated state, Sarah knew they represented wealth of the most genuine and therefore precious kind. In a world of poisoned rain, scorching heat, and ashen skies, even a single jug of water, one of the hundreds stored here, perhaps thousands, held the balance of life and death to the people of Prin.

Sarah extended a hand to touch one of the cartons. But before she could, a guard materialized from nowhere and shoved her aside.

"Keep close," Levi called from a few steps ahead, "and don't touch anything. There are things that can hurt you if you're not careful."

Only then did Sarah realize that the shelves were encircled with loops of heavy wire, the kind she had seen on a few buildings downtown: wire studded with razors that could easily slice through leather, let alone human skin.

Levi stopped. He pressed something on the wall and the air was loud with humming. In front of them was a wide ramp that led to a lower floor, and now it began to move on its own. Levi stepped on and gestured for Sarah to follow.

Sarah hesitated, frightened. Then she finally stepped on because Levi was far ahead and she stumbled, nearly falling. Terrified, she clung to the moving handrail, until she reached the lower level, where Levi was waiting for her.

He set off again through darkened aisles, then down a narrow hallway, where more guards kept watch over a battered steel door. Behind that, a poorly lit stairway led even farther downward to a series of hallways with low ceilings.

Levi stopped at a doorway. A small sign next to it read: BOILER ROOM.

"Here we go," he said. Then he opened the door and flicked a switch set into the wall.

Sarah gasped.

The blinding overhead light revealed a windowless room that was furnished sparsely, with a desk and single chair. The rest of the place was empty except for one set of shelves. Unlike the ones upstairs, however, it was not stacked high with supplies, nor was it guarded by barbed wire. Instead it was filled with books: dozens of them, battered and mildewed. Compared to the meager collection in Sarah's home, this was a veritable library.

"You kept them," was all Sarah could manage to say.

Levi smiled. "I figured since you bothered teaching me, it was the least I could do."

Sarah ran her hand over a row of bindings and this time, no guard rushed forward to push her out of the way. She marveled at the titles and names she remembered, books she had salvaged from vacant homes and looted stores many years ago and later used to teach Levi how to read: John Grisham, *The Joy of Cooking*, *American and European Furniture: 1830–1914*, *A Cavalcade of Jokes*, Stephen King, Richard Scarry. The Bible. The Brothers Grimm.

Levi had been a difficult student, moody and hotheaded. Yet he was diligent and had a hunger to learn. Within a year, his abilities had equaled and then surpassed hers. Sarah hoped that since they were both twelve, their relationship might shift into something deeper. But then Levi ended the lessons. Not long afterward, he broke his way into the Source and disappeared from the streets of Prin.

Sarah had always wondered where the books had gone. And now, she blushed as it occurred to her why he had held on to them all these years.

"Sarah," Levi said.

She turned to him, her heart pounding. He was holding out a book to her. She took it, uncomprehending.

"This was one I found especially interesting," he said. "But you only gave me the first volume. Do you have the other?"

Puzzled, Sarah turned the book over in her hands. She couldn't recall ever seeing it before. It was an academic volume, dense and impenetrable. She flipped through it, but had never heard of any of the words: "Topography." "Aquifers." "Spring flow measurements." "Hydrosphere."

"I might," she said, handing it back. Frankly, it wasn't the kind of book she liked or understood, but she had several such volumes she rarely glanced at. "It could be in my house. I'm not positive what books are there."

Levi nodded, refusing to take it. "Why don't you hold on to it?" he said. "Because I'd really appreciate it if you could find me the second volume." Before Sarah could respond, he added, "We'll talk again when you do. And by then, I just might have some more weapons in."

Sarah understood. If she could find what he needed, this meeting wouldn't be their last. And as she was thinking this, he was seizing her by the waist and pulling her close. He kissed her, lingeringly.

"Let's keep this our secret," he murmured. "All of it. All right?"

Sarah couldn't speak for a second. "Yes," she said.

Her voice almost sounded normal, even though her face was burning. She couldn't hide the smile that covered her face.

Moments later, Sarah was outside, walking, if unsteadily, away from the Source. The white of her robes seemed to give off an unearthly glow in the bright glare of spotlights that sliced across the darkened parking lot.

From a tiny window hidden high up in the Source, Levi watched as the girl was swallowed by the surrounding darkness. As before, his expression was unreadable. He thought about the past and, for a moment, almost felt sorry for Sarah.

Then he shrugged it off. She was like everyone else in this world: just a means to an end.

Levi returned to his office. There he examined the handmade maps of Prin he had drawn, the laborious approximations of its physical layout that were tacked up on his walls. They had taken him more than five years of careful study and reflected the locations of not only each of the forty-seven Excavations to date but every Gleaning, as well. Still, they had not brought him closer to what he was seeking. Frustrated, he was tempted to tear them all down.

Levi had come to Prin, drawn by a rumor of its hidden clean waters. He met Sarah, who taught him how to read. Most books he found worthless; yet one convinced him that the notion of an underground network of springs was true. All he needed was a little more time to locate it, but time was running out.

Unlike everyone else, he always knew the supplies in the Source were limited. In the last few months, they had reached dangerously low levels. He recently had doubled and tripled the workloads, driving the town to exhaustion, and increased the punishments for shirking. It was a delicate balance, squeezing the greatest amount of work out of the people before getting rid of them.

Sarah's unexpected appearance had given him new hope. If anything, he was annoyed at himself for not having thought of this earlier.

He needed the book, the companion to the text Sarah had given him so many years ago. With any luck, she would soon find it and bring it back to him, as trusting and unquestioning as a dog. And just as easily satisfied, with a little affection and a good meal.

Someone broke into his thoughts.

"Is she gone yet?"

Levi nodded, without looking, as a girl encircled his waist with her arms. She had sand-colored skin and hair, her eyes were a vivid blue, and her thin clothing fit close and tight to her figure. Her name was Michal and she was perhaps fourteen.

"Then can we eat now?" she continued.

Levi looked down at her. "Sure," he said.

The two headed back upstairs to the dining area, where guards stood watch over the ruins of the table. Even hooded as they were, they resembled wild dogs themselves, staring at the leftovers, their eyes visible and gleaming in the spill of the electric light.

"I still don't know why you put out so much," said Michal as she sat, and began piling roast rabbit onto her plate. She licked some off a finger. "I thought lots of people were coming. Why so much food for one old woman?"

Levi smiled. "You wouldn't understand," he said.

But Michal was no longer listening. She was too busy eating.

FOUR

THE NIGHT SKY WAS DARK AND HEAVY. YET AT CERTAIN TIMES, THE dense clouds parted, allowing moonlight to shine down. Someone stood by a window above the main street, gazing into the night.

Esther had been waiting like this, filled with dread, for hours. If Sarah returned home accompanied by Levi's men carrying weapons, she had no idea how she would be able to stop them. So when she spied a gleam of white coming down the sidewalk, she was relieved to see Sarah was not only unescorted, but also empty handed. Esther was so thankful, she barely noticed that the older girl was behaving strangely when she came in. Her cheeks flushed and eyes glittering, her prim sister was talking in a loud and aggressive voice, slurring her words.

"Levi didn't have any weapons," Sarah announced as she entered, before she had even removed her outer robes. Then she added snidely, "So your friends the mutants won't have any opposition. That should make you feel good."

But there was something careless about Sarah's tone, as if she was not paying attention to her words and was just saying what she believed would mollify her sister. She was not revealing what was actually going on, Esther suspected.

"Rafe's coming over in a little while," said her sister. She was folding away her robes, clearly trying to sound casual and unconcerned. "It'll just be business talk. Nothing important."

Esther nodded, as if the thought of a late-night visit from the town's leader was an everyday occurrence.

"You're right," she said. "It sounds boring. I think I'll go to bed now."

She tried faking a yawn, stretching her arms over her head. If Skar were here, she would laugh at how obvious the ploy was. But Sarah didn't even seem to notice.

Once inside her room, Esther knew enough to change into her sleeping shirt and get into bed. When she heard Rafe's knock less than an hour later, her sister checked in on her, opening the door just wide enough to let in a crack of candlelight from the living room. Esther, motionless, kept her eyes shut and breathed slowly. But once the door was pulled shut, she flew across the room, kneeling in the dark to listen.

"Don't worry," Sarah was whispering. "Levi has weapons

and is happy to give them to us. It will just take a while, that's all."

"We ain't got a while," Rafe said loudly, not whispering at all.

"Shhh," murmured Sarah. "My sister."

"We ain't got a while," Rafe repeated in a harsh whisper. "We ain't got no time to waste while Levi plays games with you. Can't you see he's just playing you for a fool?"

"You have to trust me. If you'll just be patient—"

"Don't you get it?" hissed Rafe. "The mutants ain't being patient. Next time, they gonna murder us in our own beds on account there ain't nothing we can do about it. At least not without weapons."

"Please," said Sarah. "Just wait and see."

From where she listened, Esther was now convinced that her sister knew more than she was letting on. Rafe, however, was too stupid to understand that.

"All you had to do was bat your eyes at him," he said. "Guess I was a fool for thinking anyone might still want you. Thanks to you, we're on our own."

A second later, the front door slammed.

Esther only had enough time to get back into bed and shut her eyes before the door creaked open one last time. After a moment, the door was pulled shut and Sarah walked away.

Esther counted to ten before creeping out of bed. She opened her door and slipped into the hallway. In the darkness, she sensed a faint glow was coming from the living room.

It took Esther a few moments to realize what Sarah was

doing. Although her sister kept a set of shelves full of musty books, they were now mostly for show; she rarely read anymore. Yet right now, Sarah was on her knees, searching through her collection. She worked methodically, muttering to herself as she pulled out one book after another, squinting to read their titles, then discarding them in a growing pile next to her.

Despite the care she was taking, she seemed desperate. For it was clear that she couldn't find what she was searching for.

After half an hour of watching Sarah, Esther couldn't stop a real yawn from escaping her mouth. Fearing she'd be discovered, she slipped back to bed.

But sleep proved to be impossible. With a tightness in her chest, Esther lay in the dark brooding over what she had just seen and heard, events no one trusted her enough to explain.

As the first rays of sun brightened the leaden sky, someone could be fleetingly seen darting through the shadows of Prin.

Esther was bringing supplies to her friend Joseph. She came alone; no one else in town cared to visit the village outcast, the eccentric pariah who lived on the outskirts of town, close to the Source, alone with his timepieces and cats. Even Skar was made uncomfortable by him. "The crazy one," she called him privately.

Joseph was not just one of the rare individuals in town who could read; he also kept a cluttered and moldering library that included old magazines and newspapers. The walls and surfaces of his home held dozens of watches and clocks in working order, homemade calendars, even hourglasses and a sundial. The rooms were filled with the gentle and persistent murmur of ancient gears shifting, second hands ticking, and the occasional muted chime.

Although Joseph was an old friend, this was no mere social call. For years, Esther had been skimming the supplies from her household to share with him. She sensed that if she did not do so, he would die, for he was too proud to ask for help. The girl took pains to hide her theft—pouring off the remaining water into different vessels, for instance, so it was harder to gauge how much there was. But recently, she had been bringing less because there was less to steal.

Esther chose to make her deliveries at dawn, a time when the wild dogs had long since left and the townspeople had not yet risen. But the relative cool of early morning vanished as the sun rose. It was sweaty and dangerous work to make one's way across the ruptured ground and giant, uprooted pine trees that protected Joseph's home like steel pikes around a prison, and as effectively, too. This was true even when one was not carrying a heavy armload of food and water.

Joseph and his ten cats (Malawi, Benjamin, Tiffany, Samsung, Mr. Roberts, Seven for All Mankind, Ginger, Claude, Tiger Boy, and Stumpy) lived in the wreckage of a hotel called the Gideon Putnam. Uncomfortable with people and frightened of open spaces, he had retreated there years ago; its remote location and condition scared off the curious. The lobby was a blasted ruin. One had to cross it to gain access to the stairwell, where seven flights of cracked and crumbling steps awaited.

Like most of Prin, the building had sustained heavy damage in the series of earthquakes that had flattened much of the surrounding area some years ago, and it was no mean feat to navigate it without the carpeted ground giving way or sections of the ceiling collapsing. There were entire floors Joseph dared not venture onto. Sometimes, in fact, he was quite certain the whole building was about to fall down.

Now, as he worked his way around his apartment, winding and adjusting each of his clocks and watches, Esther's signal sounded from somewhere in the building: a two-note whistle. Joseph's cats recognized it and began to call and mill about. They were fond of her, or perhaps they were just fond of the bits of dried meat she always brought.

"Joseph," Esther said as she appeared at his door.

Joseph looked as he always did: with long, unkempt hair and light-colored eyes. He was so tall, slender, and stoop-shouldered that he seemed to undulate rather than walk.

She didn't waste time with small talk. "Lately, the food payments are down even more," she said. "And the water payments are worse. This was the best I could manage." With that, she set down a gallon of water and a bag of cornmeal by the soot-filled firebowl in his hallway. "I don't know when I can bring you any more after today."

Joseph seemed to think this over and nodded gravely. The fact of the matter was, he couldn't support his brood and himself on Esther's supplies alone. He had never mentioned it, but he had long been in the habit of setting traps for the various wild animals that visited his roof and basement in order to supplement what she brought. In fact, he prided himself on his squirrel stew.

"I suppose we'll have to make do," he said. It seemed to him the right thing to say at such a moment.

Unexpectedly, she took him by the arm. When he glanced down at her, he was struck by the look of anguish on her face.

"Do you understand what I'm saying, Joseph?" she said in a low voice. "I don't know if I can come here anymore."

This was something else entirely. Esther was Joseph's only friend (his only human friend, that is) and his sole connection to the outside world. He rarely if ever left his building. To lose her companionship would be terrible for him indeed.

Esther told him about the recent attacks by the variants. She was worried that these incursions were about to be met with retaliation by the townspeople, which would only serve to fuel more acrimony. If this happened, the long-simmering tension between norm and variant would erupt into open warfare, a conflict the fragile town of Prin couldn't possibly sustain. If war began, they would all be at risk . . . even those who chose to live on the outskirts of society.

As she talked, Joseph fetched a cup of water from his desk and started to raise it to his lips.

Esther grabbed his hand.

"Joseph," she said, her voice raised in panic, "how many times have I told you? Don't drink any water but the kind I give you. You'll get sick."

She handled his cup like it was a live snake, holding it far away from her and carrying it to an open window. She was about to fling it outside, when a faint sound from below made them both glance down.

Someone was calling.

The windows of the apartment looked over the buckled remains of an asphalt field. The collapse of the neighboring building, subsequent looting, and the effects of many years of rain, sun, and wild animals had transformed it into a jungle of tall grass growing amid red clay, rubble, broken furniture, rotting wood.

Although they were far above, the two of them took care not to make any sudden movement that might draw attention to themselves. As Joseph peered out, he was surprised to see four figures below, picking their way through the shattered field. From their light-colored robes, they were clearly townspeople. A distance away, four bicycles were propped against a sagging chain-link fence.

"Do you think it's a Gleaning?" Esther asked from beside him.

Joseph shrugged. If it was, they both knew what that would signify, and it was not good.

The Gleaning entailed searching empty houses and stores, sifting through the wreckage of buildings in search of anything viable: weapons, medical supplies, charcoal, bedding, and nails. Everything was brought to the Source, where it was displayed on long tables. Levi's guards tallied the day's take and, depending on its perceived worth, added more water and foodstuffs to the town's portion. It was never very much, compared to what they paid for gasoline.

If the townspeople were Gleaning Joseph's ravaged home, that meant they were forced to reach even deeper into the outlying areas to try to meet the monthly quota. And that could only mean that Prin had been wrung dry, picked clean of anything of value.

Esther observed the people for a few moments. Chewing her fingernail, she turned for the door.

"I don't like this," was all she said.

"But where are you—"

"Don't worry. I'll be fine."

Joseph had no choice but to raise his hand in thanks and farewell. She gave a quick nod; then, without another word, she was gone.

In the lobby, she darted behind a crumbling wall and slipped out the giant gap that once held a large glass window. She slowed as she approached the backyard and hid in the dappled shade provided by some overgrown vines and bleak vegetation.

From there, she could hear faint voices and something she couldn't identify: a hollow twang that echoed in the canyon of the old hotel.

When she peered around the jagged corner, it took her a moment to locate the origin. In the distance, one of the trespassers was holding something, a ball that was dusty brick orange in color.

Now that she could see them clearly, Esther sensed that the four were not intent on anything nefarious; they were not even on a Gleaning. Whoever it was bounced the ball on the ground, once, twice, producing the strange sound. One of the others gestured at something a short distance away. It was a tall pole, with a metal ring attached near the top, with the shredded remains of a net clinging to it. The first one threw the ball at the hoop, but it fell short.

The four laughed. Within moments, they headed back across the lot to where their bicycles awaited. Soon, they were gone.

Then Esther heard something behind her and froze in place. Someone else was there.

A boy emerged from the towering, ruined mounds and stood where the four had been. By the peculiar way he dressed, Esther could tell he was a stranger. Like her, he chose not to wear the hooded robes that the people of Prin used as protection from the fierce sun. Instead, he wore a long-sleeved blue shirt and dusty jeans, with a shoulder pack that he slung to the ground. A battered, low-brimmed hat obscured his face. He had been watching the group at play, although it was impossible to say why.

He walked to the orange ball. Esther watched as he bent to pick it up.

With one hand, he effortlessly tossed the ball over his head. It landed in the hoop, the ragged net swishing. He turned to go. Before he did, though, he stopped and glanced back.

"You might as well come out," he said. "You ain't fooling anybody, hiding there like that."

His voice echoed amid the broken piles of brick and twisted metal.

From her hiding place, Esther started as if struck. She was stunned to have been spotted, and more than a little rattled. She stood poised, adrenaline coursing through her body, ready to escape should he make a move toward her.

But instead, the stranger only shrugged.

Then with one fluid movement, he mounted his battered bike and left.

FIVE

UNDER A STREETLAMP ON THE OUTSKIRTS OF PRIN, A BOY IN WHITE robes stood guard.

He shifted uncomfortably. Not accustomed to remaining still in the blazing sun for such a long stretch of time, he was perspiring heavily under his white sheets and headdress and felt more than a little nauseated. He was finding it impossible to keep his focus on the horizon. The heat caused shimmering waves of air to dance across the road, making it look as if hundreds of variants were attacking all at once. In addition, his sunglasses kept sliding down the bridge of his nose.

Early that morning, Rafe had called him together along with

a dozen others. Normally, the boy would have been getting ready for work. He had recently started a new Excavation on the eastern side of town and was preparing to spend the day deepening and widening the trench he and the rest of his team, including his pregnant partner, had just begun. Big-boned and quiet, the fifteen-year-old preferred Excavation to the other jobs in town because it was mindless and let you work by yourself.

But Prin, Rafe decided, needed sentries.

"We can't afford another attack," he told the assembled group. "So I'm putting you at each of the main roads that lead into town."

An unspoken question rippled through the crowd. Rafe seemed to anticipate what it was and held up his hands to reassure them.

"Sarah let us down about the weapons. But don't worry, you won't be unarmed. I seen to it."

That was when the boy noticed the crate by Rafe's feet, the one filled with a sorry-looking assortment of bats, corroded metal bars, and splintered table legs.

Now he adjusted his sweaty grip on the hollow steel pipe he was given and tried to imagine what it would feel like to hit someone with it.

He couldn't.

The boy guard rocked back and forth on his heels and he swiveled first to the left and then the right. A drop of sweat trickled into one eye, and he pushed his sunglasses up on his forehead so he could rub it away.

When he lowered them, he sensed a flicker of movement. Nearby, a dust-colored squirrel was watching him from the safety of some underbrush.

"Hey," he said, relieved at the distraction.

The boy set his pipe down, squatted on his haunches, and held out a hand, even though he didn't have anything to offer. He made a soft chucking sound, and the squirrel cocked its head at him, twitching its plumed tail.

The boy was glad no one else was around. Anyone in town would have tried to kill the creature, without a second thought. Unlike humans, animals were unaffected by the poison lurking in rainwater, and fresh meat of any kind was a rare and precious treat. But the sentry secretly liked squirrels and wished he had something to feed it. Maybe he had some forgotten crumbs somewhere in his clothing?

Slowly, in order not to scare the squirrel away, the boy kneeled, hoisting his robes so he could scrabble in his front pockets. One knee grazed the pipe, which rolled into the gutter, unnoticed and for the moment, forgotten.

"Ahh," said the boy at last. His fingers closed on a few gritty crumbs, which he removed and scattered on the ground.

The squirrel leaned forward on one paw, nose twitching, then appeared to make up its mind. Keeping its eyes on the boy, it darted forward in two, three quick movements, seized a morsel, then sat up and began to eat.

The boy eased back on his heels and smiled, satisfied. But after a few moments, the squirrel stopped chewing.

The tiny head jerked up and froze, black eyes staring at

some point in the far distance. Then with a flick of its tail, the animal bounded away and vanished in the tall weeds, leaving the rest of the crumbs untouched.

Still on his knees, the young guard frowned, puzzled. He glanced behind him and saw nothing. It made no sense.

But then again, he couldn't hear what was bearing down on him.

Not until it was too late.

Elsewhere, Caleb had reached the broken sign that said WELCOME TO PRIN.

The center of town itself still lay a half mile or so in the distance; he should be there within minutes. The main street appeared to be dotted with buildings, none more than a few stories high.

Caleb realized that the first thing he had to do was get water. He had nothing to trade with, but he was strong and handy; he knew he could work for what he needed.

Then he heard it.

Caleb braked and balanced stock-still, one foot on the ground, straining to identify the sound. As he did, he felt a familiar twisting sensation in his gut and a tingling in his hands and along the back of his neck.

Far away, someone was screaming.

For an instant, Caleb reeled. It was as if he was falling, tumbling backward into an abyss, a sucking vortex from which there was no escape. He gripped his handlebars so tightly his knuckles turned white, and the hot pavement beneath him started to bloom into an obliterating brightness.

Then he heard something else, a thin thread of noise that brought him back to himself. It was the sound of others shouting. Even though he couldn't make out the words, the voices seemed mocking and jubilant.

They sounded like mutants.

Could he be sure? He might be imagining things. He knew he'd been seeing them for weeks now, maybe even months. Since he first left home, he sensed them everywhere, from the corner of his eye, behind him, just around an abandoned car or bend in the road, their obscene, deformed faces silently watching him, jeering, before vanishing into nothingness. Sometimes they appeared in his dreams and when they did, he awoke in a sweat, crying out.

Several weeks ago, he had confronted mutants in the flesh, an unsuspecting group he had happened upon while they were hunting. He didn't hesitate to launch an ambush that left them unconscious and bleeding.

Now he made up his mind. Getting back on his bike, he swerved off the main road and onto a smaller street on his left.

It did not take him long to track the source of the noise. Although the screaming stopped, the other voices grew louder, providing him a rough guide to follow. He rode down one street, which led to a dead end; doubling back, he was able to find a parallel road, which led to another main thoroughfare. By now, he was so close, he was able to hear distinct voices.

"Pretty girl," said someone. This was followed by the

sound of others laughing.

With his backpack on, Caleb leaped off his bike and tossed it down in an abandoned yard, its front wheel still spinning. This was evidently once a residential block, with the remains of large two- and three-story houses on both sides nearly hidden by weeds and tall grass. Caleb cut diagonally across the last property and around to its backyard.

The yard led to an overgrown field, which bordered on the cracked parking lot of an abandoned supermarket. Caleb decided to head away from the voices. Realizing he was only one against at least three or four possible enemies, he calculated he would have to use surprise as an additional advantage. He skirted the open expanse and stuck to the perimeter, defined by an immense and straggling hedge.

As Caleb ran, his ears constantly adjusted to the thread of voices, trying to pinpoint their exact location. When he judged he was no more than fifteen feet away, he stopped. Only then did he work his way through the dense foliage, taking care not to disturb the branches around him. He noticed a small gap in the hedge. Through it, he was finally able to make out what was happening.

What he saw astonished and then repulsed him.

Five mutants stood in a loose circle looking up at a streetlamp. A boy hung from it, tilting forward at an unnatural and painful angle. His pitiful arms had been lashed together behind his back, and this rope had been tossed over the beam that extended high up the steel pole and then secured. From where he stood, Caleb could see the boy had been beaten. His face was bruised and puffy, and blood dripped from a corner of his mouth.

But what was most shocking was what the mutants had done to his body.

The boy had been stripped of most of his clothing, and his pale white skin, long unaccustomed to the burning rays of the sun, had been defaced with obscene drawings smeared in red clay. It took Caleb a moment to realize the boy had been turned into a repellent caricature of a girl, a grotesque and unspeakable travesty. A wig of sorts, made from some filthy and stringy object, sat askew on his head. The smell of wet earth was strong. The scarred and tattooed hands of the mutants were all dark, stained red with mud, and their mouths were open in harsh and mocking laughter.

The body hanged heavily, twisting a little in the breeze. At first, Caleb thought he must be dead; but when one of the mutants prodded the victim with a metal pipe, the thin sides heaved and the feet kicked feebly.

"She's pretty, all right," said one of the mutants. The rest laughed again, and one of them uttered an obscenity.

But Caleb no longer heard what they were saying. He was reaching into his backpack, searching for his weapon.

It was one of a kind. He had forged it over time and through much trial and error. Made of wood, metal, and rubber, it was the length of his forearm and had a crude wheel at the center, held firm on an axis. He kept it loaded: the six rods that fanned out from the wheel were each tipped with a shallow cup that held a jagged rock the size of a hen's egg. A taut rubber sling kept each rock in place.

It allowed him to shoot six rocks in as many seconds. He had used it once or twice, on his way to Prin. Now he prepared to employ it again.

From his hiding place, Caleb took aim at the nearest mutant, who stood facing away. He gave the wheel a sharp spin and as he did, he snapped each sling, firing off three rocks in quick succession. The first two hit the mutant in the head, and the last in the back of the neck. His knees buckled and he slumped to the ground.

As he calculated, the element of surprise had given Caleb a small but critical advantage. In the confused moment that it took the other mutants to register what had happened, he had time to take aim at his second target. He again set the wheel into swift motion and deployed his last three projectiles. While this mutant raised a hand at the last second to protect himself, it didn't matter: The rocks came too fast, all three striking his head, and he too was knocked unconscious.

Caleb was scrambling in his backpack, trying to reload, when one of the remaining mutants spied him through the dense undergrowth. She gave an angry hiss, like an animal. Then she pointed at Caleb, her mouth open in a shriek of fury like a hawk, some bird of prey, and at that, all three mutants rushed the hedge.

The first one took a running leap and dived headlong through the dense growth at Caleb. At the impact, his weapon flew from his hands and he was knocked backward and onto the hot pavement of the parking lot, the wiry and muscular mutant on top of him, clawing at his throat, his face, trying to subdue him until the others arrived.

But instead of fighting the momentum, Caleb knew enough to work with it instead. As he curled into a ball and continued to roll backward, he seized the mutant by her scant tunic, pulling in his knees until his feet rested against her stomach. Then he released his grip while violently pushing out with both legs; the mutant was catapulted over his head. A second later, she landed behind him with a sickening crunch.

As Caleb leaped to his feet, another mutant rushed at him with a rock in an upheld fist. Caleb used his elbow to strike his wrist, loosening his grip; he then swiveled, shooting out his leg and driving his heel into the mutant's knee. With a scream as much of surprise as of pain, the mutant pitched forward, off balance. Again, Caleb used momentum, this time to push the mutant farther downward while driving his knee up into his face as hard as he could. There was a satisfying crack of bone, followed by a hot gush of blood.

Caleb turned. His vision blurry, sweat streaming down his face, it took him a moment to see that the fifth mutant, the largest, was running away.

Dimly, he realized that he should let him escape.

Caleb had won this round, and he should tend to the boy who was still hanging from the streetlamp, who clearly needed his help.

But it was as if he was aflame, burning with a righteous fever that would not be satisfied until each mutant was hunted down, one by one, and made to suffer. A bloodlust was upon him. He took off in pursuit and now felt the glad fire in his legs; the mutant, a fast runner with a good head start, glanced back and the shock on his face was obvious. Caleb was nearly upon him.

The mutant swerved suddenly. He had reached a group of commercial buildings and, now frantic, he intended to escape that way instead. He clawed at the nearest wall and began to climb; Caleb leaped to grab his bare foot and only just missed. But any relief the mutant might have felt was short lived, for Caleb also began to scale the wall, moving with relentless speed.

The mutant pulled himself onto the roof; seconds later, Caleb did the same. By then, the mutant had sprinted to the far end and now balanced on the edge of the parapet; he was gauging the distance to the neighboring building. He glanced back with a look of pure panic and as Caleb ran forward, he pinwheeled his arms and took a standing leap.

Caleb didn't hesitate. He was aware that he had no clue as to how far he had to jump and that he was at least five or six floors above the ground; a misstep would be fatal. Yet he no longer cared.

He put on speed, then at the roof's edge, made a blind, running leap. He easily cleared the neighboring parapet and landed hard, instinctively rolling into a sideways somersault to blunt the impact. He came out of the roll without stopping, still running.

The mutant—only halfway across the roof—looked back.

He had a setting sun tattooed across his face; beneath it, his expression was one of shock. Yet as much as fear, there was admiration in his voice.

"You have defeated four of my best," he said. Caleb realized that this one was the leader. "Who taught you?" he called, panting.

"I taught myself," Caleb said. The hatred and contempt in his voice were terrifying.

The mutant nodded, impressed despite himself. He was cornered now; there was nowhere to run, no other buildings nearby. But as Caleb stepped forward, the mutant hesitated for only a second.

Then he jumped off the roof.

Caleb ran to where he was standing and looked down. The mutant was lucky that the alley was strewn with crates and boxes; a pile of cardboard had broken his fall. Still, Caleb was satisfied to see him limping badly as he escaped down the alley and out of sight.

It was a team of Harvesters who first saw him.

A stranger walked down the main road that led into town. The townspeople viewed newcomers with suspicion, for supplies were scarce enough without interlopers looking for more. This one pushed a battered bicycle, across which was sprawled a body, legs and arms dangling. A dirty white sheet was partly draped around it and already, dark red patches—blood? clay?—were seeping through.

Caleb was bringing the brutalized guard back to Prin.

The Harvesters slowed their own bicycles and came to a stop.

"Mutants?" one of them asked, and Caleb nodded.

The Harvesters exchanged glances as one by one, they recognized the victim. A boy gave an involuntary cry, his eyes round with shock.

"Trey?" he said in a hoarse whisper. "Is he—"

"He's still breathing," said Caleb. "Barely."

The four dismounted and fell in line behind Caleb. There was no need to ask the details; everyone understood what they needed to know. But without being prompted, one of them handed over her water bottle and another took control of Caleb's bicycle so he had a moment to drink.

By the time they approached the center of town, there were at least two dozen townspeople accompanying them. There was virtually no sound; as newcomers joined in, they were briefly told of what happened in whispers, and then the silence resumed. Without speaking, all had done the unthinkable act of leaving their jobs, and beneath their robes and headdresses and sunglasses, their faces were shocked and somber.

One of them, the guard's partner, walked up front with Caleb. At first glance, Aima seemed stoic, a sturdy, heavily pregnant fifteen-year-old accustomed to unexpected hardship. But beneath her dusty head cloth, her eyes were dark holes in an ashen face. She gripped her unconscious partner's hand, massive in her small one, and stroked it with her thumb, as if trying to will him back to health.

Word had been sent ahead of them and by the time the

procession reached Prin, Rafe and a small crowd were outside, waiting. Several townspeople managed to lift the boy and carry him into his storefront home. Once inside, Aima and her friends would wash him and tend to his wounds as best as they knew how.

Rafe was taken aback to see a mere stranger followed by the citizens of Prin. As he stepped forward to greet him, he cleared his throat and attempted to take control.

"Thank you for bringing home one of ours," Rafe said. Even to his own ears, his words sounded falsely hearty.

The stranger said nothing and merely bowed his head in acknowledgment.

"Did you see who done it?" continued Rafe. "Or did he run off before you got there?"

"I seen them," said Caleb.

Rafe nodded. "So it was more than one," he said, then turned to spit in the dust. "That makes Trey an even bigger hero. I bet he gave them a good fight with those weapons. Still, we're glad you come along when you did. Must've helped scare them off."

Rafe's voice shook and again he cleared his throat, to cover it. He was aware that everyone in town was not only staring at him; they were judging him, weighing his words.

It was, after all, his idea that guards be posted that morning, alone, and without any kind of training or backup. In retrospect, even he had to admit that perhaps it was a bad impulse. He had acted rashly, without a real plan. Without weapons, *real* weapons from the Source that idiot Sarah had promised then failed to deliver, what other choice did he have?

Now Trey's partner stopped as she headed indoors to tend to the boy. In front of Rafe, her eyes blazing, Aima spoke in a low, accusatory voice.

"Trey never fought those mutants and you know it," she said. "He's too gentle. And you sent him there alone. You sent him out there and now he's—" A sudden spasm of anger contorted her face and she pushed past him to get inside.

Rattled, Rafe cleared his throat, hoping no one else had heard. He was now aware that the stranger was speaking.

"—wonder if you could give me some information," Caleb was saying. "I have some private business to look into."

"Of course, of course," said Rafe, with a wave of his hand. He was not listening; too busy worrying what the townspeople were thinking of him, he had already dismissed the stranger to the realm of the unimportant.

But at that moment, there was a new commotion.

A small boy and even smaller girl had just arrived, and they were both talking to whoever would listen. They were breathless and shrill, words tumbling over one another in their haste to speak.

"We seen it—" said the boy.

"We was hiding," said the girl. "We heard a noise so we hid. Then we seen it—"

"There was five of them. He was shooting rocks, like this, one after another—"

"They had Trey tied to a rope. He looked bad, he wasn't moving—"

"—and he beat four. The last one tried to get away . . . but he chased him, too—"

"—five against one. He beat them all. And we seen it—"

"Five against one."

The townspeople murmured, trying to understand. Bewildered, Rafe stepped forward and leaned down to address the two, with a feeling of dread.

"Who beat the mutants?" he said.

At this, the two stopped talking, self-conscious at being the center of attention. But then, they both noticed Caleb, standing to one side. The girl's face flushed and the boy broke into a smile as he raised his finger, pointing through the crowd.

"Him. Him over there. He's who done it."

SIX

THE CELEBRATION LASTED ALL AFTERNOON.

Rafe had sent out orders, allowing everyone in Prin to take the rest of the day off from work. This was to guarantee maximum attendance—ostensibly, to pay homage and show gratitude to Prin's new hero.

The real reason was that Rafe wanted to ensure the entire town gave him credit for this turn of events.

As a result, the aisles of what had once been a supermarket were crowded. Even Sarah was there, whom Rafe had invited despite his lingering anger, as well as her misfit younger sister, Esther.

The stranger sat next to him, of course, in the seat of honor at the single table in the front of the store.

At first, Caleb was so silent and awkward, Rafe wondered if the reports of his astonishing heroism were true. For a moment, he even considered that he might be simple in the head. But when food and water were placed in front of Caleb—only he was served, as befitted the guest of honor—he started to eat voraciously. Soon, Rafe figured, he was bound to open up. And then they could get down to the real business at hand.

"We wanted to show our appreciation to you," Rafe said after Caleb slowed down. "For once, somebody not only agrees with me about the mutants . . . he ain't scared to follow through."

Caleb cleared his throat. Then he spoke so softly, even Rafe had to cock his head to make out what he was saying.

"Nobody wants to take the fight to the mutants more than me," he said. When his words were conveyed through the room, there was a murmur of approval.

"But this dinner ain't *just* about appreciation," continued Rafe. "I'd like to make you a proposition." As usual, he, too, lowered his voice, so people leaned forward. "I'd like you to stay on awhile. How about you teach us what you know about fighting and such?"

For the first time, Caleb turned to his host and Rafe was startled by the intensity of his gaze.

"Do you have any *real* weapons?" Caleb asked in his soft voice. "Any hunting knives? Shotguns?"

Rafe flushed.

"No," he said pointedly. He hoped Sarah was listening. "I'm afraid we got to take on the mutants without those. But I should add—in exchange, we're willing to put you up and feed you. How does *that* sound?"

Rafe was smiling, a bit desperately now. Caleb appeared to be thinking. After what seemed an eternity, he gave a slight nod. At this, the room began to buzz with excitement.

"But I have conditions," he said, and everyone fell silent.

This time, he looked up, addressing the entire room. "If any mutants come near town, we will attack them, and attack them hard. Any survivors will be imprisoned. There can be no contact of any kind between townspeople and mutants; if anyone is caught socializing with a mutant, they will also be imprisoned."

Now the silence was broken. Slowly, a hum of excitement in the room built to a ragged crescendo of approval. One by one, the people of Prin started to cheer, thump the floor, and bang on the metal shelves, whistling loudly. After a while, the place was utter bedlam.

Uneasily, Rafe watched this. He stood and quickly put his arm around Caleb, making sure to share in the applause.

Only one guest was not celebrating.

The person had been standing alone by the front door and now, quietly, slipped outside into the early evening while no one else was paying any attention.

It was late when Caleb staggered out onto the main street. He was full to bursting, more sated than he had been in years.

He was also exhausted, with a heavy bone-weariness. After months of hard travel, he had reached his destination, and he had been welcomed. A good night's sleep under a roof would prepare him for what he had to do.

Caleb turned onto the deserted street where he had left his bicycle, chained to a rusted parking meter. Then he froze.

Somebody was kneeling next to his bike.

Even from the back, Caleb could tell it was a young boy, small and slight, wearing a red sweatshirt with the hood drawn around his head. Gloves on his hands, he was slashing at the back tire with some instrument.

Caleb tackled the boy from behind. Putting him in a chokehold, he dragged him away from the bike. The vandal was struggling, flailing with his free hand—he was striking out with his weapon, an ugly piece of broken glass—but Caleb was able to shake it loose, then kick it away with his boot.

The two struggled in near silence—Caleb trying to subdue the boy, who continued to fight wildly, despite the obvious difference in size and strength. Finally, the smaller one managed to twist his head into the crook of Caleb's arm while seizing his thumb and yanking backward; with a cry of pain, Caleb loosened his grip and the other slithered out of his grasp, his hood ripping. The two faced each other, the boy still choking for breath, massaging his throat.

Only it wasn't a boy. It was a girl.

The girl who had been spying on him near the hoop on the pole, behind the building.

And she looked furious.

In truth, Esther was angriest with herself: annoyed that she was inattentive enough to get caught before she could even begin her task, much less finish it. She cursed herself and shot a quick glance at the piece of glass, lying a few feet away. However, the stranger caught her look and made it there first. He brought his heel down on it, smashing it with a dull crunch.

He had been staring at Esther the whole time with an unreadable expression. This, more than the fact that he had nearly strangled her, made her deeply uncomfortable.

"I seen you before," he said. "Behind that building on the edge of town?"

She returned the stare; then nodded defiantly.

"What were you doing?" he asked, indicating his bicycle.

"What do you think?" Her tone was derisive.

The stranger nodded, as if in agreement. "Why?"

He didn't sound angry or sarcastic. He asked as if he was curious about her reasons.

Esther started to reply, then stopped, confused. She had never been asked to explain herself before and now found it difficult to find the exact words.

"To stop you," was all she could say.

The stranger was kneeling, inspecting his tires for any damage. At the sight, Esther flushed with a familiar surge of resentment. Like her sister, like most of the others in town, he was ignoring her, she assumed, because she was too childish and emotional to be worthy of his attention.

But she was wrong.

"So you heard what I said in there?" He did not look at her, but seemed as if he was addressing the bicycle.

As Esther hesitated, he glanced up. She nodded.

"And I take it you didn't like any of it?"

Her face flushed with anger.

"The variants got enough troubles without you giving them more," she muttered.

The rays of the setting sun hit his face, throwing its angles into deep relief and turning his eyes into live coals. In an instant, he looked older than anyone on earth, older than anyone could possibly grow to be.

"Variants," he said.

He nearly spit the word, and Esther was unnerved by the depth of loathing that lay beneath it.

"Why do you hate them so much?" she asked. It was an honest question, more bewildered than angry. "My best friend is one and she's a good person. How can you hate someone you don't even know?"

The boy seemed taken aback by her question. *Had anyone ever asked him before?* Esther wondered. Then he spoke as openly as she had.

"I had a partner and baby son," he said. "In a town a ways from here. One morning, I was out foraging for supplies. Mutants broke in. They killed my partner, Miri, cut her up so bad I couldn't recognize her. They burned our place to the ground. And they took our son. Kai."

Protests bubbled up in Esther's throat. Before she could speak, he continued.

"One got left behind," he said. "He was badly burned, and

the others just ran away. I beat him but he couldn't tell me much. I found an empty can of accelerant, the stuff that makes a fire burn faster. Able Accelerant, that was the name. The mutant said they got it around these parts, that's all he knew. That was the last thing he said."

The last rays of sun had turned the sky as red as blood.

"That's why it's no good trying to stop me," he said. He spoke as if he had no choice. And yet, he seemed to hesitate, as if waiting for a response.

Did he want her to stop him? Esther wondered. *To talk him out of it?* For a moment she thought she had a glimpse of who he really was beneath his hatred and anger. In his own way, maybe he was as hurt and isolated as she was.

Before she could reply, the stranger mounted his bicycle and disappeared into the night.

Watching him go, Esther felt torn. His story must be true. The ghastly murder of his partner and the abduction of his child: it would be impossible to invent such horror. His pain and grief were as searing as a fresh wound, and part of her wanted to run after him, to reach out to him somehow, and comfort him.

At the same time, she believed he must have been mistaken. Obviously someone else had destroyed his family and stolen his son; some unknown variety of human monster and not the variants. The variants had no reason to kill and destroy. They may have faced difficulties and hardships, but they were better than the others because they did not covet. They did not need anything from anyone. It couldn't have been them.

Yet why would the stranger lie? His words had stirred confusion that she found hard to admit, even to herself. He had made her face the one question she had never asked herself, despite the mounting violence . . .

Why were the variants attacking Prin?

Esther heard a sound behind her and turned to see that the last of the townspeople were leaving the supermarket. Compared to the heavy spirits earlier in the afternoon, the mood now seemed lighthearted, even festive. Looking at the smiling, chattering faces of her neighbors, Esther felt sick. She realized with a fresh shock what impact the stranger's words would have on life in Prin.

All mutants will be attacked on sight, and attacked hard.

Any survivors will be imprisoned.

Anyone caught socializing with mutants will also be imprisoned.

For a moment, Esther felt dizzy. Then she gathered herself and made up her mind. No matter what doubts the stranger had instilled in her, there were more pressing matters at hand. She must warn Skar, before she came to town as usual. She had to save her friend.

But how?

It was late at night. What was more, the variants lived many miles away to the north, in the mountainous region. Esther owned no bicycle and to walk there would take more than a day.

She wheeled around, desperate.

Several people were walking toward her, indistinguishable in their white robes. Yet she recognized one of the voices.

"Where are you going?" Eli called. He sounded so jovial.

She couldn't respond. Even if she could trust him, which she couldn't, she had no way to put into words how she felt. But it did not matter, for he was not really waiting for her reply.

"Were you at the meeting?" He was as excited as a little boy. Caleb's words had given him hope and now, grotesquely, he wanted to share that hope with her.

In an instant, Esther realized what she must do. It would again require manipulating Eli, playing off his interest in her. She had done so before, when she had appealed to him wordlessly and he had understood, leading the rest of the Harvesting team away. She felt a twinge of guilt and also wondered, fleetingly, when she would have to repay the growing list of favors he had done for her.

She would worry about all that later.

"Can I borrow your bicycle?" she asked. "Please?"

Esther leaned over the handlebars, riding swiftly.

On the outskirts of Prin, she passed mountains of rubble that had once been restaurants, a shopping center, a block of offices. Behind her, the floodlights of the Source emitted a soft glow that lingered for what seemed like miles. But soon it was dark, and then darker still. Esther had only the moon and stars to light her way.

She rode along what had once been another highway, steering around abandoned cars and trucks, sodden piles of leaves and old clothing, crumpled road signs that dangled overhead from bent steel poles. Several times, she was forced to dismount and walk her bicycle around gaping crevices where the road had sheared away. Occasionally, she heard the mysterious cries of unseen animals and noticed flittering shapes that darted through the inky air. Once, a hulking form lumbered across the road ahead of her. But they did not slow her down.

Esther's mind was whirling.

She had to warn Skar. She would need to warn all of the variants of the stranger's arrival and the harsh new laws now in effect. For their safety, they all needed to steer clear of Prin.

But would they believe her? They might accuse her of being a spy, or being deliberately sent with false rumors.

After several hours, Esther paused by the side of the road to get her bearings. To one side, visible through the trees, glittered the shoreline of what used to be a vast lake. A good portion of it had dried up, exposing the parched land underneath, the skeletons of fish and birds it had digested, the occasional fiberglass cooler or hamper, destroyed. The rest of the lake was covered with a black, oozing substance as thick as a tarp and as shiny as glass. In the distance she saw a cluster of foothills surrounding a single tall peak. This was her destination.

It was nearly dawn.

Esther had been traveling for hours now and each downward stroke of the pedal was agony; her entire body trembled with exhaustion. Yet she was encouraged by the fact that although the hardest terrain was ahead, she was nearly there.

Esther glided up the exit ramp off the highway to a lesser road, and then another after that. She had only been this way once before, and that was several years ago. As a result, she made a few wrong turns.

Eventually, however, she found what she was looking for. Esther turned off the paved surface and onto a rough dirt trail that cut through the densely forested mountainside. It was steep and rocky; after several minutes, she was forced to dismount and proceed on foot, pushing the bicycle by its handlebars. She reached a withered tree with a white mark upon it. There she turned. The trail wound a bit more until it ended at a clearing, carved out of a plateau.

This was where the variants lived.

Esther had not planned to arrive at dawn, but she realized it was a fortunate coincidence. Early day was hunting time for the tribe, and the camp seemed deserted. If Skar was around, they would be able to talk in private.

From her hiding place, she softly gave their secret whistle and waited. Within moments, someone emerged from one of the many shacks grouped across the clearing. It was Skar, who glanced around, clearly puzzled. Then she noticed Esther.

Surprised yet delighted to see her, Skar ran to her friend and gave her a hug. She smiled, her parted lips revealing her little teeth.

"Esther!" she exclaimed. "I can't believe it's you! Why are you here?"

But in her haste to warn her friend and tell her all she knew, Esther had paid scant attention to her surroundings. Now, she was aware that something had changed. She stopped talking and stood still, gazing around.

When she was here before, it had only been a brief visit.

At the time, she was met with suspicion by the few variants Skar introduced her to, and so she didn't stay long. Yet she remembered what it looked like. There were makeshift shacks made of animal skins, salvaged planks, and saplings. In the center of the clearing were smoking vestiges of stick fires. Bones and other uneaten bits of animals had been strewn about, no longer recognizable.

But now, while the shacks were still there, there were no fires. Instead, Esther noticed what had taken their place.

There were large cardboard crates piled by each tent, each with crisp black lettering that Esther had trouble reading. As she looked around, her unbelieving eyes picked up other details, items that did not belong here and therefore made no sense: a clothesline pinned with dozens of shirts, pants, and dresses in bright colors and sturdy fabric. New shoes—sneakers, boots, sandals—lined up outside each door. Shiny kettles and cooking pots of all sizes. And under a canopy made from a rubberized tarp was a giant pyramid of food: oversize packages of dried beans, sacks of flour, plastic gallon jugs of water.

"What?" said Skar, puzzled. "What's wrong?"

Esther couldn't speak. Instead, she pointed to the food, the clothing, the crates.

"What—what is all this?" she said.

"This?" Skar turned and looked. Then she said, innocently, "It's food! You know, and other stuff!"

Esther looked closely at her friend now. At the base of Skar's ears and hanging around her tattooed throat and wrists were new and shiny pieces of jewelry, colorful stones and bright metals. She had never seen Skar—or any variant—adorn herself like this.

"And where did you get *this*?" she said, flicking at the bangles.

Skar touched her ears and throat, growing self-conscious and her smile less confident. "Well . . . from the Source. Like the rest of it." She gestured at the boxes as if in confused apology.

Esther nodded, very slowly.

Her mind was whirling. What did this connection, this alliance mean? The variants did not, of course, Harvest gasoline, nor was there much left to collect even if they did. So what had the variants exchanged with Levi for this massive payment of goods? What had he wanted from them? What had they done to earn it?

The sun was higher in the morning sky; the heat began to beat down. Esther had forgotten to wear her sunglasses and was forced to hold up a hand, to protect her sight. Soon, she had to shut her eyes.

All she could see was Caleb's face.

PART TWO

SEVEN

ALTHOUGH IT WAS MORNING, THE SUN BURNED WHITE HOT IN THE DIRTY yellow sky. Yet inside the Source, it was perpetual twilight, dark and cool.

To Slayd, the interior of the gigantic white building always felt like a cave . . . and he did not care for caves at all. They were damp, unwholesome places, dappled with pockets of darkness that harbored all that was unnatural, possibly deadly, and to him, disgusting. In caves, he had seen oversize spiders, patches of mottled mold growing on wet rock, snakes with pinprick eyes and pale skin, and mice that fluttered through the air with leathery wings. His skin crawled at the thought.

In many ways, Slayd felt the same way about Levi.

Although technically a norm, Levi resembled no one the variant leader had ever seen before. He was more a cave-dwelling animal than an actual human, with his black eyes, his dandified black clothing, and silver jewelry. His skin was so pale, it seemed to glow in the gloom, and it emitted a sharp and musky smell that turned Slayd's stomach.

More disturbing, Levi's skin was soft; even his bones seemed soft, revoltingly so. It was almost more than the variant could bear just to look at him, much less grasp his hand in greeting.

The two had been sitting across from one another in Levi's office, a large, trembling room with wire walls that the boy called a "freight elevator." A single electric light overhead threw deep shadows into the surrounding cavernous space. Perhaps because Slayd was the one to request this meeting, Levi kept the variant leader waiting for nearly an hour and now seated him on a smaller, inferior chair that was dwarfed by the massive desk separating them. Still, Levi continued to delay, appearing to examine some papers on his desk, a white cloth pressed to his mouth.

Slayd was keenly aware of these deliberate slights. Yet rather than be angered by such rudeness, he knew enough to hold his temper and stay watchful instead. It was clear that Levi was doing it on purpose, to trigger some sort of emotional response from him, throw him off balance. He wouldn't give him that satisfaction.

Yet even though he sat in silence, Slayd had already made

a mental note of the precise location of the five guards that surrounded them. Should the situation deteriorate, he had calculated the quickest way to escape.

When Levi finally looked up, Slayd wasted no time and got to the point.

"I'm here to request the rest of our payment," he said. "For the latest action. The one with the smaller band."

"I heard about it," Levi said. His voice was polite, almost bland.

"We've been waiting for another shipment," said Slayd, his tone as even as that of his host. Whatever game Levi was playing, the variant was more than prepared to meet him. "What arrived was less than we agreed to."

"What you did wasn't worth the full payment," Levi replied.

He was finding it difficult to look at the mutant leader. As always, Levi found everything about Slayd—his deformed features, his scarred and tattooed skin, his small and pointed teeth—freakish and repellent. He couldn't bear his sexless quality. Slayd called himself male, yet looked no different from the so-called females of his tribe: hairless, smooth-faced, and slight of build. Worst of all was his smell, which was sharp and acrid like an animal, with a tendency to linger long after he had gone. Once again, Levi pressed the cologne-sprinkled handkerchief to his face and inhaled.

Slayd was nodding. Then he bowed his head and spread his hands in an obsequious manner that Levi did not believe for an instant. "We did as you requested," he said. "We escalated the violence."

"I'm not talking about what I requested," replied Levi. He realized his tone was harsher than he intended, revealing too much; he softened it. "I'm talking about the stranger. I understand he defeated you and four of your best single-handed."

"Ah," said the mutant leader. Again, his air of polite apology seemed false to Levi. "But we did not know he was coming."

At this, a slight frown creased Levi's forehead. "Even so, I'm surprised," he said. "Five against one? I can't imagine that should be so hard to handle."

Slayd shrugged. "My people and I had specific instructions, and those instructions did not include taking on another. Especially one who turned out to be so skilled a warrior."

"But everyone knows you people are the best fighters," said Levi, persisting.

Again, Slayd shrugged. "That may be," he said. "All I can suggest is that perhaps my people might work harder in the future if they were paid the full amount. And maybe even a bit more."

Levi now rocked back in his chair, silent.

The variant watched him, making sure his expression gave nothing away. If Levi was changing the terms of their agreement, then he would counter and change them too. There was, he thought, no harm trying.

"Well," said Levi after a moment. "That's certainly a conversation we could have further down the line."

Slayd frowned, annoyed by this evasion. "We are—" he began, but Levi cut him off.

"But the truth is, I'd only consider increasing your pay if

you people managed to do a better job," he said.

Slayd felt his face flush with annoyance.

"I told you, we did everything that was asked," he said, his control slipping. "Two of my people were seriously injured as a result. If you pay us more goods, perhaps it would *begin* to make up for the loss to my tribe. It would certainly not cover what we have lost in goodwill with the people of Prin by attacking them, the reasons for which you never once explained. That alone is worth an increase."

Levi didn't even look at Slayd now, finding that his patience was wearing thin. *Explain?* he thought, with disbelief. *It would be like justifying yourself to a dog.* Instead, he ignored the remark.

"I am not only talking about the *recent* attack," said Levi. "It's everything. What about that other job from before? The job I asked you to do far from Prin?"

But Slayd was shaking his head. "Why do you mention that now? We brought you the child," he said. "We fulfilled our end of the deal. What else was required?"

"You were supposed to kill *both* parents," replied Levi. "You told me the father survived. I'm surprised, Slayd. I thought you people were capable of handling such a simple job."

The variant leader smirked.

"We are," he replied. "But it was not my people who carried it out."

"I don't understand," said Levi.

Now Slayd was grinning, relishing the look of confusion on the norm's face. "It was another tribe. They made the mistake. Not my people."

"But—" began Levi, and this time, he was interrupted by the variant.

"I hired them," Slayd said. This time, he did not bother to hide not only his triumph, but also his anger—anger at Levi's rudeness, his condescension, and presumed superiority. "It was too far for my people, too much trouble. Not worth what you offered."

"And you paid these others . . . out of the fee I paid you?" said Levi, his voice rising. He, too, had dropped the veneer of politeness, the pretense of civilization; he was openly furious. "You dare to attempt profiting from the jobs I give you by hiring others?"

"Profit?" The mutant seemed to spit out the word. "When my people are starving? You dare to call that a profit?"

Incensed, Levi was about to rise and call for his guards. But with the remarkable self-restraint that had served him for so many years, he instead remained motionless.

Levi realized he was foolish to respond emotionally to what was a business disagreement. True, any norm alive would be angered by the effrontery of the savage in front of him. Such arrogance was unacceptable and at some point, Levi would make certain to pay it back, harshly and many times over.

But not quite yet.

As much as it pained him to admit it, Levi still needed the mutant leader. Since the Source had started running out of food and water, Slayd and his tribe had been critical in helping Levi carry out his plan. He had to drive the people out of Prin. If the residents believed they were making the decision to leave themselves, it would lead to a cleaner and simpler transition than if he were to try using force. With control over an endless supply of water, Levi would then be sole owner and occupant of the town. All he needed was for Sarah to bring him the missing book, which would tell him exactly where to dig. Until she did, Levi would have to endure Slayd's insolence.

Levi was aware that Slayd was watching him and so he forced himself to smile. Then he chuckled, as if enjoying the punchline to a good joke. At this, the mutant visibly relaxed, and in doing so, missed the involuntary twitch in the norm's jaw.

"Of course," Levi said, "perhaps I should be taking all of this as a compliment. You seem to have picked up a few of my tricks, Slayd. Why shouldn't you hire others to do your dirty work for you?"

Slayd inclined his head in acknowledgment. "Any comparison to you is a compliment we do not deserve," he murmured. "But as to the subject of our payment. May we possibly assume . . . ?"

Levi nodded. "The balance will be paid in full as soon as you leave. With an extra half case of water thrown in."

He noticed with distaste that even though the mutant leader kept his gaze lowered, he couldn't control his jubilation. Slayd was grinning openly. Now he got to his feet, his hand extended, but Levi remained where he was, his elbows propped up on his desk and his fingers steepled.

"All of this is on one condition," Levi said. "Will you and your people be ready for another excursion soon?"

"Certainly," said Slayd. "Can we also assume . . . ?"

"I will raise the fee," said Levi after a moment. "One half case of clothing, one of grain, and one of water." He watched as a look of stunned happiness crossed the mutant's animal face. The effect was both grotesque and comical. "But this one must be special," Levi added. "I want you to use something different than the usual clubs and stones. This attack needs to be much more . . ." He traced something ineffable in the air with his pale hand and let the sentence hang, unfinished. "Do you understand what I mean?"

The mutant smiled. Then the two shook hands.

Slayd was escorted to the door. He was given back his knife, his bicycle. After checking to see that no norms were nearby, he pedaled back toward the variant camp miles away. Jubilant at the thought of the extra payment, he relished his victory over the clever and arrogant Levi. It would make for a good story to tell to the village elders that night, he thought.

Back at the Source, no one saw him go. Not even Levi watched from his hidden window.

He was too busy calculating his costs. True, he did not anticipate the bonus he had just promised to Slayd. Even so, in the long run, the terror he had purchased with a handshake would be a bargain even if it were two or three times the price paid. For fear was like fire, a powerful force that could sweep unchecked through a town and drive everything living from its path.

And if all worked out as planned, that was exactly what was going to happen.

* * *

The plume of smoke rose almost imperceptibly in the midday sky. Without even looking, Esther knew it was there. But instead, she pedaled harder and tried to keep her eyes trained on Sarah, who rode her purple bicycle in front of her.

That morning, using a combination of guilt and begging, her sister had managed to talk Esther into taking part in the Harvesting they had both been assigned to. She even managed to find a bicycle for her. Resentful at having to work at all, Esther was nevertheless aware that she was down to her last warning, and any more work violations would result in an automatic Shunning.

"Hurry up," Sarah called over her shoulder, from far ahead. Her voice was anxious. "You're going too slow."

But Esther found it difficult to ignore the signals, which had been coming all day. They had begun early in the morning and at least in Esther's eyes, had become more and more insistent, reproachful. Helplessly, she peeked upward. Although she knew it was impossible, she was sure she could smell the far-off smoke, the pervasive scent of damp and rotted pine branches tossed onto a fire.

It smelled like a rebuke.

There had never been a day when Esther had not scanned the horizon for such signs. Long before the recent tensions in town and the growing ugliness between townspeople and variants, the secret code was how she and Skar had always communicated.

The signals were few and simple, meant to convey only the

most basic and crucial information:

Meet me now. I am returning to my home. All is well. I need to speak with you. The situation is urgent.

But Esther's surprise visit to the variant camp had changed how she felt about her friend. She did not know why. All morning, she had been struggling to sort her jumbled thoughts about seeing the goods from the Source and make sense of her churning emotions.

Skar had little to say when pressed for information. She had always been this way, the kind of person who bent to authority and accepted what was going on around her without doubt or question. Unable to give any satisfactory answers to Esther's questions, she instead tried to placate her friend and change the subject, which only made Esther angrier. It was the first time the two girls had ever quarreled or parted on bad terms.

Even now, Esther couldn't stop thinking about it.

By now, she had lagged far behind the others, despite Sarah's best efforts to shepherd her. She bicycled hard and soon caught up with the group. Besides her sister and herself, there were three others on the Harvesting team, all girls a year or so older than Esther. One of the girls, thin and haughty, was named Rhea; she was the team's Supervisor. When Esther joined them, panting, Rhea glanced at the others and raised an eyebrow, and everyone laughed.

Sarah, blushing furiously, gestured at Esther to stand near her.

"Where were you?" she hissed. Esther only shrugged.

Today's destination appeared to be what was once a large

field that lay to the side of the highway. Over the years, the sun had hardened the land, which was now covered with an intricate network of fissures and cracks. Strange pools of relatively clean, white sand were scattered across the field at intervals. The remains of a large building, once resplendent, sagged in the distance, past a broken sign reading SKYVIEW LINKS. A windowless structure, no more than a large metal shed, stood closer to the highway. Its doors were held fast with chains and heavy locks.

"In here," said Rhea, nodding at the shed.

The shack was most likely a garage, the kind of structure that housed cars, motorcycles, and other gas-filled vehicles. Judging from the heavy scuff marks on the doors and the locks themselves, it was obvious that others had tried here without success. But today, the team had brought a crowbar with them. After repeated efforts by all five, they succeeded in smashing open the locks.

Inside, the team found a row of boxlike vehicles. They were not much bigger than bicycles, only with four wheels, and were clearly meant to carry two passengers on their cracked leather seats. The side of each vehicle contained a rusted metal cap.

Elated, Rhea and her team tried to unscrew the caps in order to get to the gas inside; but the job was harder than they expected. And even once they managed to pry them off, it turned out that the tanks were nearly empty. For all of their time and effort, they collected no more than half a bottle's worth of gas.

Throughout, Esther attempted to participate. She dutifully

took her turn with the crowbar, tried to open the tanks, and helped coil away the rubber tubing once the small amount of gas had been Harvested. But her mind was not on it.

"Try to be friendly," Sarah implored her in a whisper. Their work done for now, the team was on a break, sitting in a loose circle in the shade of an abandoned truck in their dusty robes and eating the meager lunch they had brought. The air was heavy with humidity, a sure sign of an oncoming storm. "They're not so bad. Try talking to them." But Esther made a face.

"About what?" she whispered back.

Sarah shook her head hopelessly. Then she turned back to the others and made a great show of listening as she laughed and nodded.

Esther couldn't understand why her sister bothered. It was apparent the three others had little use for Sarah and even less for Esther. Not that she minded; as far as she could tell, their conversation was worthless, less interesting than the droning of bees. One girl boasted about her recipe for wheat porridge. Another described a tattered bedspread stolen from a recent Gleaning and how it matched her one curtain. And then there were the endless, tedious anecdotes about their men, for all three were partnered.

When the gossip turned to partnerings, Rhea pointedly leaned close to the other two girls and whispered. After a moment, the three shared a harsh laugh, glancing sideways at Sarah. The older girl acted as if she was in on the joke, smiling and bobbing her head, even though it was clearly at her expense.

At seventeen, Sarah was an old maid, long past the age of

partnering. What made it odd was that she had never attempted to find a partner, despite the fact that over the years, many boys in town had expressed interest in her. Rafe in particular pursued her, to no avail. It seemed as if her sister had been waiting for someone special, Esther thought. But who?

The girls' chatter became faint as Esther tuned it out. In its place, she heard someone else's voice: Caleb's.

In her mind's eye, Esther could see his face, the set of his jawline, the haunted expression in his dark eyes. And although she despised what he had said at the town meeting, she now realized things might not be as simple as she thought. She also remembered how he spoke to her afterward, directly and openly, and how he listened to her, *really* listened in a way no one ever had before, not even Skar.

The inane drone of the girls' voices cut into her thoughts. Esther was jerked back to reality and with it came the realization: *She didn't want to be here anymore.* She looked up at the sky, where her friend's smoke signals had been. The clouds had thickened and grown darker.

She made up her mind and stood.

"Esther?"

She was already across the small parking lot and hoisting her bicycle by the handlebars when her sister grabbed her by the arm.

"What are you doing?" Sarah whispered. She sounded panicked.

"I have to get out of here," said Esther. But her sister refused to let go.

"Please," she said in a low voice. "Just a few more hours, until the rain passes. I promise, once we're in the shed, I'll keep them away from you. But if you go now, it'll be over for you. I won't be able to save you."

Esther attempted to shake her off. "It's never as bad as you say it's going to be. Shunning's only for people who are sick or for *real* criminals." She had one foot on a pedal and was trying to take off.

"But that was before. These are Levi's new rules. And you know there's no way that Rhea isn't going to report this. She's been waiting for the opportunity all day."

Esther glanced over at the other girls. They were still sitting where they were, watching her with their mouths open in shock. And it was true that Rhea was staring at her with an appraising look, a faint smile on her face.

"Please, Esther." Although she kept her voice down, Sarah couldn't keep the desperation from her voice. "You're going to get Shunned. And no one will be able to help you."

But Esther had broken free and was pedaling away, as fast as she could. The town was five or six miles away. She would have to hurry before the rain came.

EIGHT

"HIT ME," CALEB SAID.

He stood in front of a red-haired boy, with one arm extended and relaxed, palm facing out. The boy was a husky fourteen-year-old, stocky and exceptionally strong; he figured it was the reason he was chosen. Eager to prove himself, he tensed up his arm and punched the open hand as hard as he could.

The boy was surprised and then embarrassed to see what little effect it had. The stranger barely registered the blow. He was about to ask for a second chance, but Caleb had moved on to the next person in line, a sturdy girl with close-set eyes.

"Hit me," he said to her.

Seven townspeople were lined up in the large, echoing room that had once been a bank. They had been excused from their various jobs for this first round of training and now stood in the thick heat and humidity of the November day, their arms by their sides, awaiting instruction from the stranger who was going to teach them how to save their town.

The red-haired boy was especially excited to be included in the first group. Like everyone in town, he was familiar with the details of the stranger's victory over the five mutants. He knew of his impressive fighting skills and his strange new weapon, which was capable of firing several rocks in quick succession.

The boy looked forward not only to learning from Caleb firsthand, but maybe even following him into battle. He and his partner had sustained serious damage to their storefront home in the recent mutant attack, their windows smashed and much of their stored goods destroyed. Since then, he had been hungering for revenge. Today, he had come half expecting to be handed his own weapon, given instructions on how to use it, and maybe even led to the mutant camp for some kind of showdown.

But he had been surprised. So far, the lesson was nearly all talk. What's more, most of what the stranger had to say was downright bewildering.

"I can't teach you how to fight," Caleb said at the very beginning. At this, everyone shifted on their feet, glancing at one another and murmuring. "Fighting isn't in your hands or your feet, and it isn't about getting hold of some fancy weapon. Mostly, it's in your head."

The boy with the red hair wiped sweat off his brow as he mulled over these peculiar words.

By now, Caleb had worked his way to the end of the line. Everyone had punched or slapped his hand—some harder than others, some less eagerly, some clumsily. The boy brightened up at this part of the lesson; this was what he had come to do. He assumed Caleb would now get down to business, would talk about the techniques of hitting and fighting and pick out and praise the strongest participants. Maybe he'd even spar with the best student and again, the boy felt his hopes rise.

But once more, he was surprised.

"Fighting isn't a game," Caleb said. "You should only do it because you have no other choice. And you've got to know that your enemies aren't just stronger than you. They're smarter, too."

The boy frowned. He was not quite sure he followed what Caleb was saying. He was also not sure he liked the sound of what he was hearing.

"To win, you've got to keep your mind clear," continued Caleb. "You've got to see the situation as it is and use every advantage you got. But you can't keep a cool head if you put your feelings into your fists."

He turned to the red-haired boy, who was now examining his hands. "For instance," he said, "I could tell by the way you hit that you're impatient and you want to fight." Caleb imitated the boy perfectly, his eager stance, the overly enthusiastic punch. "You want to prove to me and everyone here that you're strong."

There was suppressed laughter down the line and the boy frowned, trying to understand what had been said and if he had just been insulted. But before he could say anything, Caleb had moved on to the next person in line, the girl with the close-set eyes.

"You think this is some kind of game," he said to her. "It's like you don't even think the threat is real." The girl giggled, then blushed, staring at the floor.

Caleb moved to the next person. "The way you hit tells me you're mad, maybe at me," he said to the boy, a hulking sixteen-year-old. "You don't like being told what to do." The boy looked startled; then he glowered at the stranger, his fists clenched.

Caleb continued to work his way down the line. He stopped in front of each person and told each one what he thought he or she was feeling:

You're scared. You think you know better. You care too much about pleasing others. You're bored.

When he was done, Caleb turned to face everyone, his expression serious. "Think about what I said," he said. "Try to leave your emotions at home. And I'll see you back here tomorrow."

At first, the red-haired boy darkened with anger. But when he thought it over, he was astonished. It was amazing that the stranger could know so much about him by just a single punch to the hand.

By the look on everyone else's face, he knew he was not alone. Feeling a first glimmer of understanding, he stepped forward to speak his mind.

But he was stopped in his tracks.

Without warning, a gust of wind swept through the broken windows that surrounded them, swirling grit and paper across the room. Everyone simultaneously glanced outside.

Overhead, the sky had changed to a deep and unnatural green and purple. Then, it seemed as if all the air was violently sucked out of the room; shards of broken glass rattled in their wooden frames, some snapping off and sailing into the street.

Caleb moved deeper into the room and everyone followed. They stood against the back wall in order to get as far away as possible from the gaping windows and open door.

Even if the red-haired boy were to speak now, no one could hear him. For with a deafening crack of thunder, a bolt of lightning split the darkening sky.

A moment later, rain began to fall: fat drops freely splashed through the broken windows, forming puddles on the marble floor. Outside, the drops marked the dusty ground vividly, faster and faster. They covered the hardened dirt with dark spots before converging and turning into deadly pools of mud and water.

Half an hour later, the storm was still raging. Looking onto a deserted street, Esther watched the steady downpour from the decrepit lobby of Joseph's home, the Gideon Putnam Hotel.

When the first drops had begun to fall, she leaped off her bike and wheeled it into the nearest building, thankful for any shelter at all. Even so, she was aware of the heavy sound of rain as it thrummed on the sidewalk and splashed through the gaping windows and doors, soaking the faded carpet. She moved deeper into the building interior, making certain to avoid the walls, which had begun to weep moisture.

She berated herself again for not thinking, not planning.

It was a stupidly close call. Moments earlier, an unlucky gust of wind could have driven the downpour straight at her, through the broken glass of the front door. She knew all too well what a single raindrop could do if it found its way into your eyes, your mouth, or a scratch on your skin that hadn't healed. First came the bone-crushing fatigue and telltale lesions; then headaches and fever. These were followed by severe stomach pains, vomiting, and delirium.

After that, she was not exactly sure what happened. For no one had ever been allowed to stay in town once the symptoms appeared.

Esther had been on her way to the school, where she knew Caleb was staying, when the storm hit. Now she had to wait until it was totally spent before she dared to continue on her way.

Whenever it rained, the people of Prin pressed close to their windows and watched the storm. They couldn't help it: from the safety of their homes, they found the risk, the presence of death, fascinating.

But not Esther. As usual, she turned her face from it.

That was when she saw Joseph.

Her friend was standing across the lobby, carrying an empty plastic bucket. As ever, he was accompanied by a cat. Both boy and feline stared at the intruder with a look of astonishment.

"Esther," Joseph said.

Esther felt a pang of guilt. So much had happened recently that she hadn't told him. Now she had only run into him by accident. She noticed what he was carrying.

"You're not going to get rainwater with that, are you?" she exclaimed.

"With what?" He looked down at the bucket. "Oh, no, I—"

"Because it can kill you," she said. "Do you remember what I told you? Do you still have any of the water I gave you last time?"

"Yes. Yes. I do."

"Then will you please drink that instead?"

As she watched Joseph first attempt to hide the bucket behind his back and then a column, Esther realized too late that she had spoken in a sharp voice. *I must sound like Sarah*, she thought. "I'm sorry I shouted," she said, touching him on the arm. He felt thinner than usual, and so she dug deep in her shoulder bag. At the bottom, she found what she was looking for: the lunch she had not eaten at the Harvesting, a container of boiled rice and beans. "Take this."

"Are you sure you want to—"

"Yes. Please."

Smiling his thanks, Joseph received the gift. Then he placed it on the floor in front of the cat, which began to eat.

Esther watched for a moment. "I wish I had more."

Joseph shrugged, then shuffled his feet. "Would you like to come upstairs? We can have a proper visit."

"I can't." Esther spoke with real regret. "Once the rain stops, I've got to see someone. I'm sorry."

She turned to check the progress of the storm and was startled to make out her image reflected back to her in the cracked glass door.

Esther leaned forward and examined herself. She squinted, trying to imagine that she was seeing herself for the first time, as if she was a total stranger.

As if she was someone like Caleb, for example.

Esther had never done this sort of thing before. There was a full-length mirror at home, but she almost never glanced at it. In fact, she associated primping and fussing with Sarah, so much so that not caring about her looks had become not just a matter of pride, but an easy way to irritate her sister. She was amused by how agitated she could make Sarah by something as simple as not combing her hair.

But now that Esther was studying herself, she was rattled by what she saw.

She saw a girl in boy's clothes—jeans and a sweatshirt—that hung off a bony frame; she saw watchful eyes that seemed too large and dark in a thin face. There was a smudge of dirt on her chin, which she tried to rub away with her sleeve. Her hair, dark and unruly, was cut unevenly, at different lengths, and it stuck up on top. Esther frowned and tried to smooth the cowlick down; it wouldn't obey and she gave up.

Then she turned sideways and tried to examine her figure, pulling her sweatshirt close.

It was no good, she realized with a sinking heart. She was

simply not appealing, not the way other females in town were. She lacked the curves and softness of some of the girls, the gracefulness of others, even the dainty femininity of her sister.

For a moment, Esther stared at her reflection in the glass and despaired. Then she turned to her friend, who had been watching her with a bemused look on his face.

"Do you think I'm pretty?"

Joseph started, then seemed to consider the question. After a few moments, he looked up. "You're Esther," he replied.

Esther smiled. Although at that moment, she would have given anything, anything at all, to change her looks, she realized that there was nothing she could do about it. She couldn't, after all, change who she was.

She walked over and kissed Joseph on the cheek. He recoiled, as she knew he would, but she didn't care.

At last, the rain started to let up. Esther waited until she was sure it wasn't a false alarm. Then she saw a rainbow—the indisputable sign that the coast would soon be clear—stretch across the sky.

"I'll see you soon," she said.

After a final, vain attempt to make her hair lie in place, she wheeled her bicycle out from the hotel lobby. Her hood drawn around her face, Esther took off through the glistening streets for the school, a half mile away.

There were many shattered windows on the ground floor of the building. It was no trouble for her to reach in, unfasten the latch, and enter.

She made her way down a hallway, lined on both sides with dusty and dented metal lockers that gaped open. She picked her way through trash, mounds of paper, and broken light fixtures. Along the way, she passed empty classrooms, rusted water fountains, and abandoned stairwells.

When she rounded a corner, she noticed something written on the wall, and curious, stopped to examine what it was. Primitive drawings and words, little pictures of hearts with arrows through them, and initials were carved into the plaster. She was able to spell out the words and letters with difficulty:

mikey + lissa. e.h. + a.t. j-bo and k.k. 4ever.

They made no sense to her.

Caleb sat on the creaky cot in his room. He had been given these accommodations in the school, a dank, gray two-story building, as a reward. When Rafe first showed him the place, he assumed that the stranger would take the largest room, the auditorium, for his lodgings and had it furnished accordingly. By Prin's standards, such a dwelling—with its high ceiling, scuffed wooden floors, and tall windows covered with thick wire mesh—was luxurious, even palatial.

But after living outdoors for so many months, Caleb no longer trusted open spaces. Instead, he thanked Rafe, whom he was beginning to find irritating and overbearing. Then once he was alone, he searched the building until he found a room more to his liking: a classroom off a secondary hallway, with dusty blackboards still attached to the walls and desks and chairs pushed to one side in a jumble. Satisfied with its size and location, Caleb transferred all of the furnishings and supplies Rafe had the townspeople provide.

He thought about those people and his students, as well. He had taken the job for practical reasons only, as a way to stay in town. But he found he liked the teaching more than he expected.

On his rickety bed, Caleb drank from a plastic jug of water. Lowering the bottle, he glanced around and for the first time took in where he was.

The tables that were pushed against the wall were much too low to sit in front of; and the chairs piled on top of them were small as well, perhaps coming up to his knee. He looked up and noticed strange pictures tacked to the wall, faded, mysterious illustrations that were curled from too much humidity and mottled with mildew:

A white goose in a bonnet read a book to a little boy and girl. A cat walked on its hind legs, wearing green boots. Three bears confronted a small girl with yellow hair.

Around the wall, close to the ceiling, were the remnants of a long strip of paper. Caleb could barely read, but he realized with a shock that the torn banner was printed with the letters of the alphabet.

This was a room for little children.

Children like Kai. Soft, sweet Kai, with his mother's serious eyes and his sudden smile.

His son.

The images seemed to reproach him, a silent reminder not to forget why he was there. Caleb squeezed his eyes shut. Then he opened them again.

Someone was in the hall.

Caleb seized his backpack, hanging over a chair. He took out a sap, a small, heavily weighted leather pouch, which he hid in his hand.

But he realized he would not need it.

A girl in a red hooded sweatshirt stood in the doorway.

It was the girl he had first seen at the ball court, the angry one who had tried to slash his tires. The pretty one, he thought now, pretty if you looked at her the right way.

"Hey," she said. She was appalled to find she was blushing and she tried to cover it by scowling. "I'm Esther."

"I'm Caleb," he said. "What can I do for you?"

Esther couldn't meet his eyes, and so she plowed ahead, staring at the floor.

"I came to . . . I wanted to say I'm sorry."

"Uh-huh," he said. "What for?"

"For . . ." she started, then trailed off. Apologizing didn't come easy to her and this was harder than she thought. "Because I messed up your tire."

Caleb considered her words.

"You didn't really mess it up," he said.

A smile flickered across her face and at last she raised her eyes. "I would have, if I had more time."

Now it was Caleb's turn to smile. "I bet," he said.

Esther cleared her throat. "And . . . I'm sorry about your family."

Caleb's face grew serious and he nodded.

That was all Esther came to say. It felt right to apologize for what she did and to express her sympathy. After that, there was no real reason to stay; yet for some reason, she couldn't break away. She lingered for a moment, hoping Caleb would speak, but he was as silent as she was. So she started to go.

"Hey?" he said.

Esther turned back.

Caleb had his hands in his pockets and averted his gaze; she was surprised to see that he was so ill at ease.

"You think it's safe around here?" he finally asked. He indicated his black bicycle, leaning against a wall. "I'd like to keep that outside, case I need to get somewhere in a hurry. Think that'd be okay?"

"Sure," Esther said. "If you want, we could put it out back. That way, nobody would see it from the street."

Together, they headed farther into the school, Caleb pushing his bicycle next to him and Esther navigating. It was not just one building but a series of them and she had never been inside before. Still, her sense of direction was good, and she felt they were heading the right way.

As they walked side by side, the two talked. Esther was especially shy at first. The only person she really spoke to was Skar, and they had been friends for many years. She found it was easier when they weren't looking at each other. Mostly, they took turns asking questions, listening as the other spoke: about growing up, their homes and family, and the people they knew.

Soon Esther was so caught up in the conversation, she

stopped paying attention to where they were and began choosing turns and stairways without thinking. When they reached the end of a large hallway, she frowned. She spun around, confused, as she tried to get her bearings.

"What's wrong?" Caleb asked.

Esther didn't answer at first. "I don't know how we got here," she said. She pointed down the echoing corridor, which seemed as long and broad as a highway. "I think we're supposed to be down at that end."

Caleb smiled. "That's easy," he said. He mounted his bicycle in one fluid movement. "Hop on."

When she realized what he was proposing, Esther hesitated. Then she met his eyes and made up her mind.

His back wheels didn't have the standing pegs the variants used, so Esther perched on the seat. She held onto Caleb, who pedaled standing up. When they reached the far end of the hall, Esther saw she had been right; there was a door that led to a courtyard in back. Caleb slowed, then stopped. He took her hand and helped her off the bike.

"Thanks," she said. "That was fun." She held the door open for Caleb, and he wheeled his bicycle through and rested it against the brick wall. Esther realized it was a word she had only ever used with Skar: *fun.*

As the two returned to the classroom, Caleb seemed thoughtful.

"Who's Levi?" he said. "And what's the Source? I've heard people talk about them, but not so as I could understand."

Esther couldn't imagine anyone not knowing, but she

explained as best she could. Caleb listened, squinting as he took it in.

"They got more than food and water in there?" he asked, after she was done.

"What?"

"At the Source. He's got all kinds of stuff, right?"

Esther shrugged. "I guess."

"Do they ever trade with anyone else?"

"Like who?"

"Mutants. Because I'm looking for something. Something you start fires with."

Esther was puzzled. Then she remembered his recent tragedy. The mysterious fire. The death of his partner and the kidnapping of his son.

And before she was aware what she was doing, Esther found herself opening up even more to Caleb. She told him what she'd found when she visited the variants' camp—that Levi was supplying them with goods. What they were doing in exchange for this payment, she had no clue. And she realized too late that she didn't know what Caleb would do with this information.

Caleb listened, gazing downward without speaking. Then he looked up.

"How do you get in the Source?" he asked.

"I don't know," Esther said. "I never been inside."

"You think I could?"

"Depends," she replied. "Why are you asking me?"

"Because. You know everything else."

Esther glanced up at him. She wasn't sure if he was teasing or if he valued her opinion. *Maybe both*, she thought. *Because he was smiling.*

"I can't answer that," she said. "But I think you'll end up doing what you want, anyway."

"Probably so," he said. Just then, Caleb's attention was directed to the window. He walked over and peered out. Breathing onto the filthy glass, he rubbed a circle with his elbow. Although the rain had stopped, a form covered in shiny black clothing—a hooded slicker and galoshes—was striding across the street. Whoever it was headed toward the school.

"That's one of Levi's boys," Esther said, from behind him.

"How do you know?" he said.

"No one else has gear like that."

Caleb thought about it. "Better hide someplace."

"Why?"

Caleb looked at her. "You know how to fight?"

"Oh," she said. "Well, I—"

"Wait there."

There was a closet in the back of the room. Esther opened the door and disappeared inside.

The stranger had already entered the room. It was a boy, probably in his mid-teens. His ensemble gave him a bizarre, animal-like quality, as if he was something not completely human.

"Levi wants to see you," he said.

"I'm Caleb. What's your name?"

The boy in black didn't answer; he cocked his head, confused.

"You got to come to the Source," he said.

"Why?" Caleb asked.

The visitor paused again. It was as if he had never been asked anything like this before. He seemed to be blinking stupidly behind his hood.

"Come tonight, before the sun goes down," he said.

"What if it rains again?"

But the boy had turned and, seemingly unnerved, was tramping out.

Watching him go, Caleb shook his head, amused. "Well," he said. "Looks like I'm going to the Source, after all."

"I guess so." Esther emerged from her hiding place. She was smiling, too. Then her expression grew serious. "But if you go, be careful."

The emotion in her voice surprised both of them. Before he could respond, she spoke again. "Maybe I'll see you around. I'm usually in the fields, near the tracks."

Then Esther turned and ran from the room and down the hall. In no time, she was at the front door of the building.

But before she could leave, she heard Caleb calling after her:

"See you, Esther."

Rather than bring a sense of coolness, all the rain had done was make the late afternoon heat feel more oppressive. The air was now thick and muggy and even more difficult to breathe.

Caleb shifted on his feet. He had been waiting for over an hour outside the Source, standing on the steaming asphalt of the parking lot. There was not much to look at. Weeds and tall grass grew freely in the cracked surface. Beneath his feet and stretching as far as the eye could see were fading parallel lines, painted in white. A few featured remnants of a crude drawing: a stick figure seated on a half-circle.

Caleb pushed back his hat and raised his sunglasses to wipe his face; he was perspiring freely. He was more than aware that he was being made to wait on purpose; it was an obvious ploy, Levi's way of establishing the balance of power between them before the two had even met. Yet it didn't succeed in making Caleb feel intimidated. It only made him impatient.

He was aware that there were laborers working nearby; he had passed some sort of worksite on his way in. From where he stood, he could hear the faint sound of picks and shovels hitting the ground. It was a rhythmic sound, hypnotic in this heat, and he closed his eyes, momentarily lulled.

Something snapped him out of his trance.

He blinked, not certain if he was seeing things. There seemed to be an apparition emerging from the Source. And it was heading his way.

From where he stood, it first appeared to be a single creature, some large and misshapen organism floating toward him in the hot, shimmering air like a mirage.

As it approached, it was easier to see that it was a group of people. One walked in front. Another, hooded like the messenger from before, walked by his side and held out a large black umbrella, to shield him from the sun. Two more hooded figures, presumably guards, flanked them.

The leader wore no headgear, revealing that he was pale, luminously so, almost like the underbelly of a frog. His pallor was accentuated by a shock of dark hair that fell over his forehead and his black clothing.

To Caleb, it was clear what this was meant to convey. In a world where everyone had to be swathed in white against a deadly sun, such a wardrobe was a show of strength, a taunt to the elements, a way of being above and better than the heat.

Caleb assumed this must be Levi.

"Greetings," the leader called as they got within earshot.

Farther back, another guard held a second umbrella over a girl, who picked her way with difficulty across the broken surface on thin-soled sandals. She was fair-haired and impossibly pale, as well; she was perhaps fourteen or so. She wore a meager, turquoise-colored top and shorts, her white midriff exposed. A gem-like stud in her navel glinted in the sun.

The group stopped at a reasonable distance from Caleb, not getting too close. The two guards continued to keep their umbrellas raised, shielding Levi and the girl from the sun. Caleb noticed what looked like weapons at the belts of all four henchmen, a chunk of plastic and metal that he had glimpsed beneath the raingear worn by the messenger.

That Levi was both so physically protected and so attentive to his appearance made Caleb assume he was weak. Yet Caleb was also aware that there were other ways of being strong than through sheer physical might.

One way was to be clever.

Levi stared at him for a long moment. His sunglasses were made of a mirror-like material that wrapped around the top part of his face, rendering his eyes unreadable; and Caleb was unable to see his full expression. Yet the boy's mouth opened slightly with what appeared to be surprise, even fascination. Then he regained his composure.

"I'm Levi," he said.

He didn't bother to extend his hand; he kept his arms by his side, one thumb hooked in his front pocket. Caleb didn't offer up his own.

"Caleb," he said.

For a second, the other boy's face seemed familiar, but Caleb dismissed it as a play of shadows.

"This is Michal," Levi said, with a casual, almost indifferent nod to the girl. She gave him an eager smile.

"Good to meet you," Caleb said.

"Care for some water?" Levi said. "It's clean."

Caleb smiled. How could he say no? The simple offer established that Caleb was now in Levi's debt and must be grateful.

"Sure," Caleb answered.

Levi gave a short nod to one of the guards, who tossed a blue metal bottle at their guest. It was actually cold. Caleb acknowledged his thanks with a slight tilt of his head. Then he uncapped it and drank.

Levi was watching him; behind his glasses, he almost seemed amused. "Keep it," he said as Caleb offered the bottle back. Not caring that this put him further in his host's debt, Caleb slid it in his backpack.

"Whereabouts are you from?" Levi said. "You're not from around here, are you?"

Caleb shook his head. "I've been traveling a long time," he said. "I come from beyond the mountain range to the north."

There was a moment's pause. Then: "Don't know the area," Levi said blandly. Pleasantries over, he got to the point. "I've heard things about you from my boys."

"Is that right? What kinds of things?"

"That you single-handedly fought off the mutants. And that now you're officially protecting Prin."

Caleb shrugged. "It's not official. And it's just for a little while."

"Don't sell yourself short," replied Levi. "It's impressive. And the town needs help. I could only do so much for them." At this, he lifted one hand, dismissively. Silver glinted on three of his fingers.

Caleb shrugged again. By now, he was aware that the other boy seemed to be studying him, as if waiting for some kind of response. He had no idea what it was supposed to be. He had been waiting for the right moment to inquire about the accelerant when his host gestured across the parking lot, in the direction of the work sounds Caleb had heard before.

"Would you let me show you something?" Levi said.

It was clearly not meant to be a question, Caleb thought. Levi had the ability to make people not only obey him but also feel as if they worked for him too, even when they didn't.

In a way, he admired such manipulative skill; it made him feel clumsily physical by comparison. He was willing to bet Levi could also read well, something he could barely do. If you could only combine Levi's brains with his fighting abilities, Caleb thought idly, you'd have a perfect leader.

"Okay," he said. "Show me."

Levi snapped his fingers at the guard assisting Michal. He stepped forward, abandoning his charge, in order to hold his umbrella over Caleb. Exposed, the frightened girl had no choice but to run to Levi, clinging to his arm for protection from the sun.

Levi strolled across the parking lot, followed by his entourage. Caleb followed, curious, and grateful for the shade.

By the time they reached the end of the asphalt, the sounds of people at work were so close, Caleb could make out the grunting of individuals, the shouts of a Supervisor, the rasping of metal on rock. Levi stopped in front of a chain-link fence strung with barbed wire that seemed to encircle the entire parking lot and gestured at Caleb to look down.

On the other side was a deep trench. It was the only one of at least three such pits scooped out of the earth that surrounded the parking lot, one after the other. Each represented a tremendous amount of effort; they were deeper than the height of two men and at least three times longer than that.

Toiling in each trench were a dozen townspeople of every age. Some used picks to break up the rock and packed earth beneath their feet; others shoveled up what was excavated and tossed it behind them. There, the youngest workers filled plastic buckets with the dirt. At the end of each trench was a primitive pulley, where the children attached the buckets to a dangling rope. They were then pulled to the surface by two other workers and their contents disposed of.

It was appalling, backbreaking work, all the more so because of the weather. The day's rain had turned each trench into a vast and treacherous pit of mud and rainwater, and so everyone wore protective gear: rubber hip boots, gloves, plastic face masks. Caleb couldn't imagine how unbearable it must be to work in such clothing in this heat.

What's more, as far as he could tell, it all looked utterly pointless.

"This is what we call the Excavation," Levi said. "It's one of the fair trades we've devised here in Prin, for the goods I dispense from the Source. It's a system that's been working very well."

"For who?" Caleb couldn't help asking.

"For everyone," Levi replied. He sounded sincere.

"I see."

"I know what you're thinking. That it seems to have no purpose. But that's where you're wrong."

Levi stepped forward, out of the shade of his own umbrella and into Caleb's. As he did, he took the umbrella from the guard, who backed off. The two boys were now standing very close to one another; their faces were mere inches apart and Caleb would have stepped back, if it wouldn't have been so obviously rude.

Levi addressed him in a voice so soft that even Caleb had

trouble making out the words.

"They're digging for something," he said. "Something important. Even precious. No one can know what it is, because they wouldn't understand. Look at them. They're animals." He indicated the guards and Michal with a glance that was dismissive and contemptuous. "When I find what I'm looking for—and I will—I'm going to need help with it."

Caleb nodded, just listening. Levi never raised his voice yet still managed to speak with absolute conviction. He stared into Caleb's eyes, which Caleb noticed were the same shade of gray as his own. He heard something resonant in the boy's voice. Had he heard it before? All of this threw him for a second.

"Do you have any family? A partner?"

Caleb was jolted back to reality by this question.

"I did," he said. "Once."

Levi was nodding as if in confirmation. "There's an opportunity here," he said at last, "but not just for anyone. It's for someone who thinks big, someone who can rise to an occasion. Someone who's like me."

After a long pause, Caleb answered, finally understanding what was going on. "You're offering me a job."

Levi remained motionless, not even blinking, his face still close to Caleb's. "That's one way of looking at it."

"Who said I want one?"

"You're already working for *them*." He almost spit out the word; it took Caleb a moment to realize he was talking about the workers in the pit, the people of Prin. "Why are you wasting your abilities?"

"I told you. That's just for now."

"What I'm offering you isn't a job. It's a future. Don't you want one of those?"

Caleb hesitated before he shook his head, this time with certainty. "That's not why I'm here."

"No? Then why are you?"

"I want to find who killed my partner and stole my boy. That's why. And that's it."

Levi's remarkably pale face flushed. Briefly, he shook his head no, as if he couldn't accept what he'd just heard. "You're better than that."

"Am I?"

"Yes. I can tell. You want to build something positive. Revenge will just leave a bad taste."

"Maybe it's not revenge. Maybe it's justice."

Levi shrugged away the difference. "That's a lonely road," he said.

He turned and beckoned to the girl, who had been waiting beneath the other guard's umbrella. She pointed to herself, startled, and Levi nodded, impatiently. Smiling, glad to be of service, Michal moved forward.

But before she could reach the shade shared by the two boys, Levi raised a hand to stop her. Then he turned back to Caleb.

"You wouldn't have to be lonely here," he said. "I'd make sure you had friends. Right, Michal?" He raised his voice. "You'd be Caleb's friend, wouldn't you?"

Caleb looked at the girl. Michal was sweating, her pale

skin already turning pink in the bright sun. She couldn't hear everything that Levi had said, so she simply nodded with pathetic eagerness, desperate to please.

"More than friend," Levi added. He raised his voice so she couldn't miss the insinuation in his voice.

The guards did not miss it either. As they guffawed lasciviously, Michal's face froze and her eager smile faded.

Levi turned back to Caleb. "You could start a new family," he said. "You'd get over your old one in no time."

Caleb felt sickened by not only what Levi was offering, but his blithe assumption that it would please him. He stared coldly at the other boy.

"No thanks," he said.

For the first time, Levi seemed off guard; Caleb thought he could see him blinking rapidly behind his sunglasses, as if to regroup. Then Levi waved the girl away, back to the shelter of the guard's umbrella.

He now gestured behind them, to the massive building looming in the near distance.

"You don't know the things I have in there," Levi said; "clothing. Furniture. Gold watches." He seemed less sure of himself now, his voice beseeching. "If you worked for me, I'd make sure you had your fair share of whatever you liked. There's more in there than you could ever want."

Caleb paused. "Actually, there is one thing I want."

Levi waited for him to tell him.

"It's an accelerant," Caleb said. "For setting fires. It's called 'Able.' I was told it could be found around here."

Levi paused for a second. Then he shrugged, as if to say, what did this have to do with me? He seemed to have lost interest, as if he had just found out that Caleb was a less worthy person than he imagined. "As far as I know, we've never stocked it."

"You never sold any to mutants?"

"Of course not. From time to time, we've done a little trading, but just the necessities. Deer meat for water. That sort of thing."

Caleb nodded. This might explain what Esther saw at the variant camp. "Have you ever been robbed?"

Levi smiled and then shook his head, as if charmed by Caleb's naïveté. "That's ridiculous."

But Caleb wouldn't let it go. "Do you mind if I take a look inside? It's not that I don't trust you. I'd just like to see with my own eyes."

Levi stared at him for a moment; then he smiled. "Of course," he said. "It's the least I could do."

He said a few words to his guards; then everyone turned around and headed across the parking lot, back to the Source.

Inside, it was impossibly cool and dark. It took Caleb's eyes several moments to get adjusted to the gloom. He was aware that Levi was waiting for him before he took off through the cavernous space.

"Stay close," Levi called over his shoulder. "It's easy to get lost in here and I don't want to waste your time."

Yet Levi walked at a deliberate pace down the endless aisles. Caleb wondered if this was intentional, a way of showing off his wealth. Certainly, he had never seen so many supplies in his life.

A single crate, he reckoned, could feed a family for months.

Levi stopped and turned around.

"This is where it would be," Levi said, nodding over his shoulder. "Household supplies. You see?" He pointed at the crates stacked high on the oversize shelves. "This is where we keep all the solvents and flammables. We have turpentine, floor cleaner, bleach, hydrogen peroxide, ammonia. But I'm afraid not what you're looking for."

"Can I?" asked Caleb, and Levi nodded, stepping aside.

Caleb scanned the shelves. Although he could barely read, he knew how to spell "Able"; still, it was laborious work. And after close searching, he had to admit that Levi was correct; nothing by that name was there.

Levi walked him to the door. "Well," he said, "I'm sorry you weren't able to find what you were looking for. But you know where I am in case you change your mind."

"I won't," replied Caleb.

Levi hesitated. "In that case," he said, "you might consider trying down the road a ways. There's another town where I heard they trade with the mutants. If you follow the main road to the east, it's at least a full day's ride. I suggest getting a start first thing in the morning."

Caleb nodded his thanks and, without a handshake or another word, was gone.

Levi watched from his hidden window until the other was out of sight. Then he immediately headed back downstairs, to the main warehouse floor.

In one aisle, a hooded guard braced a stepladder on wheels and another stood on its top step, craning to see onto a high shelf.

"Found it yet?" Levi asked.

The guard grunted an affirmative and handed something down, a crate with a name stamped on its side. It took two guards to carry it.

"Hurry up and bring it this way," said Levi. "I want you to put it in my office." He was glad his boys never learned to read.

For although he would never admit it, certainly not to his underlings, Levi was nervous now. Maybe for the first time.

"Make sure," he said, "that he's gone by morning."

NINE

When Caleb emerged from the Source, it was late afternoon.

He headed out of the asphalt lot toward the main road. He bicycled through the center of town, passing townspeople on their way home from work. He wasn't sure of his exact destination, but he sensed it lay on the north side of town.

I'm usually in the fields near the tracks, Esther had said.

As he approached the bleached land that lay beyond a cluster of abandoned office buildings, Caleb dismounted his bicycle and wheeled it next to him. It was pointless to ride; the ground was littered with broken glass and scraps of old metal. Far away, he could just make out the glint of train rails mostly hidden by overgrown and sun-bleached grass.

By now, the sun was setting, sending blinding shafts of light from the horizon. Caleb shielded his eyes with one hand as he scanned the desolate expanse. Other than the rusted hulk of a truck, a soiled and rain-bloated sofa spilling stuffing, and the charred remains of a bonfire, he saw nothing.

Then his glance flickered back to a small copse of trees in the distance.

They had lost most of their leaves and their branches were bare and skeletal in the November twilight. But even in the fading sun, he could make out a patch of color amid the black limbs.

It was a red hoodie.

From where she sat, Esther watched as Caleb wheeled his bicycle toward her. Although no one ever came to the fields, she had recognized him the moment she saw him, no bigger than a speck on the horizon. She was surprised by how quickly her heart began beating; it almost hurt and she forced herself to look away. She waited until he was below her before she trusted herself to speak.

"Hey," she said.

"Hey."

He stretched up a hand, but refusing his help, she jumped down. She smiled up at him, but his expression was serious. He wasted no time in pleasantries.

"I just came to say good-bye," he said.

Whatever Esther was about to say froze on her lips. The sense of shock was like a physical blow, sharp and unexpected.

"Why?"

"The thing I'm looking for isn't here. Levi told me about another town I should try. It's a day's ride away, so I have to leave in the morning."

"But . . . what about Prin?"

"They'll have to do without me."

"But they'll want you to stay." Esther couldn't help herself; the words sprang unbidden to her lips. "*I* want you to."

She blushed, and Caleb also averted his gaze. Then he spoke, as if addressing the ground:

"We still have all night."

Together, they headed across the field and back onto the main street. But instead of going into the center of town, Esther turned the other way. They walked along the crumbling sidewalk, following a tall metal fence for several blocks until they reached a gate. A rusted sign hung overhead. Esther couldn't read most of the words but knew it was a place where people once buried their dead. Although it was nearly dark, they went inside.

Along the way, Esther and Caleb talked. They followed the broad pathway, which was covered with white gravel and gave off a faint glow. They passed rows of tombstones that had been defaced or toppled by vandals. Crosses, angels, and obelisks lay smashed and cracked on their sides. The path looped its way through the trees and past the dried remains of what seemed a large fountain, edged by wooden benches. They sat on the one that wasn't broken.

Esther felt Caleb tense up beside her. "What's wrong?"

She heard it as soon as she spoke. There was a rustling sound close by, and the rattle of gravel. An overhead cloud shifted, revealing silhouettes moving in the shadows around them.

"Dogs," said Caleb. He raised his voice, and the forms seemed to hesitate. "We're okay, but we should probably get back."

He and Esther stood, stamping their feet as they did. Wild dogs wouldn't attack two people, especially if they walked slowly, making noise as they went. Still, the hair on Esther's arms stood up; if fear had a smell, she hoped the animals couldn't detect it. She and Caleb retraced their steps, following the white pathway until they emerged back on the main street.

Caleb insisted on walking her home. She gladly let him, and together, they headed through the center of town. When they reached the Starbucks, she turned to face him.

"Goodnight," she said. She didn't want to say good-bye.

Caleb said nothing. He just reached out and held her hand for a second, then pulled away.

Esther opened the door and turned to say something else. But he was gone. All that was left was the sound of his bicycle disappearing into the darkness.

Esther was running down an empty road.

She was playing Shelter and, for once, she was winning. Jubilant, she could see the safe place, the large cardboard box, in the distance. It sat incongruously in the middle of the highway, straddling the double lines that seemed to go on forever under a hot yellow sky.

Yet as she got closer, her legs started to move slower and slower. Each step felt as if she was fighting her way through deep sand and she panicked at the thought of losing, of someone else getting there before her.

Soon she couldn't move; she attempted to thrash her arms and legs, but they were pinned down by their own weight. The ground began to crumble and collapse beneath her; she was breaking through the earth and would soon be swallowed by it, buried alive.

Someone grasped her by the hand. She clung to her rescuer and struggled to break free as he lifted her from her grave. The caked dirt fell from her face and she could see who it was.

Caleb.

He was saying something to her, something urgent. To not give up. To keep fighting.

Then, as if from far away, she heard a cry . . .

Esther jerked awake in the darkness, her heart pounding.

It took her a moment to realize she was safe at home, in bed. But far away, a girl actually was screaming.

She rose and crossed into the dark living room. When she peered from behind the curtains, the first gray light of early morning revealed two cloaked forms hurrying down the sidewalk, carrying bundles.

Esther checked to make sure her sister was still asleep. Then she dressed and stole down the stairs and into the street. Far ahead, she noticed that the two people had been joined by another. She followed them for several blocks, until they turned onto a side street. The three were apparently on their way to the home of Trey and Aima, which was once a store. The opaque glass door still had the words "dry cleaning" painted on it. Now, it gaped open and light spilled onto the sidewalk.

This was where the screams were coming from.

Unnoticed, Esther stood in the open doorway, stunned by the noise and activity. Inside, the sobs and shrieks were deafening. Bleary-eyed females, robotic with fatigue, nevertheless moved around the room with purpose, carrying towels, plastic jugs of water, blankets. Although the air was stifling and dense with smoke, one of them tended a blackened fire bowl in the corner of the room, tossing chunks of wood onto the leaping flames.

The crowd parted for a moment and Esther could see what was happening.

Aima squatted in the center of the small room, clutching the edge of the laminated counter. To Esther, she was unrecognizable. Her soaking nightdress hiked up, her monstrous belly suspended over her knees, she was white-faced and gasping, her hair plastered across her face. Two females kneeled by her side, supporting her, and again, she screamed.

Esther, horrified, couldn't speak.

Aima threw back her head, causing the cords in her neck to stand out like ropes. She strained powerfully, her teeth clenched and her hands white-knuckled on the edge of the counter. Something dark and wet shot from beneath her and was caught by one of the waiting females. At the same time, there was a loud gushing sound, as an eruption of clear liquid and bright red blood splashed onto the dirty tiled floor. Moments later, there was the thin, reedy cry of a newborn. The others closed around Aima, murmuring as they tended to her.

But something was wrong.

One of the girls gasped and another flinched. Something was said in an urgent whisper, followed by a muffled exclamation.

"No." Aima's voice was faint, but it rose above the clamor. "No! It can't be!"

Esther craned her neck, trying to see what was wrong. But the person closest to her swiveled around, her hands slick with blood and afterbirth. She noticed Esther for the first time, and her eyes blazed with anger.

"Ain't nothing to stare at," she hissed. "It was born dead."

Esther recoiled.

Everyone in the room, even Aima, was suddenly aware of her. Silence fell, and all of the females turned one by one to stare at Esther. Stammering apologies, she stumbled backward out of the room, nearly tripping on the doorsill. When she was outside, the opaque glass door was pointedly pushed shut behind her.

Esther stood alone on the sidewalk, thinking about what she had just seen. She was deeply rattled.

It was not just the sight of childbirth that bothered her, although the violence far exceeded anything she could have imagined. Nor was it her rude exclusion from the circle of women, a secret society that had never wanted or welcomed her.

It was born dead, the girl said.

Yet Esther had heard it cry out.

Instead of going home, Esther retreated to a darkened doorway where she could see Trey and Aima's home. There she waited to see what would happen next. She leaned against the side of a building and felt her eyelids droop; she was about to pass out on her feet. She was ready to give up and head home when the door across the street opened, spilling light onto the sidewalk as a figure exited and walked away.

Whoever it was carried something bundled in her arms.

Esther used the tracking skills she had learned from Skar to attempt to follow undetected. Oblivious, her target hurried through the darkened streets, sure of where she was going. Once, she glanced around, as if sensing she was being trailed. Esther melted into the shadow of a streetlamp, and satisfied, the other girl continued.

Onward they walked, the robed girl in front, Esther half a block behind. They reached the outskirts of town, past the Source looming huge and white in the early morning light, and still the female continued. She turned off the road and cut through the land beyond the gaping pits of the Excavation, picking her way across the precarious open wasteland made up of the debris of collapsed buildings.

Occasionally, she shifted the bundle in her arms.

At last, she arrived at what appeared to be her destination. It was a massive oil tower, a giant steel tank set high atop four spiderlike legs. Weather and time had eaten away the letters once painted on its side, and the metal was corroded with rust and rot. A spindly ladder made its way to the top. At its base, the female finally set down her bundle.

Esther stepped out of the shadows. "What do you aim to do with that baby?"

The female started violently and cried out in fear. When she saw who it was, her expression changed to one of utter disbelief.

"You followed me?" she asked. It was Sian, an older girl Esther knew only slightly. "All the way from town?"

Esther nodded. "What do you aim to do with that baby?" she repeated.

Sian shook her head dismissively.

"It ain't no baby," she said.

She stepped aside and Esther could see the child. It was tiny, much smaller than she had imagined. It whimpered, then beat at the air with its minuscule legs and arms. The blanket fell away and in the early morning light, Esther could see its sex, which was a misshapen lump, neither male nor female. Its nose was nearly flat, little more than slits in its broad face. Its eyes were far apart, bulging, and lavender in color.

It was a variant.

Esther, stunned, tried to make sense of it.

"So you're just leaving it out here to die?" she asked.

Sian shook her head with a mixture of disgust and pity. Then with her robes hiked up, she took hold of the ladder and began to climb, an orange T-shirt clenched in her teeth. When she was more than halfway up, she tied it to a rung with a clumsy knot. Then she made her way back down.

"This way, they know," she said.

"You mean the—" Esther started to ask, but the other girl cut her off.

"The fathers don't want to know. And the mothers want to

forget. So this is how we figured it out with the mutants, long ago. It works out the best for everybody."

Esther couldn't take her eyes off the baby. It had found its thumb and sucked on it.

"It's a secret only the mothers know," said Sian. She stared at Esther, her voice hard. "And now you do, too."

Esther headed home, walking down the center of the road that led to town. The sun was already well in the sky and she was aware that she risked being detected by a crew on its way to work. Yet she was too exhausted and confused to care.

She was thinking of all the couples in town and how so few of the females ever managed to become pregnant. Of the few dozen who carried a child to term, most of their babies were born dead.

Or at least that was what everybody was told.

Now it seemed the truth was both simpler and more complex. Her suspicions had been right, all along: Variants weren't animals at all, but humans. That the mothers of Prin kept this secret was something she couldn't have begun to imagine.

Still brooding, Esther walked home down the center of the street. Although the sun was visible above the horizon, it was too early for anyone else to be out. She was not aware of the bicycle until it had pulled up beside her. The rider in robes and dark glasses jumped down, removing the scarf that covered its face.

"Esther." It was Eli, his face flushed and eager. "I saw you from my window and wanted to talk."

She smiled back politely and he fell into step next to her, pushing his bike. They walked like that in silence for a few moments. He seemed to want to say something, but each time she looked at him, he merely blushed.

"Esther," he began again.

When she glanced at him, he cleared his throat. Then he awkwardly reached over and, to her shock, took her hand. His skin was rough and dry; his palm seemed the size of a dinner plate. She stared at him, uncomprehending.

"We known each other a long time," he said. Esther could see her distorted reflection in each of his sunglass lenses; she looked confused and exhausted. "And you got to know how I feel about you. I guess what I'm saying is, I want to be . . . I was hoping you might think about me becoming . . . your partner." He finished in a rush, his face red.

Esther was speechless.

Yet why should it be a surprise? At fifteen, Esther was past the average age for partnering. Still, she could have three or four good years ahead of her. And Eli had always been kind and generous. In a town that treated her like an outsider, he had never made any secret of his affection for her. And even she had to admit, she may have encouraged him by asking favors.

Now Esther stared at him critically, as if seeing him for the first time. Eli was not tall, but he was strong and healthy. He had thick, wavy hair, a nice smile, and dark brown eyes. His voice was deep and pleasant, and he was a hard worker, dependable and considerate. She could do a lot worse than to become his partner.

Yet she felt nothing beyond an acknowledgment that he was a good catch. Was that reason enough for her . . . or for him, for that matter? Was she so wrong to expect something more from a decision she would have to live with for the rest of her life?

Eli had stopped talking and seemed to be waiting for her to respond. Yet Esther found her thoughts were not on the boy in front of her.

She was thinking of Caleb.

Esther pulled away her hand. "I can't tell you right now," she said. "I'm sorry. I just can't."

Eli stared at her, clearly disappointed. Then he tried to smile.

"Sure," he said with forced heartiness. "I can understand that. A girl needs time to think this kind of thing over."

As she walked away, stiff with self-consciousness, Esther could feel Eli's eyes following her before she heard the sound of his bicycle heading off. But she was still rattled.

If she were paying more attention, she might have noticed that although the sun was well over the horizon, there were no other townspeople outside, on their way to work. Instead, the streets were empty. It was not until she entered her building and crossed the empty storefront to reach the stairs in the back that she noticed that something was odd.

Esther paused. The building around her felt different somehow. Every nerve ending in her body told her that.

Her first thought was of her sister. Esther hesitated at the foot of the stairs, her hand on the banister.

"Sarah?" she whispered.

And with that, they were upon her.

Two townspeople lunged down the stairs and sprang at her. Although startled, Esther was able to leap backward and avoid their grasp. But she was not prepared for the two others who now rushed in from the street, blocking her escape. One of them seized her by the arms; another struggled to bind her wrists behind her back with an elasticized cloth cord that had black metal hooks at each end. Esther struck out, kicking and punching, but she was only one against several and was quickly overpowered.

"What are you doing?" she screamed. Her mind was whirling; was she being punished for finding out about Aima's baby?

No one answered. Rafe walked in, his expression unreadable.

"Rafe!" she screamed. "Help me!"

But a vile-tasting rag was stuffed into her mouth. Esther couldn't speak; she could barely breathe. The last thing she saw across the room was Sarah, clinging to the doorframe, her hand to her mouth. Her face was white with shock and anguish.

With arms tied behind her, Esther was dragged from the building and down the street. When she stumbled, she was yanked back up by her elbows. It was a long, hot walk.

When the group stopped, they were in the middle of what had once been a large lake on the outskirts of town. The ground under their feet was dusty red clay, baked hard by the sun and littered with trash. The shoreline was edged by dead willows and more than a few dozen motorboats that balanced lopsidedly on their hulls, long since drained of any gasoline.

A rickety bridge spanned the narrowest part of the lakebed, cinching it like a belt.

The five people who surrounded her were identical in their reflective sunglasses and face scarfs. Only Rafe spoke.

"You know why you're here," he said. "We got word you left your work detail. You got anything to say?"

Esther swallowed as the realization sank in: It wasn't about the baby after all. The situation seemed so unreal that only the pain of the rubberized cords biting into her wrists told her this was not a dream. "It was Rhea, wasn't it?" she said in a low voice. "She hates me and my sister."

"It don't matter if she hates you or not," said Rafe. "Was it true what she said?"

"I worked hard on the Harvesting. You could ask anyone else who was there."

"You're not answering the question," Rafe replied. "Did you leave your work detail or didn't you?"

When she didn't answer, he nodded his head. "That was what I thought."

Esther glanced at the others in open appeal. They must have been thinking what she was: that no one in Prin had ever been Shunned for anything less than illness or a serious crime. Never for something as minor as skipping work detail. Rafe was just following Levi's new rules without thinking, and for that, Esther found him more contemptible than ever.

Two of her neighbors refused to meet her gaze. It was clear that none of them was going to help her in any way, to speak in her defense or ask for mercy.

"Esther," said Rafe. "You are hereby Shunned from Prin."

He nodded, and one of the others fumbled to undo her bonds. Another handed Esther a nylon backpack which she took, numbly. In it, she knew that there would be supplies meant to last a week or so.

For an instant, Esther sensed that this last person was viewing her with regret, even sympathy. But the moment passed and whoever it was joined the others, who stood together, watching in silence.

In a daze, Esther walked across the lake surface and toward the rising sun.

On a grassy patch behind the bank, the seven townspeople surrounded Caleb. He was in the middle, holding a long, wooden stick with an angled end, the word EASTON printed along the laminated shaft.

Caleb addressed one of the students, a tall boy. "Tell me what you're going to do," he said.

"I'm going to go with the motion of the push and see where it takes me," said the boy.

Caleb nodded. Then he raised the stick and used it to shove the boy in the right shoulder. The boy grabbed the stick with both hands and pushed back.

Caleb shook his head.

"No," he said. "See how you're fighting back? You're pushing *against* the motion. I want you to go with it instead and see where it takes you." The tall boy nodded, brow furrowed with concentration.

This was the second day of class and the boy with the red hair was surprised; things were going much better than before. Somehow, he had absorbed some of Caleb's earlier verbal lessons. Now he was focused on the actual basics of fighting.

That morning, they had spent three hours on punching. The boy hadn't realized there was so much to learn and how little he knew: how to make a fist to best protect your thumb and knuckles. How to aim for a distance a hand's width beyond your intended target to maximize the impact. How, if you lacked arm strength, you could use speed to compensate. How to increase your power by stepping into the punch with your entire body. How to relax your body until the instant you threw the punch.

Now Caleb lifted the staff again. "We're going to try it slowly," he said, "and this time, don't fight it. Relax and try going with the motion." As he pushed the stick against the tall boy's left shoulder, the boy allowed himself to be guided backward, his body twisting.

"Where is your right arm going?" Caleb asked.

The boy gestured: It was swinging inward.

"Now make a fist with it. Think about using that natural movement and using it to help you punch inward. Again."

The two repeated the move, and this time, the boy succeeded in turning the attack into a roundhouse punch.

"Do you see what you're doing?" asked Caleb. "By going with the motion, you're decreasing the damage to your shoulder. At the same time, you're using it to generate an unexpected attack, from the other side."

As the tall boy thought this over, everyone else in the circle murmured. "Thanks," said the tall boy, beaming with excitement.

Caleb glanced at the sky; the sun was almost overhead and he made a quick calculation. After he had worked with everyone in the circle, he would have only a short time to teach basic self-defense moves. Then he would devote the afternoon to beginning techniques in slingshot, sap, and short club.

With any luck, they would be finished by sundown.

He knew he was going quickly, much too quickly, for his lessons to be truly useful. If they could even remember what he was teaching them, his students would have to practice each move for many weeks, hundreds if not thousands of times. Only then would their new skills start to become automatic and, therefore, any help at all. But even the best of them would be nothing more than mere beginners: eager, perhaps, but clumsy and unskilled.

To learn to fight well took months, even years of training. And he had spent little more than a day with them.

It was the best he could do. He should have left Prin already, gone that morning. Yet at the last moment he decided to stay a day longer. He unexpectedly felt obligated to these people and wanted to leave them with at least a fighting chance to protect themselves.

There was another reason that was even more important. He had to see Esther again.

"How are we doing?"

Caleb looked up; Rafe stood in the doorway of the bank.

His hands clasped behind his back, he rocked up and down on his heels, checking out the class. Caleb noted the *we* in his question. This was the first time the town's leader had deigned to show up. While learning to fight was something for others to do, Rafe seemed happy to share the credit.

"*We'll* get there," Caleb replied.

Rafe gestured for Caleb to approach him. "What's your guess on how long it'll take?" he asked in a low voice. "How many days do you think?"

Days? Caleb thought. *More like months.* But he didn't say it.

"Hard to figure," he replied.

But there was no time to keep talking. The red-haired boy had seized the staff and was using it to prod the others, with a bit too much enthusiasm, in an attempt to drill them in the technique they had just been taught.

"More slowly," Caleb said, walking back to the group. "It's not a natural reaction . . . you have to feel it first. Let me show you . . ."

It was sunset. His pack strapped onto the back of his bicycle, Caleb stopped in the street outside the building marked STARBUCKS. He didn't want this to be the last time he saw Esther. Yet how in good conscience could he ask her to join him?

He looked up at the second-floor window, half open and framed by a fluttering white curtain. He called up, just loud enough to be heard.

"Hey?"

After a minute, a girl came to the glass and looked down.

Wearing a flowered bathrobe held close to her throat, she looked haunted. This must be Esther's older sister, Caleb thought. He raised a hand to get her attention.

"Is Esther at home?" he asked.

At the name, the girl winced. There was a pause during which she did not reply. She untied the curtain, which fell and covered the window. Then, just a shadow, she walked away.

Caleb rode on, disturbed. Although he knew he should be leaving, the weird encounter made him want to see Esther more than ever. So, as evening deepened, he continued to search for her.

He headed along the main street of Prin, glanced down alleyways, passed the meeting hall, the old parking garage, the bank. By now, the streets were largely deserted; most people were home from work. Whenever he saw anyone, he asked, "You know Esther? Where she might be?" Each time, he got the same response: averted eyes, an evasive shrug, an unpersuasive no.

Heading down one street was a group of stragglers. They stopped, recognizing Caleb. Some were in awe, too shy to speak. He asked them the same questions.

"Any of you know Esther? Where she might be?"

One girl found the courage to respond. "She's gone."

"Gone?" Caleb said. "What do you mean?"

"She's just gone," the girl said. "For good."

The others glared at her. One tugged at her sleeve, whispering that they'd be late. But it was clearly an excuse.

"But where did she—" Caleb started to ask, but they were

walking away, the girl shooting him an apologetic gaze over her shoulder.

Caleb stood there, still straddling his bicycle. Now he found the idea of leaving impossible. Despite what the girl said, he couldn't believe it was true. Esther would never have left without telling him. And where would she go? So he did the only thing he could, continue his methodical search for Esther, up and down the streets of Prin.

Eventually, he made it to the railroad tracks on the outskirts of town. The tree where Esther had perched, watching him, was empty, as were the surrounding fields. It had been many hours; by now, the horizon was touched with pink.

He glanced up. Outlined by the rising sun, someone on a bike had crested a nearby hill and stood looking down at him. The face was obscured by a black hood.

Another one of Levi's boys, Caleb thought. What did he want?

At that moment, the sun shifted, momentarily blinding him. Still, he could see that the boy's arm had risen, in what appeared to be a wave.

Caleb raised his hand in response. As he did, he blocked the light and perceived the truth: The boy was holding a fiberglass hunting bow and drawing back the string.

There was a hissing sound, and Caleb felt a sudden blow. He stumbled, and a moment later, heat blossomed across his shoulder, surrounding the feathered shaft embedded in it.

TEN

THE DAY BEFORE, THE HEAT HAD BEEN INESCAPABLE.

It not only beat down from the sun; it radiated up from the concrete and oozing tar. The air itself shimmered with arid heat, forming waves that danced across the horizon.

Esther was not prepared for such relentless exposure.

Even with her thin hoodie tied closely around her face, her lips and nose were soon chapped and blistering. She did not have sunglasses, and the ceaseless glare was excruciating to her unprotected eyes. And although she was wearing sneakers, the bottoms of her feet were burning through the thin rubber soles.

Only now, an hour since she had left the boundaries of Prin, did the full impact of what had happened hit her.

She had only enough supplies to last a few days, she realized, and no weapons, no tools, and no shelter. She would never see her home again or climb her stairs or sleep in her bed. She would never see anyone she knew again, neither Caleb nor Sarah.

At the thought of them, Esther felt a flicker of hope. But a moment later, she recalled with a sinking heart that anyone who helped a person who was Shunned incurred the same sentence as well.

Except for the variants.

Variants had no need for the laws and regulations of the town. They followed their own rules and meted out their own justice.

With a pang, Esther recalled that she and Skar had parted on bad terms. Moreover, she knew that she had ignored her friend's desperate attempts to contact her. But Skar had never been the kind of person to hold a grudge; surely, she would forgive Esther when she found out the trouble she was in and convince her tribe to take pity on her.

By now, it was midmorning. On foot, it would take Esther until sundown to reach the variants' camp, but at least she knew where she was heading. She took off for the foothills that lay on the horizon.

Mostly, she ran at a swift trot, ignoring the agonizing blisters that formed on her feet. Even so, it was not until the sun was disappearing over the horizon that she saw the poisoned black lake glittering ahead of her. She veered from the roadway, hurdling the low metal fence and plunging into the deep undergrowth.

After the bright heat of the highway, the relatively dark and dappled forest was a relief. Esther toiled up the steep hillside, passing the tree with its faint white mark. As she neared the camp, she went slower and more cautiously. Every several minutes, she gave her special, two-tone call. Soon, she was at the edge of a small meadow, the last clearing before the final ascent to the variant camp. She was about to repeat her call when the whistle was returned. From across the meadow, she saw a flicker of movement as Skar stepped out from the trees.

"Esther?" Skar called.

The girl emerged from her hiding place and the two ran to each other. As Esther hugged her friend, overwhelming relief and exhaustion caused her knees to buckle and she almost collapsed.

"What happened?" Skar asked. Concerned, she led Esther to a flat boulder, where the two sat. "Every day, I have been signaling you and you haven't responded. I was worried you were still angry with me. But now, I see something else was wrong."

Esther nodded. "I'm in real trouble," she said in a low voice. Then in a rush, she explained everything that had occurred.

Throughout, Skar listened without speaking, her expression unusually grave.

"So I need your help," Esther concluded haltingly. She

was aware that her normally talkative friend was not saying anything, and she found this disturbing. "Please. I need you to ask your tribe if I can stay here."

Biting her lip, Skar dropped her gaze.

"It is not so simple anymore," she said at last. Then she looked up at Esther. "Why didn't you answer my signal before? I wanted so much to explain to you face to face. Then you would understand my situation."

"What do you mean? What situation?"

Skar held out her arm.

Esther glanced down. Her friend was still wearing the meaningless assortment of silver bracelets and wristwatches that she had on the last time. But beneath the jewelry, there was something new, something different.

Among the familiar whorls and patterns written on Skar's skin in scar tissue and ash, there was a vivid new line that snaked its way around and up the forearm, from the wrist bone to elbow. The wound was so fresh, it was still dark red with clotted blood and was framed by an angry ridge of pink, inflamed skin. One could still make out the dirt that had been rubbed into the cut, to maximize the scarring.

Esther stared at it, uncomprehending.

Skar was smiling. "I have a partner," she said. Then she giggled, covering her eyes and mouth with both hands as a deep blush stole over her face.

Esther was speechless.

She was not sure why she was so stunned. After all, she and Skar were both fifteen, more than old enough to be partnered.

Yet in all the years they had been friends, Skar had always behaved like the younger of the two. She had always looked up to Esther and in many ways, was like a little girl, one who giggled and occasionally played with a castoff doll and still sucked her fingers when she slept.

"It happened so quickly. I was not expecting him to ask," said Skar. "I meant to tell you when I saw you. But I was too surprised when you showed up at my home. And you were so angry, and then you left so fast. You didn't give me a chance."

Esther nodded slowly. This was true, she realized.

Now she swallowed hard. "Your partner," she muttered. "Does this mean you have to ask him for his permission?"

Skar shook her head. "Not for his permission. But his blessing."

Esther allowed Skar to take her by the hand and to lead her deeper into the woods. Soon, they reached a small clearing; the moon had come out and by its light, Esther could make out a nearby stream.

Skar turned to her. "Please try to understand. If it was only my decision, you know I would do anything you ask," she said, giving Esther's hand a final squeeze. "But now, I have someone else I must consult." Then she put her hand to her lips and gave a warbling cry, like a dove.

There was a long silence as the two girls waited. Finally, a solitary variant emerged from the forest.

Skar let go of her friend's hand and went forward to meet him. The two conversed in faint yet urgent whispers. Esther could not make out what they were saying, although it appeared to be an argument. But soon, Skar seized her partner by the hand and tugged on it to bring him close.

"This is Esther," Skar said. She could not hide the anxiety that creased her brow. "And this is Tarq."

The variant boy stared at Esther with open hostility. Although he was the same height as Skar, he was husky and outweighed her by a few pounds. In addition to the triangle he wore on his bicep, his dark skin was covered with other vivid tattoos and scars: stars, moons, the depiction of a hunt. His short tunic was cinched with a leather belt studded with metal, and he wore a plastic wristwatch and several pairs of sunglasses on colorful cords around his neck.

"What are you doing in these woods?" was the first thing he said.

Any polite greeting Esther was thinking of froze on her tongue. "This is neutral territory," she said stiffly.

"But you are Shunned," he said. He spoke not with concern but with hostility. "If anyone were to search for you, this is the first place they would try. Your presence can only bring trouble for my partner."

He stared at her in an open challenge. Esther didn't answer and lifted her chin, matching his antagonistic gaze.

Skar was anxiously looking from one to the other.

"Esther is my oldest friend," she whispered to Tarq. He said nothing at first, but a muscle in his jaw twitched. He had one arm draped around Skar's shoulders and Esther noticed that he now squeezed the nape of her neck possessively.

"And I am your partner," he said. "It is dangerous to be seen with norms. Especially one who has been driven out by her own people."

He raised his head and gave a high-pitched whistle. Moments later, it was answered by a second whistle far away, then a third and then a fourth. Skar glanced up, and Esther could see both panic and concern flash across her face.

"Forgive me, Esther," Skar said. "I want to help. But my people are nearby. If they see you here, they—"

But Esther was not there. She had already slipped back into the forest.

By now, the moon was high overhead. Dizzy and disoriented, Esther did not know where she was going. Still, she continued mechanically placing one foot after the other as she followed the faded double yellow lines; they seemed to go on forever as they bisected the abandoned two-lane highway.

She was filled with rage at the people of Prin. She loathed their cowardice, their blind obedience, and their pettiness. *They were responsible.* Esther's body pulsated with fury, and her churning emotions acted as fuel and provided a rhythm that drove her on as she continued mile after mile down the highway.

Esther stumbled. She had been traveling since dawn that day, and she was close to collapse. She did not recognize any of the landmarks around her, casting long and ominous shadows, but she seemed to be on the outskirts of a small town. When she reached a shopping plaza, she had no choice but to stop for the night.

There were several possible shelters, but Esther was careful about which one she would choose. More than most, she was aware of dangers any unfamiliar building could hold. Many were structurally unsound, with rotting floorboards and ceilings. Any collapse could carry with it a deadly surprise, releasing hidden pockets of stagnant rainwater. Others were infested with roaming hordes of territorial animals, whether they were fire ants, rats, oversize spiders, or snakes. Still others teemed with massive patches of mold and fungus that could make you ill just by breathing their foul air.

After investigating a diner, an eyeglass store, a pharmacy, and a jewelry store, Esther found something that seemed promising, the final business in the block of buildings. It was a large, open space with windows that were mostly intact. In the dim light, she could see that empty metal racks lined the walls and adorned wooden islands. It was, she decided, a clothing store.

Esther picked her way across the trash-littered carpeting to the back. There was a smaller room here, with open booths built into the back wall, side by side. Each held a wooden bench and a full-length mirror. One still had a tattered curtain, which Esther pulled shut behind her. There, after a quick meal of bean cake and water, she curled up and attempted to sleep.

Despite her exhaustion, Esther was too keyed up. Although the store was deserted, tiny sounds kept disrupting the silence: the skittering of claws across wood. A sudden flurry of paper, and a loud squeaking. She tossed on the hard and tiny bench, attempting in vain to find a comfortable position.

Then Esther froze.

There was another sound, but it was not that of an animal. It was much too heavy, much too deliberate. Someone was in the outer room, and he was walking as softly as he could, trying not to make any noise.

In the dark, Esther sat up as she kept her eyes trained on the thin curtain, illuminated by moonlight that streamed in from the front room. She put on her sneakers and gathered up her bag, her muscles tensed to spring.

The footsteps were getting closer. Within seconds, they seemed to stop a few feet outside her booth.

A tiny shadow appeared at the lower corner of the curtain. Esther stared at it. Then suddenly, it extended and sharpened, as a skeletal claw reached out to touch the fabric.

Before it did, Esther ripped the curtain back.

A hulking creature was standing there in filthy and tattered robes. His eyes glittered in an emaciated face encrusted with dirt.

He said something guttural that she could not understand. Then without warning, he lunged at her.

Esther tried to push past him. He was no more than bones floating within his billowing robes, yet he was surprisingly strong as he clawed for her bag. She kicked him in the knee as hard as she could, and he let go for a second, allowing her to dive past. Then she was running through the outer room, leaping through the broken window and into the parking lot.

That was when she noticed that she was not alone.

In the moonlight, she could see at least a dozen skeletal forms moving through the stores and buildings of the shopping plaza. Esther stopped in her tracks. At first, they seemed like spirits of the dead, supernatural creatures from one of the stories Sarah used to read her many years ago. But then, she realized what was happening, and the truth of it was almost worse.

There was nothing left and yet they were obeying a routine they could not shake.

They were attempting to Glean.

She knew they were only people, boys and girls her own age who had been driven mad by hunger, desperation, and exposure. But their hunger was frightening because it seemed unthinking, inhuman, and insectlike.

She took off as fast as she could.

The air was cool and it was a relief to run, to put as much distance as she could between herself and what she had just seen. Yet the night was full of other potential dangers, sounds and shapes that she could not identify. When the moon retreated behind a thick covering of clouds, Esther was plunged into total darkness. She knew she should stop; to risk injuring herself would be stupid. Yet she was beyond caring. She stumbled on a broken piece of roadway and fell hard on her hands and knees.

Esther broke down and cried.

This time she did not do so out of anger or frustration. Instead, she cried because of her foolishness. She cried because she thought she could get away with breaking the rules, and she could not. She cried because, as a result, all was lost. At last, fatigue won out. She lay on her side, curled into a ball; and blessedly, she fell asleep.

Several hours later, Esther awoke on the side of the road, half in the gravel-studded shoulder and half in an overgrown field that bordered the highway. Overhead, the sky was gray with the first light of dawn. Her face was pressed to the concrete, which was still hot, tiny pebbles cutting into her cheek; and despite the scent of gasoline baked into the road, there was a thicker smell, sweet and nauseating, that overpowered it, catching in her throat and making her gag. The air pulsed with a heavy and constant drone as she found herself staring at a piece of broken glass, a shard of deep blue lying inches away.

Beyond it, something gleamed white. It was a branch stripped bare of its bark, a piece of wood bleached by the sun. But as her eyes focused on it, Esther realized what it was.

It was a bone. And attached to the end was a battered sneaker.

For as far as she could see, human remains littered the ground. There were hundreds of bones and bone fragments, most softened by exposure to near dust, animal teeth marks and knobbed ends alike eroded away to nothingness. All were human, still clad in the tattered remains of jeans and T-shirts, wrapped in moldering robes. Still others were fresher, heaped piles that stank of decay and were all but invisible beneath an oily black coating that shifted and shimmered in the early light. It was in fact flies, hundreds of thousands of them, busily eating, mating, laying eggs, and dying. They were responsible for the ceaseless drone that filled the air.

For this was the rumored place where the sick went when they had been Shunned from every community and driven away from the living. It was the place where people went when there was no more hope, no more life. It was the Valley of the Dead.

And Esther had ended up here as well.

She would run from it in terror, if she could. But she barely had the strength to breathe, much less move. As the first rays of sun began to heat and thicken the air around her, she felt the life force within her starting to ebb. She closed her eyes and saw a brilliant red that pulsed more and more faintly, in time with her heart.

But above the droning, Esther heard another noise, faint but real.

Something was in the bushes that lay beyond the highway's shoulder. Esther opened her eyes to see what it was, but it was still too dim. Then she heard it again.

Someone was coughing.

Esther raised her head. The sky was imperceptibly brighter, and by its modest light, she could make out a small figure huddled against a tree.

Shakily, Esther got to her feet. She stumbled closer and saw that it was a girl, wrapped in dirty robes, sitting up and watching her.

The two gazed at one another without speaking. Even in the dim light, Esther could see the extreme pallor of the girl's face, and the feverish light in her eyes. If she stood any closer, she knew she would also notice the telltale sores, the lesions that covered the face and limbs of the afflicted.

"Where are you from?"

The girl's voice was cracked and dry, like an autumn leaf. It was so tiny, Esther had to strain to hear her.

"Prin."

The girl nodded. "I was there once," she said. "A long time ago."

Esther hesitated. It was dangerous, she knew, to be close to someone who had the disease. In Prin, no one even spoke to the afflicted; once the lesions appeared, they were driven out of town, as Esther had been. But without food and water.

It made no sense to waste precious supplies on the dying. Yet now Esther reached into her bag. Taking out her water bottle, she uncapped it, and handed it over. The girl's eyebrows went up in a question and Esther nodded. Then the girl reached out her hands. When Esther touched them to help her lift the bottle, they were hot and papery.

The girl drank deeply, the muscles in her throat working. She drank until the bottle was nearly finished, then she pushed it aside and sighed.

"Thank you," she said. She sounded much, much better, but neither girl was fooled. "Where are you headed? You got a home?"

Esther shrugged. "I did."

The girl nodded. "It all lasts so short, don't it. Here and gone. Well"—her eyes flickered to the side, as if to indicate all of the horror that surrounded them—"there's a place for you here, if you want it."

She closed her eyes. Within moments, she was breathing deeply. In sleep, her face was eased of its pain and tension and Esther was surprised to see that she looked her age. She was no more than nine or ten.

Esther got to her feet. Then she put her backpack over her shoulder.

It all lasts so short.

And no matter how bad things were, she was still alive.

The sun was now visible in the eastern sky. If she set off now, she should be back in Prin by evening.

ELEVEN

At the same moment in Prin, a figure lay exposed to the morning sun, writing in agony. Instinctively, Caleb grabbed the fiberglass shaft where it entered his shoulder. He could not risk having the arrowhead break off, lodging in his body. So he pulled it out in one swift motion and flung it away.

Then he realized his terrible mistake. Without the arrow to keep it plugged, the wound began to pump blood. Soon the front of Caleb's shirt appeared black and glistening, and dark crimson began to pool on the packed earth beneath him. Caleb's hands were stained red as he pressed hard against his chest, trying to stanch the flow that wouldn't stop.

It was so early, teams on an Excavation had not yet shown up. He was far from the main roads, miles from the center of Prin. His only hope was to somehow ride into town to get help.

But when Caleb took his hands from the wound, a fresh bout of blood bubbled up through the soaked and torn fabric. He pressed his hands over it, felt the fluttering pulse underneath.

Then he noticed something out of the corner of his eye. Across the parched field, past the metal tracks long overgrown with weeds, there was an abandoned truck that sagged on dusty wheels. Next to it, a small person was picking its way toward him.

It was not the hooded guard, the would-be assassin from the Source. It was bundled in a pale blue sheet, its head covered. Caleb felt a surge of relief. He tried to half rise.

"Esther!" he called.

"Don't be scared!" it responded, and his heart sank.

It was female, but not the one girl he desperately wanted to see. As she came nearer, a strange, heady smell, like that of a thousand flowers, seemed to shimmer from her. When she crouched next to Caleb and saw all the blood, the girl gasped.

"I didn't think he'd really do it," she murmured.

"Who? And who are you?"

The girl pushed the sheet away from her face. To Caleb's blurred vision, she was as unreal and exotic-looking as an animal from a dream: pale, with golden hair and strange blue eyes. He noticed the glittering rings on the girl's fingers, the chains and bangles that dangled from her slim wrists.

"You're from the Source," he said. "Levi's girl. Michal."

Caleb fumbled on the ground for the arrow, which was sticky with his blood. "Keep your distance."

Michal glanced at the arrow, then back at Caleb.

"I don't blame you if you don't trust me," she said. "I should have warned you."

"What do you mean?"

"After you left, I heard the guards talking. Levi told them if you weren't gone by yesterday, to come after you. I kept an eye on the guards. And this morning, when one of them left with a weapon, I followed him."

Caleb cut her off. "It doesn't matter," he said. "I need to get to town. Give me that."

At first, the girl looked baffled. Then Caleb seized the cloth that protected her and started tearing it. When she realized what he was doing, she helped him to unwrap it. Then she wadded up one piece and pressed it against the wound. He used the other strip to bind the bandage against his shoulder.

She got to her feet, having grabbed him under the arms. The effort of standing caused him to almost lose consciousness; his eyelids flickered in his pale face.

"Hold on," Michal told him; "this is going to hurt."

With difficulty, she managed to help hoist Caleb onto his bicycle seat. He was sweating and his teeth were gritted, but he said nothing.

Then Michal wheeled him across the scorched field, trying to avoid the stones and ruts. It was slow going; his weight made the bike difficult to steer and they had to stop every few feet to keep him from sliding off.

When they stopped for what felt like the hundredth time, Michal spoke up.

"It's too far," she said. "We won't make it."

The girl was clearly unused to physical exertion. Dressed in skimpy clothes, she was sweaty and red faced as she gasped for breath. Caleb knew she was right.

Desperate, he looked around. Visible in the distance was the Source, and a sudden idea came to him.

"You could bring me back supplies," he said. "Fresh water, bandages."

Michal frowned, staring at the ground, weighing something in her mind. Then she looked up.

"I should take you there," she said. "It'll be safer."

Caleb glanced at her sharply. "What do you mean?"

"I got my own room. Past the loading dock."

"What about the guards?"

Michal shook her head. "They got cameras everywhere. But when I left, I shut off the ones along the back. No one will notice if we hurry."

She seemed sincere. Yet it felt like insanity to Caleb to go to the very place where his intended executioner was.

He noticed that blood was soaking through the makeshift blue bandage. Plus, he was having trouble breathing and his skin felt cold and clammy. He had no choice but to trust Michal.

"All right," Caleb said finally.

As the sun rose, the two continued their slow and painstaking way across the field toward the gleaming white building in the distance.

When Caleb came to, it was dark and cool. For a moment, he had no idea where he was.

Then the memories came stuttering back as scattered and disjointed images.

The sun blinding his eyes. The hooded guard appearing on the horizon, raising his hand. Then the split-second understanding of what was about to happen, when it was too late . . .

He jolted upright, but a deep pain radiated from his upper chest, and he gasped. It hurt to breathe and he couldn't move his left shoulder.

"You're awake," said Michal.

She was sitting beside him, wringing a washcloth into a plastic basin. Without her jewelry and makeup, she looked years younger, like a little girl.

"Where am I?"

"You're in my room," she said. "Don't worry . . . no one never comes in here."

"How long have I been here?"

"I found you this morning. Now it's long past sundown."

She handed him a cup of water. As Caleb drank, he glanced at Michal's quarters. Everything was not only new, but impossibly clean: the bed, the silky quilts and pillows that covered it, the rug on the floor. The walls were decorated with glossy pictures hung in frames, not just images torn out of magazines; and scented candles burned on the bedside table.

He had been changed into a fresh shirt and underneath it, he could feel the crackle of medical gauze and tape.

He shook his head. "You're his girl," he said. "Why are you doing this?"

Michal blushed and glanced down. "Levi disrespected me." Her voice was so low he could barely make out what she was saying. "He . . . he offered me to you. In front of everyone." When she looked up, Caleb was startled by the flash of rage in her eyes.

"He thinks I'm worthless," Michal said. "But I'm not."

She stood. "I heard what you said that day . . . that you're looking for your son. Well, a few months ago, somebody brung a baby here. It was real late, but I could hear it crying. Levi wouldn't let nobody near it. Not even me. But it's still here, somewhere. And I know how to find out for sure."

Caleb had been staring at her. Now he swung his legs to the ground. With difficulty, he stood and grabbed his pack.

"Show me," he said.

Moments later, they were outside her room. The girl moved through the darkened corridors and down a back stairwell. Aware of where the cameras were, Michal was careful to take a circuitous route, yet one that was not so unusual that it would arouse suspicion.

Caleb trailed a short distance behind. Each breath he drew was agony. Yet he ignored his discomfort and focused on navigating his way through the treacherous terrain without being seen.

Occasionally, Michal ran into a guard. When she did, she

stopped to flirt with each one, touching the boy on the arm, laughing, leaning close. To Caleb, it was the oldest and most obvious trick in the world; nevertheless, he was impressed to see that it always worked. Each time, he was able to make his way past the guard, unnoticed.

Soon, he and the girl were in the basement. In the hallway, he waited behind a cluster of pipes that ran from floor to ceiling as Michal slipped ahead to a battered steel door that lay ajar, halfway down the hallway. A sign attached to it read SECURITY.

She disappeared behind it for a moment and reappeared, frowning. "There's supposed to be a guard here." Then, she made up her mind. "That's where you need to go. Look careful, but be quick. I'll be out here in case anyone shows up."

Caleb nodded, and slipped inside the room.

At first, he was puzzled by what he saw. It was a small and windowless office, a scuffed cement cube painted gray. A set of dusty metal shelves held pieces of forgotten equipment; above it, a clock on the wall read an eternal 2:47. In the center of the room was a large table that supported a bank of twenty or so small screens.

Caleb approached.

Each screen showed a flickering image in grainy black and white. It took him a moment to realize that these were different locations within the Source: the front door, the loading dock, the dark aisles with their endless shelves of crates, Levi's office. As Caleb leaned closer, he was stunned to see that these images were moving: *A guard walked past a closed door. Levi leaned back in his chair. Another guard carried a box across a room.*

And in one screen, a toddler sat on the ground.

The image was so grainy, it was hard to make out. The child had its gaze downward and appeared to be studying something on the ground. Then it clapped its hands, laughing, and for an instant, raised its head.

Caleb gave an involuntary cry and leaned forward, his palm on the glass screen. If this were a window, he would smash through it now, to reach deep into the past, to grab hold of what he had once possessed and then lost.

His son.

Kai.

"Miss?"

Outside the security room, Michal jumped and whirled around. A guard stood in front of her, hulking and anonymous in his black hood. A moment ago, she had thought she heard something and went to investigate. She was unaware that in the echoing hallway, the sound was in fact coming from the other direction.

Badly startled, she laughed. Even to her ears, it sounded false and hollow.

"You scared me," she said. That much was true. She tried to sound playful and again, failed miserably.

"What are you doing down here?" Without being able to see his face, it was impossible to tell what the guard was thinking, feeling.

Her mind raced. "Levi sent me," she said at last. "He

thought the camera on the front door was broken. He wanted to know if there's still a picture."

The guard grunted.

"Let's go check," he said, and turned to go.

She grabbed hold of his arm. "I already did," she said. Then she gave him a tremulous smile and tilted her head, opening her eyes wide and softening her expression.

It always worked.

But this time, something was wrong.

He stared into her face for a long moment. Then he pushed her away.

"What are you playing at?" She could see his eyes, small and suspicious, glinting through the holes in the fabric.

Michal drew herself up haughtily. "Nothing," she said.

She could feel his eyes on her back as she sauntered away. She only prayed they were talking loudly enough for Caleb to hear and that he had had time to take cover.

In truth, she was trembling with panic.

Caleb heard the voices in the hall and froze. He could not make out what was being said, but even so, he sensed the alarm in Michal's voice, pitched high and shrill.

She was talking that way to warn him.

There was nowhere to hide in the tiny room, so sparsely furnished with its table and equipment. Even as he glanced around, the dented metal door was swinging open and he ducked behind it, flattening himself against the wall. The moment the guard entered, Caleb managed to slip around the door.

He was not expecting to find two more of Levi's men in the narrow hallway.

They were on their way to some sort of break, their defenses down; one had his hood partly pushed up so he could tear into a piece of flatbread with his teeth. The other glanced up and for an astonished second, locked eyes with Caleb.

But Caleb was already on the attack.

Sprinting forward, his adrenaline overriding his pain, he raised one elbow and rammed it into the throat of the second guard. Choking, the boy staggered backward against the wall and slid to the floor with a thud.

The other guard, bread falling from his open mouth, let out a roar and rushed at Caleb. Caleb bent forward, digging his injured shoulder into the boy's gut. Grabbing his hood, Caleb flipped him over his head, slamming him on the floor. As he lay there, dazed, Caleb kicked at his holstered weapon, freeing it from his belt and sending it skittering across the floor and under a rusted radiator at the end of the hall.

Caleb had bought himself a few precious seconds, enough time to escape; but he forgot about the guard inside the security room, who now came barreling out, as hulking and enraged as a wild boar. Caleb scrabbled in his pack for anything that might stop him. The moment before the guard reached him, his fingers closed around something.

Perfect.

Caleb whirled his arm in a roundhouse punch and smashed a rock into the center of the guard's hooded face. There was an audible crack, and with a scream, the boy reeled backward, clutching his nose. As his legs buckled beneath him, it was easy to grab one knee, yank it hard, and twist; this sent him crashing to the ground. Blood spurted from his nostrils, splattering his robes and the cement floor.

Caleb was halfway down the hall, heading for the stairs. There was only one thought on his mind.

Kai. Kai was alive and somewhere inside the Source.

But where? On the main floor, he ran through darkened aisles, surrounded on both sides by towering shelves stacked high with cardboard boxes. The pain in Caleb's shoulder pulsed powerfully in time with his heart; but the sensation seemed far away, as if it belonged to someone else.

Ahead of him and high above, he saw something glinting, light reflecting off glass from some distant source he couldn't yet place. Instinctively, he headed toward it.

Caleb reached the entrance to a wide ramp leading upward, with handrails on either side. It was a peculiar thing, unlike any he had ever seen before, almost like a mountain road inside a building. Caleb hesitated. Behind him, he could hear the heavy steps and distant shouts of Levi's guards. They were searching for him through the aisles, spreading out across the vast floor. Making up his mind, he raced up the surface and into the darkness.

At the end, he paused to get his bearings. By the echoing void that surrounded him, Caleb sensed he was now in a large and empty space, devoid of shelved goods. As he moved forward, his eyes adjusted to the gloom. Soon he noticed a faint glow in the distance. He was in a cavernous room marked by giant rectangular columns, and he moved from one to the next until he reached the source of the light.

It came from a small, box-like space seemingly carved out of the back wall and exposed, doorless, to the larger room. Two guards stood on either side. The bottom half of its three walls seemed to be made of some battered metal; upward, they were thick chain link, the kind you would see on a fence or cage. Inside, Caleb could partly glimpse what seemed to be a desk; the light came from a lamp. Occasionally, a boy's hands moved into view and then away.

Caleb removed his backpack and took out his weapon. Then he loaded it with all the ammunition he had left: three rocks.

Placing it on his shoulder, he aimed meticulously; there was no room for error. He fired once, hitting one guard in the temple with a loud crack. As the boy sank to the floor, Caleb shot again, but this time, his aim was off; he only grazed the shoulder of the second. The guard looked up: Caleb followed with a third shot that cleanly hit the space between the boy's eyebrows, just above the bridge of his nose. With a grunt, he also dropped to the floor.

The room was now undefended as Caleb stood before its threshold.

Levi was behind his desk, papers strewn in front of him. Alone, the pale boy was paler still as he stared at his intruder. For an instant, fear and confusion flickered across his features. Then he acted as if nothing unusual was happening.

"Caleb," Levi said. "What are you—"

Caleb gave the other no opportunity to speak. Like a

hawk after a mouse, he lunged across the wooden surface that separated them. Using both hands, he grabbed Levi's lapels and dragged him across the desk, scattering everything that lay in their path.

With newly found strength, Caleb lifted the other boy clear of the desk; he felt the black fabric strain and rip under his hands. Then he threw him down onto his back on the floor, straddling and pinning him to the cement.

"Where is my son?" he shouted.

Levi's hand moved. He attempted to lift a meager weapon, a thin, decorative utensil with a blade too dull to cut but pointed enough to stab. Caleb seized the slender wrist and twisted it; with a cry, Levi dropped the weapon and it clattered to the ground.

The two remained locked, one under the other, both breathing hard. The pain in Caleb's shoulder had spread down his arm, weakening his grip; still, he did his best to ignore it.

Even in the losing position, Levi maintained his composure. Caleb had to restrain himself from crushing Levi's throat. Instead, he grabbed the small weapon on the ground beside him and placed the sharp tip against the side of the other boy's neck. He took grim pleasure in noting that the pale blue vein there was pulsing wildly, betraying the boy's show of cool.

Caleb pressed the tip of his knife in deeper. A bead of blood welled up, the bright red in shocking contrast to the white skin.

Through a fog of emotion, something clicked in his mind.

The fire. His house, burning to the ground, with Miri trapped inside. A freakish mutant attack, as senseless as it was deadly.

Kai, seized from his cradle. After so many months, most likely dead or gone forever.

What Esther saw at the mutant camp: goods from the Source.

And now, his baby, under this roof.

"You hired the mutants," Caleb said. "To kill my partner, to kill me. You paid them off, to steal my boy. And now, you have my son. And you still want to kill me."

Levi was watching him, saying nothing. It was like they were playing a game of dare.

"Why?" Caleb said. "Just tell me why."

When there was no reply, Caleb forced the blade even deeper into Levi's neck. Blood started to run, dripping down and pooling on the cement floor.

Levi stopped struggling. Ever practical, he knew there were to be no more secrets—not if he wished to live.

He looked away from Caleb and into the distance, into the past.

"I shouldn't be surprised you managed to survive," he said. "You were always the stronger one. You were always lucky. That's what this was about."

Caleb started, confused, and his hold on the knife wavered.

"What are you talking about?" he asked.

Levi turned his gaze back to him. "That's why they gave me away. Because even though we were both so young, you were clearly the only one worth saving."

Caleb sat back, stunned. Part of his mind fought what he

was hearing even as the words started to make a terrible sense.

"You're my brother," he said at last.

"I was," Levi said.

No longer pinned, the boy in black sat up and got to his feet. He managed to keep his poise and walk back to his desk.

"I don't blame them, really. At least not anymore." As he spoke, he took a handkerchief from a drawer and dabbed at the blood running down the side of his neck. "As you know, keeping one child fed is virtually impossible, let alone two. Why wouldn't our parents keep the stronger, younger boy and cast out the sickly, older one? That is what animals do, isn't it?"

Still on his knees, Caleb was finally able to answer.

"That's not what they told me," he said, his voice catching. Inwardly, he was reeling with disbelief; the idea that they were related was obscene, unthinkable. "They told me you were ill. They said you died years ago."

Levi smiled; it wasn't a pleasant sight.

"As far as our parents were concerned, I did die," he replied. "Happily for me, some animals behave better than others. Strangers pitied me, and took me in. I was never strong. But even as a small child, I knew how to use people, how to make them do what I wanted. Soon, I started to build a new family, to make friends. Or at least collect acquaintances."

As he spoke, Levi had begun to clear up the mess on his desk. He stacked papers, put his writing utensils back into their container, arranged files, restored order. Caleb, mesmerized by the boy's actions and words, made no move to stop him.

"Of course, between us, what I was really doing was cobbling together an army. Or would you call it a gang . . . a posse? Well, a group of boys, anyway, strong and I'll admit not very smart boys who nevertheless respect power almost as much as they like having their bellies filled on a regular basis. You've met some of them—or at least they've encountered you."

He gestured at the door, outside of which the two guards still lay motionless in a heap.

"They followed me when I came to Prin, five or six years ago," Levi said. "I always knew I was smart. But it wasn't until I came here that I learned how to read and improve myself. Suddenly, I understood what potential there was . . . not just for scrabbling together an existence day to day, but for real power. I planned how to break into this building, and with my army's help, I eventually succeeded."

His workspace orderly, Levi once more assumed a position of authority. He sat behind his desk.

"And my boys have been good scouts, as well," continued Levi. "They've brought me back things from not only Prin, but places far beyond. News, mostly. But also goods, trinkets, pretty little things they thought would amuse me. Like Michal."

Caleb looked up sharply and Levi laughed.

"But most important, my guards managed to find out what I *really* wanted to know all these years . . . and that's what became of you."

Levi rubbed his temple. For a moment, his expression seemed haunted; traces of pain and longing appeared as deep lines etched around his mouth and eyes. Then they disappeared, like shadows.

"They knew where you were," he continued. "They told me you had partnered and had a son. Again, you were lucky. I've tried to father an heir many times, with different females. And yet I can't."

Levi's voice, normally so controlled, broke at this last statement. And as Caleb looked at his brother, he finally recognized the similarities in their faces, things he had sensed at their first meeting but couldn't name.

"Once I knew where you were," Levi was saying, "I decided to take from you everything, just as everything had been taken from me. Most important, I would have a son, a true heir, one linked to me by my own blood. One who will carry on what I'm about to achieve."

At last, Caleb found the strength to stand. He leaned forward on the desk in front of him. Only the whiteness of his knuckles revealed the intense emotions roiling inside of him. He looked into his brother's eyes.

"You can't have him," he said.

Levi nodded. Then he reached behind him to a panel embedded in the wall and pressed one of three buttons.

The room shook.

Caleb looked up, startled. Behind him, two large metal plates, the doors to the office that had been hidden in ceiling and floor, were sliding shut like jaws in a mouth; the two boys were quickly trapped in the small space.

Then, with a grinding of ancient gears, the entire room began to move. Through the wire mesh walls, it was clear that they were advancing down a dirty brick shaft.

"Use your head," Levi said. "The boy's much better off with me than he would be with you. What have you possibly got to offer him?"

"I'll kill you first," Caleb said.

"Go ahead," Levi said. "When the doors open, and they will any second now, you will be greeted by all my guards. I know you can handle a few mutants waving rocks; I'm not so sure what your chances will be against eighteen of my guards carrying Tasers. Especially if I'm dead. And where will *that* leave the boy?"

With a sudden lurch, the room came to a halt and the huge doors behind Caleb began to grind open again.

"Forget the boy," Levi said. He sounded so sensible, even wise. Like a big brother, in fact. "It'll be easier for you—for everyone—if you're far away."

"I'm not going anywhere," Caleb said.

Now the doors opened. Four hooded guards burst in and surrounded Caleb. Levi held them off with a raised hand.

"Very well," he said. "I can't force you to leave. But I have my own plans, bigger plans than you can ever understand. I asked you to join me in them before, but you refused. So now I will not tolerate your interfering in them. You can stay if you want. But if you do, you are not to lift one finger to defend the town or its people from the mutants again. Do you understand?"

Taken aback, Caleb hesitated. "What I do is my own business."

Levi shrugged. "If you disobey me, no matter where you are, I will hear word of it from my boys. And the moment I do, I will kill your child. Do I make myself clear?"

Caleb was furious—and flabbergasted.

"You would do that . . . after all the trouble you went through to track him down? Even after you tell me you—"

But Levi cut him off. *"Do I make myself clear?"*

Caleb nodded, uncomprehending. When Levi gave a signal his guards seized Caleb and started to drag him out. This time, he was reminded of the pain, which had returned worse than ever; he could not resist even if he wanted to.

In the main room, the guards dragged Caleb forward on his knees. He kept his face impassive, refusing to give them the satisfaction of knowing he was in agony. But he could not keep the blood from dripping from his shirt again, leaving a glistening red trail.

"Enjoying yourself?" one asked.

Caleb gritted his teeth as they yanked him around a bend. Ahead, he saw that the giant main door of the Source was open, revealing the tarry black sky.

The guards picked him up and threw him outside. Caleb landed hard on his hands and knees, scraping himself on gravel and broken glass.

His backpack and hat were thrown after him and landed nearby. Next to them fell pieces of his weapon. They had been ripped from each other and scattered, like a squirrel's bones from a cat's mouth.

Caleb was about to pick them up, when he sensed a guard standing above him.

"This is for the others," he said.

He was holding the weapon all the guards wore, the plastic box with two wires at the end that crackled with blue fire. Caleb was trying to crawl away when the guard rammed it into the small of his back. He screamed as a bolt of white-hot electricity erupted through his spine and exploded in his brain, seeming to set everything in his body on fire. He dropped to the ground, immobilized.

Nearly unconscious, he heard the three guards walk away, chuckling. The door of the Source creaked and then slammed shut.

Caleb lay there, motionless. It was as if his entire body had been scorched from within. He felt blood from his wound seeping into the hot, baked earth beneath him. It was all he could do to open his eyes. Still, the physical pain was nothing compared to his emotional anguish.

All along, it was one person who destroyed his family.

It wasn't the mutants after all. For months, he had blamed them; poisoned by his rage and hatred, he had worked obsessively to track them down and destroy them.

Mutants.

For the first time, Caleb was struck by the ugly word, one he had used a thousand times without thinking, and he winced. For they, the variants, were nothing but pawns, poor and pathetic; had it not been them, Levi could have found someone else desperate and hungry enough to do his bidding.

The variants weren't responsible; it was his brother. The

person who was in a real sense closest to him, his own flesh and blood, had set out to destroy him . . . and very nearly succeeded.

When Caleb thought of the months Levi must have taken to plan and carry out his campaign, his mind reeled. Levi's revenge was no impulsive act done in the heat of anger. It was carried out with clear eyes and cold calculation.

If what Levi said was true, he had been brutally wronged in childhood. Still, Caleb couldn't imagine lifting a hand or plotting against his own brother, especially a brother who was innocent of any wrongdoing.

Caleb's only sin was the fact of his birth.

Levi waited until they had gone. Then he got up and retrieved the small dagger that had dropped to the floor.

After wiping the blade clean, he placed it back on his desk, next to the matching penholder and leather blotter. He discovered that he was trembling and breathing fast, nearly hyperventilating. He had waited years for this moment, this long-anticipated revenge on his younger brother; and his victory was all the sweeter in that he had won it by his wits alone.

Caleb's days as the town's savior were over. Prin would need a new hero. And that would be easy enough to arrange.

Levi knew he should be glad. Yet, strangely, he was not.

One thought continued to nag at him: Somebody must have told Caleb about the boy. That meant someone, like his parents so long ago, must have betrayed him, someone he had trusted and housed and fed.

Levi called together a meeting of his guards.

Now he leaned against the wall, watching as one by one, his guards were tied to a steam pipe against the wall and questioned. Assisting in the interrogation was a tool from the gardening and patio aisle, a black wand filled with fuel. When a button was pressed, a small flame blossomed out from the top. As the smell of butane mixed with and then was overpowered by the stink of charred flesh, the basement of the Source echoed with screams that no one could hear from the outside.

Levi watched not because he enjoyed it; in fact, the constant weeping and pleading wore on his nerves. He had to make sure his instructions were being followed; he could not be certain that his guards would do their job. The very one asking questions, after all, would soon be the one interrogated by his peers.

While a clumsy system, it had always served its purpose before. Yet after an hour, no one had confessed to anything. By now, Levi was tired of not only their tears and moans, but the glimpses of their squinched and sweating faces, only partly hidden by their hoods. They looked as pink and helpless as cornered mice. It sickened him.

Exasperated and impatient, Levi was about to begin the cycle of interrogation once more, when a guard, shaking, separated himself from the group.

"I hate to say it . . ." His voice was almost inaudible. "But when the stranger come down to the basement, there was someone who came out of the security room only a second before." He swallowed hard. "It was your girl. And she was acting funny."

Levi stared at him. He felt almost faint with anger: the gall of the guard to try saving himself with such a blatant lie! Yet the more he thought about it, the more it made a hideous kind of sense. If he had been betrayed, why shouldn't the treachery be of the worst, most intimate kind? That was the story of his youth: Wasn't his childhood trust paid back with cruelty and abandonment? So now, wasn't it likely that he had been forsaken by the person who had always said she loved him?

Levi kept his voice calm, revealing nothing.

"You better be right."

He ended the session.

Levi returned to his office, any sense of jubilation forgotten. Yet as he sat alone, brooding, he felt strangely content. Once again, the world had proven itself to be the way he had always known it to be: faithless and cold. It was reassuring.

He would search Michal's room himself.

TWELVE

BY DAWN, CALEB REACHED THE SCHOOL.

He fell against the front door and leaned upon it, breathing hard. It had taken nearly everything he had to walk back. He was light-headed from blood loss and thirst, and exhausted from fighting. When he closed his eyes, he could still feel the lingering shock of the electrical current surging through his body.

He stumbled toward his schoolroom, and took two faltering steps over the threshold.

Then he saw her.

Esther looked thinner than ever, her face burned by the

sun. His shock giving way to joy, he moved quickly to her. But he could only go so far before his legs buckled, and she had to catch him before he fell.

Caleb was almost unrecognizable: dusty and bloodied, shivering in the heat. He clung to her as if he was drowning, and she led him to his cot, where she eased him down. Then she fetched water to clean his wounds and for him to drink.

Esther's own journey here had been as much a hardship. Escaping from the Valley of the Dead, she had eventually found discarded robes in an abandoned van. She put them on over her clothes, and they both protected her from the sun and shielded her identity. The irony was not lost on her: Now that she was Shunned, she was finally dressed like one of the people she had long disdained and who had exiled her. By the time she reached the school late that evening, she was not able to remove the robes fast enough.

To her disappointment and misery, the schoolroom had been empty.

Esther was never good at waiting. Unable to sleep, she paced up and down the room all night, glancing out the window and door, listening in vain for the sound of Caleb's footsteps.

And now that she was alone with him, her relief was replaced by fury at the people who did this to him, as well as the need to cherish and make him well again. She had come here seeking his protection, but now she realized he needed hers just as badly.

"What happened?" she asked, once he had stopped drinking.

Caleb told her, haltingly. He spoke of seeing his child, the revelation of Levi's kinship, and his terrible retribution for their parents' neglect, hiring the mutants to carry out the dirty work he would not do himself. At last, when there was nothing more to say, he buried his face in his filthy hands.

And he cried.

Esther could not bear to see it. She alone understood that Caleb wore a tough exterior, a mask to protect what was important and precious inside; she knew this because it was what she did as well. For him to drop his guard meant that he no longer had the strength to fight off his despair, and she felt his pain as keenly as she felt her own.

She reached out and grabbed his hands.

They were icy cold and she wrapped her own hands around them, trying to give him her warmth and life, the way she knew variant shamans did to the dead. Her thumbs traced the ridges of blisters on his palms, the rough and bruised skin along his knuckles. Then she pressed her palms against his, and their fingers intertwined.

She raised her eyes to his face, at the stubble built up over days. Then she looked into his eyes and felt herself overwhelmed by his intense gaze, which mixed relief with gratitude and something more. As he caressed her hand, she lifted her fingertips to his face, tracing his cheek to his chin, then toward his lips.

"It's going to be all right," she whispered.

But something had shifted inside her, a strange new emotion moving into the other. Her desire to ease Caleb's suffering had been joined with another desire, one even more powerful, like two streams meeting and converging in a riverbed, mingling in a current against which she had no strength.

She had never known this feeling before.

Her fingers found his lips, which moved together and pressed against her fingertips, so softly she could hardly feel it. Then he kissed them again, this time harder; and at the pressure, she felt her body tremble.

"Caleb," she said, his name meaning everything she could not say.

Then their lips were on each other's, at first brushing there, like a question. Each applied more pressure, first quickly, then lingeringly. Esther closed her eyes, feeling only his mouth, his hands clasped in hers.

It was the first time she had ever kissed anyone. And it was different from how she imagined it would be, better, more dizzying.

Esther knew Caleb had been partnered, so he had kissed another, done more than kiss. And he was older than her, by more than a year. Yet she yearned to be closer to him and so she parted her lips, sending him a signal, indicating he could do the same. She was not certain but thought he understood, the way you did when someone opened a door, then walked away, saying it was safe to enter, you were allowed.

His tongue was softer than she expected, and warmer, and smooth. It filled her mouth, exploring, and she let it. Then she responded, pushing her own tongue to meet his, and each teased the other a little. It was the most delicate and intimate thing she could imagine, comparable to nothing.

Then the kiss ended. And as the two pulled away from one another and smiled bashfully, Esther suddenly felt so much older, years and years older, than she had only a few moments before.

As for Caleb, he was stunned by the tenderness he felt toward Esther. It was the first time he had touched anyone since his partner's death, the first time he had allowed himself to open up and care for anyone.

He put his hand on Esther's head and caressed her jagged hair. Esther must have cut it herself, he thought. It even resembled her, in a way: sharp in appearance but delicate to the touch.

"Tell me what happened," he said.

Unemotionally, she told him the facts of her Shunning, her journey south, and what she had encountered. She was now a fugitive in her own town; if she were discovered, it would mean certain death for her and anyone who harbored her. When she finished, Caleb knew they were on their own. They were deprived of the people they loved, the places they knew, protected by just each other and the brick and broken glass of the school.

"What do we do now?" she asked him.

"Stay here," he said.

"For how long?"

"Forever."

Yet, even as they huddled together, they could hear something happening outside. Without speaking, Caleb got to his feet, followed by Esther. Holding hands, they approached the window and stood there, looking out at the street with a new feeling of dread. For in the distance, they could hear a sound that neither of them could place. Then, they recognized what it was; and the realization sent a deep chill through them both.

It was the baying of wild dogs.

On the far end of Prin, the townspeople tried to flee, but it was no use.

A dog had his teeth buried in the leg of a girl as she kicked at it, vainly attempting to drag herself into a doorway; her white robes were torn and soaked through with her blood. Two other dogs set upon a boy who was on his way to a Gleaning. Swerving, he fell off his bicycle into the dust of the road, where another dog slashed at his arms as he tried to shield his face.

Other dogs were galloping and lunging at anyone unlucky enough to be trying to escape. There were at least two dozen of them in all, skeletal and cringing beasts that were nevertheless fast and strong, crazed now with the bloodlust of the hunt.

Behind them, their owners, Slayd and three of his warriors, surveyed the road and gave commands.

Slayd was not without misgivings. He and his tribe used these dogs to hunt wild animals, never people. Yet Levi had been clear: He wanted something different, more terrifying.

The variant leader noticed someone attempting to crawl to safety under an abandoned car and whistled three of the dogs over. He made a soft, chucking sound and the animals obeyed.

It was the red-haired boy from Caleb's class, one of the town's handful of trained protectors. All week, he had been practicing his punches and club work; but what good was a small leather sap or even a metal pipe against three wild animals? One of the dogs seized his ankle. As the boy screamed and tried to fight it off, the others managed to drag him out.

There was a flurry of canine bodies as they piled on, the sounds of growling and snapping, and the piercing shrieks of the boy. When the screams abruptly stopped, Slayd whistled the dogs over. They did not want to obey at first; a variant warrior had to go to them, brandishing a club to break them up. When the dogs joined the rest of their pack, their eyes glittered madly and their muzzles were stained red.

The townspeople who were lucky enough to have been indoors watched from windows. A few who had been attacked were able to stumble to safety; others were somehow pulled or carried inside, bloodied and torn. But there was no way to warn the rest of the town. People could only look on, listening to the sounds of mayhem as Slayd and his men continued their bloody way toward the center of Prin, their pack of dogs roaming ahead and freely attacking anything that moved.

Yet one boy stood, unmoving, by the side of the road.

It was Caleb.

As one by one the people of Prin grew aware of his presence, word started to spread. He was their protector; only he could save them from this latest calamity. His backpack held his weapon, the terrible instrument that could strike down five men in as many seconds. Surely, he would use it now, take it and spring into action.

He will help us. He will protect us.

Yet their certitude turned to confusion, then doubt, then sheer panic and disbelief. As the devastating attacks continued, Caleb still didn't move. He remained frozen in the eye of a hurricane, the mindless blur of maddened dogs and snarls and screams, the desperate attempts of people trying to escape. Caleb had been drawn there by the instinct to protect. Yet he knew he could do nothing without risking the life of his son.

In the near distance, hidden behind a dusty truck, Esther also stood, motionless and white faced.

The townspeople shifted their attentions from Caleb. There was a sudden commotion from the other end of the street. It was the agonized howl of a wounded animal.

A wild dog lay in the gutter, its legs kicking feebly as it attempted to bite the feathered shaft that protruded from beneath its ribs. It gave up, muzzle smeared with its own blood; and as the scrawny body gave a final shudder, the brown head lolled back, mouth and eyes open in death.

Striding into the center of the chaos was Levi.

He was flanked by six of his boys, faces covered by their black hoods. Three carried loaded hunting bows. When one spied a wild dog, he took aim and fired. Already, they had shot six or seven, and the air was full of the screams and yelps of dead and dying canines.

As he approached, Levi's eyes caught Caleb's for a moment. He smiled faintly, before turning to a guard.

"That dog," he said, pointing down the street.

Slayd and his men were the last to notice what was going on; the variant leader appeared stunned when the largest dog of the pack, the animal closest to his side, let out a sudden yelp and collapsed at his feet.

He whirled around and with a look of utter shock, saw Levi and his men twenty feet behind him. Two of the hooded guards had their bows raised, aiming directly at him.

"Levi!" he shouted. "What are you—"

But Levi cut him off. "I give you and your tribe ten seconds to get out of Prin," he said.

Slayd's look of confusion turned into one of pure hatred. There was no way to comply with any kind of dignity. With a quick nod to his men, he and the other variants sprinted down the street and were soon gone.

The people of Prin, unaccustomed to good news, were moving about the street in an impromptu celebration. The ragged sound of cheering carried all the way up into the apartment above Starbucks.

Inside, Sarah was getting ready to join them.

At last, there was something to be happy about, after Esther's Shunning, something in which to lose herself. It was a welcome distraction to select the right colored robes to wear, a soft pink that flattered her increasingly pale complexion. Now, she combed her hair one last time in front of her small mirror.

Earlier, when she had heard the first reports of Levi's victory from her open window, she felt almost dizzy with pride. As she recalled the lingering kiss he had given her that night in the Source, Sarah shivered, closing her eyes. She only wished Esther was there to share this moment.

For she had a gift for Levi, something that would all but ensure her future with him.

Sarah took it out from under her bed. It was the book he had asked her to find: *Topographical and Hydrospheric Tables of the American Northeast*. The words meant nothing to her. All she knew was that he wanted it, and so she had found it. It was as simple as that.

She had spent dozens of hours searching in vain, wasting early mornings as well as long nights after working all day. She had picked through the crumbled remains of the town library and pored over the thousands of waterlogged and deteriorated books that filled the shelves of a large store off a Prin side street. Stubborn though she was, she nearly gave up hope; it was like trying to locate a single pebble in a giant field.

But after racking her brain, she was able to remember where she had found the first volume. During a sudden rainstorm years before, Sarah had been forced to take refuge in a cluster of crumbling buildings called "College." In a basement, she had stumbled upon a cache of books. Squatters were burning the texts to ward off vermin. When Sarah asked, they allowed her to take a few volumes. She later used them to help teach Levi how to read.

Sarah had retraced her steps to the basement, now deserted. And, miraculously, she had found the companion book, charred and mildewed but still readable, on its long-forgotten shelf.

Sarah anticipated telling Levi the details of her search. She would have to phrase it so it didn't sound like she was bragging; that would be unseemly. But he was sure to understand and then compliment her on her cleverness, her resourcefulness.

It was not only her own future she was considering. Levi was the only one capable of making and bending the rules of Prin. Once the two of them were partnered, he would surely listen to her entreaties and lift the sentence on Esther, overruling Rafe. Then her sister would be allowed to return.

Once outside, Sarah found that the streets were thronged with people, hoarse with shouting. She found she didn't mind. Laughing, she allowed the crowd to bump against her, guiding her along, as she hugged the book to her chest. More and more people joined them, and together, they surged forward in a delirious mass.

Everyone rounded a corner, and there, partly visible through the crowd, was the boy they were looking for.

"Levi!"

Sarah's voice was drowned out by all the cheers, the shouting. She pushed her way forward through the crowd, intent on reaching him.

"Levi!" she called again. Jubilant, she waved the book at him. "I've got it! I found it!"

As she squeezed her way through the packed bodies, there were fresh cheers around her as Levi climbed onto the hood of a battered SUV. Now that he could be seen by all, he turned and waved at the townspeople. Was he acknowledging her?

There was a gap in the crowd and Sarah stepped into it. She was almost there; he must be able to see her now. But at that moment, Levi was leaning forward, helping someone from the street clamber up onto the car beside him.

"Levi!" By now, Sarah's voice was hoarse.

And then she froze.

Levi was pulling close a girl. She was young: impossibly, cruelly young, with golden hair and gleaming skin revealed by tight, thin clothing and set off by jewels that sparkled at her throat and on her arms. Levi paused to kiss her, then turned back to the crowd, accepting their cheers, their love.

Sarah could not breathe.

She let the crowd surge around and then past her. They were all screaming now. They were surrounding the car and rocking it back and forth, banging on the metal in rhythm. Laughing, Levi clung to the girl as they swayed perilously, as one with the crowd.

No one saw Sarah standing there. No one could sense the thoughts that whirled around and around in her head.

Levi had a girl: someone far younger than she was, someone far prettier. With a dull shock, Sarah realized, *And he probably always did.*

Which meant that he had used her.

It was as simple as that, and as heartless. He sensed she could help him, and so he played off their shared history, manipulating her feelings for him. He lied to her to get what he needed.

Afterward, did he and the girl laugh at her behind her back?

Sarah thought about how she had behaved at her dinner with Levi, how she simpered and flattered, and her face burned at the memory; what she felt now was worse than any physical pain. And when she thought of her fantasies about becoming his partner, her dreams of sharing the Source with him, the shame was like a dagger twisting in her chest.

Humiliated and heartbroken, she turned away from the spectacle.

But she didn't go empty-handed.

She was still clutching the book, the one he wanted and which she had come so close to handing over. Her eyes hot and dry, Sarah vowed to herself that she would never give it to him now, not even if he were to beg for it on his knees.

It wasn't much comfort. But for now, it was all she had.

The celebration was nearly over. The townspeople began to head to work, walking in animated groups of twos and threes.

Among them, Rafe was nearly drunk with pride. He had actually shaken Levi's hand and congratulated him. And Levi even listened to him, a handkerchief pressed to his mouth, as he made some of his suggestions for how to improve worker efficiency in the Excavation. Levi seemed to take him—him, Rafe!—seriously, and this had softened his view of Levi as a heartless tyrant. Rafe now hoped there could be a good working relationship between Levi and the town, ideally with Rafe himself as a go-between. This would solidify his quest for another term as leader, if he could survive to run for it.

He became aware that farther down the street, a lone individual was leaning against a mailbox. It was someone who hadn't come to the rally and honored the town's hero; and at this thought, Rafe felt a wave of righteous indignation.

When he got closer, he saw it was Caleb.

Rafe's feeling ripened to one of outright disgust. He walked up to his former champion.

"Coward," he said.

People on either side of him looked up. Caleb didn't move.

Behind Rafe, a girl was hissing. "Why didn't you help us?" she yelled.

Then someone in the crowd bent to pick up an empty plastic bottle. He threw it at Caleb and it bounced off his chest.

"Coward!" he shouted. There were scattered boos and curses.

Another person tossed a clod of dirt at Caleb, who still didn't move. The fact that he didn't defend himself infuriated the townspeople. One at a time, then more and more, they stopped to pick things up from the ground and threw them at him: dented cans, sticks, a dead pigeon.

Soon, at least twenty townspeople surrounded Caleb, safe in both their numbers and their anonymity. Jeering, they pushed him one way, then the other.

"Not so brave now, are you?" said one; and another spat in his face.

Rafe felt emboldened enough to yank off his own hood, exposing his face.

"Why don't you just turn around and get out of town?" he yelled, loud enough for the people in the back of the mob to hear. "And you best not show your face here again, if you know what's good for you!"

For an instant, the brown eyes met his own; and Rafe recoiled, taken aback by what he saw. For Caleb seemed neither frightened nor ashamed. Instead, his eyes blazed with a hatred Rafe had never seen before.

The boy staggered backward, wishing he hadn't yelled quite so loudly. Yet he sensed that Caleb wasn't angry with him, or with the people of Prin.

Caleb turned and, without a word, walked away.

There was no sign of Esther, yet he refused to believe she was not somewhere nearby. Then he noticed a flicker of movement from an alley.

She was there, lurking in the shadows. Their eyes met; hers were full of questions. He was about to call to her, then stopped.

Several townspeople had caught up and flanked him. Caleb only had time to flash a warning to Esther before he was led away from her, in the direction of the highway.

PART THREE

THIRTEEN

ANOTHER TOWN MEETING WAS ABOUT TO START IN THE ABANDONED restaurant in the center of town, the one with the yellow arches looming high on their steel pole. However, unlike the last time, the air was festive and Rafe himself had trouble hiding his exultation.

Several days had passed since Levi and his men came to the town's rescue during the latest attack, and the event had had a miraculous and lasting effect. Since then, there had been no fresh outbreak of violence, no new, senseless ambush of the town and its work teams. No one had even seen a mutant anywhere near the town's limits. They seemed to have been frightened off for good, gone from the face of the earth.

With one glorious and decisive rout, Levi had put an end to the terror that had gripped Prin.

Now Rafe had different news to share, news that was even more exciting and significant. It was a plan he had had a hand in creating and helped make happen with his cleverness and quick thinking. It was crucial that as many of the townspeople as possible were present so he could explain it to them properly. He needed an enthusiastic majority of the town to vote the right way—namely, the way he wanted them to.

He had promised Levi nothing less.

By now, he had been invited to the Source no fewer than two times. He and Levi had established a good working relationship, he thought. It was almost too good to be true.

As he raised his hand for attention, it occurred to Rafe that his recent dealings with Levi reflected well on him. Right now, as everyone in the room began to settle, they were staring at him with open admiration and respect, something they had never done before.

It was an intoxicating feeling, one he wanted to last forever; and with any luck, it would.

If the townspeople did as he suggested, it would cement his relationship with Levi. Rafe wondered what this might mean for him: a new position at the Source? He might be made some sort of assistant, maybe even Levi's second-in-command; and the thought of this made him shiver.

As always, he spoke softly, so the others were forced to lean in. "As you know, I been in discussion with Levi these past few days," he began.

The room murmured its approval. After the decisive way Levi had vanquished the mutants, even those who once distrusted him were now his supporters. Rafe was happy to see that some of the biggest doubters—he ignored the inconvenient fact that he himself had been one of them—now banged on the laminated tabletops as enthusiastically as the others and stamped the ground with their sneakered feet.

"He's done made a very generous offer to us," he continued, "one that I helped him think up." It dawned on him that no one would know if he stretched the truth. "But I don't know how long he's willing to keep it on the table."

He paused, and as he knew they would, everyone stopped fidgeting and hung on his words.

"He's willing to buy Prin from us," he said at last, his voice unintentionally cracking with excitement. He cleared his throat and tried again. "He wants to take the whole mess right off our hands. What do you all think of that?"

There was a moment of silence as everyone in the room digested his words. Then at once, they all began talking.

"What do you mean, buy Prin?" called out a girl holding a younger child in her lap. "If he buys it, where we gonna live?"

"We need to find a new place, obviously," said Rafe. This was an easy question, one of the four or five he had anticipated. "Someplace bigger, better. Because let's face it—we done picked this whole area clean long ago. There ain't nothing left for us here, especially after the mutants smashed the place up."

"But they ain't attacked in a while," said one boy. "Maybe they done coming after us." He sounded hopeful.

Again, this was something Rafe had anticipated.

"They only stopped on account Levi drove them off," Rafe said. "How many times do you think he's willing to do that?"

"Heck, if he wants it, I say he can have it," a boy shouted, and several people laughed.

A girl raised her voice. "What's he gonna give us in return?"

"He's going to pay us in water and food supplies," said Rafe. Again, it was an easy question; the meeting was going exactly as he had hoped. "I did some hard bargaining and here's what we come up with. He's willing to give each household half a crate of water and six months' worth of flour, mixed grain, beans, and salt. I say that's more than fair . . . supplies like that should last all of you a long, long time."

Again, people started talking all at once, trying to shout each other down. Rafe was glad to see that most in the room were on his side: nodding their heads, arguing with their neighbors.

However, there were more than a few who looked like they had reservations about the idea. Some were shaking their heads in disagreement. Several were deep in thought, frowning and thinking hard. They worried him the most.

One of them was an older girl, who sat huddled on top of a table, her back against a window. She spoke up.

"If there's nothing left here in Prin, why does Levi want it so bad?"

Rafe hadn't thought of this. And, in truth, he didn't really know.

He ignored her and tried to steer the discussion back to more comfortable ground, questions he knew the answer to and wished more people were asking.

"This is the kind of opportunity we been waiting for," Rafe said, more loudly than he needed to. He could feel a trickle of sweat start to work its way down the back of his neck. "Now we can head out and find ourselves a new place, a place to build on. In fact, we can start sending scouts as soon as we vote tonight. We—"

"You didn't answer her question," someone called.

Before Rafe could pretend he didn't hear and continue talking over this interruption somehow, another voice called, "Answer her question!"

Rafe licked his lips, trying to think of a way to get control again. People were starting to murmur, and doubt and skepticism rippled across the faces in front of him.

Trying to stave off disaster, he screamed, "I told you, this deal ain't going to stay on the table unless we act fast! He's being more than generous . . . he don't have to offer us nothing! We should be grateful he even wants to do business with us in the first place!"

But by now, others were frowning and shaking their heads, looking at the girl who spoke.

"She's right," a boy said.

The others sitting at his table were nodding in agreement.

"Prin ain't much, but it's our home," added another girl.

"Got to have a better reason to leave it than a few months' worth of food."

Rafe was stunned that the mood had so quickly shifted and he was at a loss as to how to regain the upper hand.

"I say, let's vote on it!" someone yelled, and there was general agreement.

Rafe swallowed hard, his mind reeling. Although he had called the meeting with a quick resolution in mind, that was now the last thing he wanted. If he allowed a vote, it was obvious which way it would go.

"Now, this was just an informational meeting," he said. "Just to get the facts out. We'll be scheduling a vote at a later time."

He adjourned the meeting soon afterward. He stood by the door, stopping people to cajole or joke with them, trying to recapture some of the enthusiasm he had seen just minutes before. But even he was forced to admit it was a lost cause.

Desperately, all he could think was: *What would Levi say?*

A lone figure neared the Excavation.

Disguised by her robes, Esther averted her face from those who passed.

She had spent difficult days and nights, trying not to be noticed in the streets she knew so well, sleeping in abandoned storefronts and surviving on whatever supplies she could steal. Throughout, she was haunted by what she had seen happen to Caleb. Why had she stood by as he was insulted and spat upon? For the thousandth time, she rebuked herself for not rushing forward when he was being led away.

She had not seen Caleb since.

Esther had to find him; but she could not risk being found within the town's limits. She knew that to ask for help was both foolhardy and dangerous. She would not have come to this Excavation site if she had had another choice.

Even though it was crowded with abandoned cars and trucks, the asphalt area surrounding the Source was too exposed; it would be suicide to approach that way. Instead, Esther took the indirect route, circling far around and through the back fields. Creeping through the tall grass in order not to make any rippling movement, she was able to get close to the trench. Soon, she could make out the rhythmic clank of shovels hitting dirt and rock and the voices of workers calling to one another.

Esther lay motionless in the grass, only a few feet from the pit, with her eyes shut so she could hear better. As the team members yelled to one another, she found she could identify who each person was and she started to keep a silent tally of who was there.

"Break time," called a voice. "Lunch."

With her belly pressed low to the ground, Esther listened to the clatter of tools being tossed aside as one by one, the workers pulled themselves up over the ledge. She pictured how they looked, with their robes caked with dirt and clay. Most of them were probably retrieving their nylon backpacks, stashed in the backseat of a car or truck to keep them safe from wild animals. Now she imagined them pulling out bottles of water and plastic containers of porridge and beans, yanking down their masks and chatting with each other as they headed off to the relative shade of a small copse of trees nearby.

The last person to leave the pit took a moment to sit on the edge. Esther heard him knock the soles of his sneakers together to dislodge the red clay. Having tracked who had left, she was fairly certain who it was. More important, she was desperate enough to take the chance.

"Eli," she whispered.

The boy looked up, and Esther waved him over. When he saw her, his face broke into an unbelieving smile beneath his mask.

"Esther?" he said.

With a quick glance to see if anyone else had noticed, Eli exited the trench. Esther had already retreated into the tall grass. He stooped low and made his way toward her through the sun-bleached weeds that grew as tall as his waist. When he reached her, she was kneeling, almost completely hidden by the towering blades. Eli took off his gloves and pulled down his mask so he could speak.

"What are you doing here?" Although he seemed overjoyed to see her, his face was creased with worry. "If the others catch sight of you—"

"I know." She took a deep breath, then plunged ahead. "I need to talk with you. It's real important."

A flush broke over Eli's face and he stared at the ground, smiling hard.

"I was hoping you'd make up your mind soon," he said, his voice husky. Then he cleared his throat and looked up at her. "I can talk to the others. That Rafe, he's just full of air. If I go see him first, he's bound to see reason."

Esther stared at him, confused.

"What?" she said.

As usual, Eli wasn't listening. He reached for her and, to Esther's shock, took her hand firmly in both of his.

"We'll get that sentence thrown out," he said. "We'll see this through together. I promise you that."

Esther jerked her hand away before she realized what she was doing; too late, she saw the look of bewildered hurt flash across his face. Inwardly, she cursed herself yet again for her clumsiness, her rashness.

"I'm . . . I'm sorry," she stammered. "I can't be your partner. But that's not why I'm here. I need your help."

Eli looked as if someone had hit him, hard, when he wasn't expecting it. He stared into the distance, shaking his head. Then he laughed, mirthlessly.

"Help?" he said. "You tell me you won't be my partner, but you still say you want my help?"

Esther swallowed hard. "I—I'm sorry," she stammered again. She had blundered every step of the way, she realized now.

Yet she still needed him, and any help he could provide.

"I'm sorry to have to ask you. But I don't know who else to go to. You're pretty much the only person in Prin who's ever been nice to me."

Eli snorted. "And look what good that's done me."

He was still gazing off, blinking hard, his eyes bright. Yet without looking at her, he seemed to be softening.

"What is it you need me to do?"

Esther was overwhelmed with relief.

"It's Levi," she said. "He's been using the variants somehow . . . getting them to attack the town so he looks like a hero."

Eli nodded, pursing his lips; he appeared to be thinking. "He wants to buy Prin," he said. "That's what Rafe says, anyhow."

"We can't let him," said Esther.

"Well, I don't know that it's such a bad thing, Levi buying us out," he said. "Prin ain't got much left for the rest of us, anyhow. If he wants it so bad, why shouldn't he have it?"

"It's not just about Prin," she said. "It's Caleb I'm worried about."

At the mention of his name, Eli's face froze.

"Caleb?" he repeated.

Esther sensed trouble, but she plunged ahead regardless. "I need you to find him for me. I know he's been told to get out of Prin. But Levi's got his baby and I know he won't leave until he gets him back. I'd look for him myself, but I can't."

But the boy cut her off and Esther was stunned by the fury in the otherwise mild brown eyes.

"Your friend," he said, spitting the words, "got what he deserved. He ain't nothing but a coward. If only I'd have known what kind of trash you liked, maybe I would have stayed clear of you from the beginning."

Esther put her hand on his shoulder; this time, he was the one to jerk away. "You played me for a fool for the last time."

He started walking away, the grass swishing in his wake.

"Eli!"

But he did not turn around and soon was gone.

Esther sighed and sank back on her heels. She knew there was only one person now she could possibly approach, the only one (save for Joseph, whom she loved but knew was helpless in an emergency) who would even speak to her.

And it was the last person she ever wanted to ask for anything.

The sun was dipping low in the western sky by the time Esther stood outside the ruined mansion.

Unable to ask where the Gleaning crews were working that day, she had been forced to figure it out herself. Without a bicycle, she had canvassed much of the town on foot, searching up one long street and then the next for the familiar, purple-framed bicycle parked outside.

It was agonizing and time-consuming work, all the more so because she had to stay alert to the sound of work teams riding past. Yet at last, she had found it, on a street of broad lawns and large houses that was once considered exclusive. It lay in a tangle of other bicycles that leaned against an enormous uprooted tree in a large yard overgrown with weeds.

Behind the bicycles curved a long circular driveway that seemed to have once been picked up and wrenched by massive hands. The house itself resembled the face of an old giant, broken and toothless and blind. All of the windows were shattered or missing, and vines grew freely over the gaping chasm where the roof once stood.

It was almost dark; soon, the Gleaning crew would emerge, get on their vehicles, and head home with their haul. Esther squatted behind a toppled tree, rested her aching legs, and listened.

She did not have to wait long.

She heard voices, and then a person in filthy robes appeared at the door. It was a girl, talking to someone behind her. Four others stepped out onto the sagging and dilapidated porch, carrying a few filled plastic bags. It was an insignificant haul for such a large house. Esther assumed this was not the first time the mansion had been Gleaned.

One of the five called to someone still inside. "You go ahead," Esther heard from the depths of the house. The four clipped their robes close to their legs and mounted their bicycles. Then, carrying their meager haul, they pedaled off into the twilight.

Moments later, Esther stood in the doorway.

She could not hear anything stirring; and she ventured in, picking her way along a makeshift path that wound its way through piles of sodden trash, dead leaves, and the broken remains of furniture. By the dim light, she could see she was standing in the ruins of what was once the entryway, with rooms leading off on the left and a hallway in front. Next to it loomed what was left of the stairway, disappearing into the murky darkness.

"Hello?" she called.

The cavernous living room was down two steps; by the far wall, the ceiling had partially collapsed, crushing two of the eight windows with heavy wooden beams. As Esther edged down the steps, something skittered through the trash and disappeared into the pile of bricks that was once the chimney.

She gave an involuntary start when she saw someone across the room. Whoever it was huddled against a destroyed sofa, its head bowed nearly to its knees.

"Sarah?" Esther called out.

There was no response. Then the masked figure raised its head.

"Esther?" said Sarah.

For an unguarded moment, the joy and disbelief were naked in the older girl's voice. Then she caught herself and, once more, assumed her usual fretful, nagging tone. "What are you *doing* here?"

"I need to talk to you," replied Esther.

She had been steeling herself for this conversation, one she had a premonition would go badly, the way they always did. "It's important. What are you doing?"

Sarah made a dismissive gesture and stood, leaning against the wall. "I was just resting," she said. "Did the others see you? They were only here a moment ago. Oh, Esther, how could you risk coming back like this? Why don't you ever *think*?"

Already, Sarah was talking to Esther as if she were a little girl. And even though Esther struggled to stay calm and focus on what was important, she instead found herself clenching her fists so hard, her nails dug into her palms.

"I need you to help me," she said in a low voice.

"Help you?" said Sarah. She laughed, but the sound of it

was mocking. "I tried to do that. Didn't I? I warned you again and again, and you refused to listen to me. So how can I help you now that you've been Shunned? It's too late, Esther. It's much too—"

Esther cut her off. "I need you to find Caleb for me."

At this, Sarah fell silent for several moments.

"I see," she said. "And was this why you came back to Prin?"

"Yes," said Esther. "I—"

"No, no," interrupted Sarah. "I want to make sure we both understand this. This was why you're risking not only your life . . . but my life, too. Because that's what you're doing here, dragging me into this. You're risking both of our lives to save that boy. That stranger." Her accusation stung Esther, who stood in silence, taking it. "When did he arrange all this with you? Before you left? Did he tell you he loved you, make promises to you?"

"No," muttered Esther. Her face was hot with anger and embarrassment. "It's not like that. He—"

"You know what I think is sad?" said Sarah, almost to herself. "That boys say anything they want just to get something. And girls always believe them." Her voice caught for an instant, but Esther could not tell if she was about to laugh or cry. "I can't say I blame you. He rides into town and impresses everybody, and we all fall for it. Then he deserts us when we need him the most. And now you're willing to risk everything just to save him."

Esther couldn't stand it anymore.

"Well, you know what *I* think is sad?" she shouted. As much as she hated them, tears of anger stung her eyes and she tried in vain to wipe them away. "That for the first time in my life, I need help. And the only person I can ask is you."

Esther turned to go. But as she crossed the threshold, some impulse made her turn around and look back.

Her sister had pulled off the scarf that covered her face.

Esther was shocked by Sarah's appearance. The dim light threw long shadows across her features, making her look gaunt and ancient. Her cheeks were sunken and her normally rosy skin seemed gray. Only her eyes glittered in the dark, too brightly, like obsidian.

"Sarah? Are . . . are you all right?" Esther said.

Sarah's head dropped forward and she again sagged against the wall. Quickly, her younger sister was by her side, kneeling next to her. Esther reached out to touch Sarah's arm and recoiled at the heat coming off of it.

Her sister was burning up with fever.

"You're sick," she said stupidly. She tried to touch Sarah's forehead, but her sister pulled away.

"No," Sarah said. "I'll be all right. I just need to rest."

"Come on," said Esther. She was on her feet. "Let me get you home."

"I can't walk," whispered Sarah.

Esther reached down to pull her sister up by the hands, but she was unable to stand. Esther then grasped her under the arms and tried to hoist her to her feet; but as Sarah's arms were raised yet again, the sleeves of her robes fell back, revealing the bare skin.

That was when Esther noticed the lesion.

It was round and small, no bigger than a child's thumbnail, purple and pink and glistening halfway between Sarah's elbow and shoulder.

Esther recoiled, her hand to her mouth.

Both of them knew what that lesion represented, and the fever and the weakness, too. Soon Sarah would be found out and driven out of Prin.

Esther refused to think of it. All she knew was that right now, she had to get her sister home and into bed.

Without speaking, she reached to lift the older girl. But Sarah pulled away.

"Don't," she whispered. "I don't want you getting sick, too."

Esther hesitated. Then with a start, she thought of something that hadn't occurred to her before.

She'd given her water to the dying girl on the highway, had even touched her hands. That was days ago. And yet she was still alive and well.

That decided it. Ignoring Sarah's protests, she half guided and half carried her outside, propping her on her bicycle seat. Then with her sister's arms wrapped weakly around her from behind, Esther gripped the handlebars and pedaled standing up. She had not gone half a mile before she was drenched with sweat—not only from exertion, but from the heat radiating off her sister's thin body, pressed against her back.

Once they were home and she had helped Sarah up the stairs and into bed, Esther went into the kitchen. She had never prepared so much as a cup of powdered milk before, and now she glanced in despair at the meaningless utensils and bags of grain and flour stacked on their shelves, the unopened bottles of water. She was relieved to find a plastic container that still had the remains of rice porridge in it, leftovers from the night before. Scraping it onto a clean plate, she carried that and a glass of water into her sister's room.

Sarah was sitting up in bed. In the soft glow of her bedside candle, she looked almost normal and for a moment, Esther felt an irrational burst of hope. She sat by her side, placing the glass into her hands.

"Here," she said, with false brightness. "You'll feel better."

But Sarah did not drink. Instead, she took the glass and played with it, turning it around and around in her hands as she stared down at the bedcovers. Then she looked at Esther.

"I let you down," she said. "I think I let down all of Prin." There was a tremor in her voice. Then she bit her lip and looked away.

"Don't talk," said Esther. It panicked her to hear her sister talk this way. She held the plate of porridge in her lap and now, she lifted a spoonful of the meal to Sarah's lips, to keep her from saying anything more. "Just eat something. You need to eat."

But Sarah was shaking her head.

"You were always so willful," she said. "You never trusted anyone, even when you were little. You hated this town. I thought you needed looking out for, no matter how much you despised me for it. Turns out I was the idiot all along."

Her eyes were shining, and Esther was horrified to see that that her older sister—always so proud, controlled, seemingly perfect—was on the verge of tears.

So many feelings came rushing at Esther, it was impossible to make sense of them.

"I never despised you," she stammered. "You're my sister. You're the smartest person I know. The smartest person in the whole town."

Again, Sarah shook her head. "Book smart, maybe," she said. "But I was stupid enough not to notice what was going on, right under my eyes." She gave a low laugh, but there was no warmth in the sound. "And now here you are, in the same place. We're two idiots, you and I."

"What do you mean?"

Her sister said nothing, her lips pressed together as she gazed at the wall. "We're two idiots," she repeated under her breath, as if to herself.

Esther suddenly understood.

Levi. The way her sister always stuck up for him, even when others in town turned against him. Her dinner alone with him at the Source, and her strange behavior afterward. The fact that she had stayed single, despite the offers.

Sarah spent her entire life waiting for the boy she had always described as just a friend from childhood, nothing more. And Esther was too young and self-involved to notice.

Now she felt a wave of sympathy overwhelm her, as well as a crushing sense of sorrow.

"Caleb's not like that," Esther said. "I don't know what happened between you and Levi. But Caleb is a good person."

She hesitated to tell her sister the truth about Levi, then made up her mind. "Levi is trying to do something with the town," she said. "What it is, I'm not sure. But he told Caleb if he interfered anymore, he'd kill his baby." As she spoke, she could feel her sister's eyes on her, wanting her words to be true.

Sarah took a moment to digest her sister's words. Then she was reaching beneath her, fumbling under her blanket and quilt, and Esther instantly set down the food, concerned. Sarah pulled something out from beneath the futon mattress.

"This was what Levi wanted all along," she said, "so it must be important somehow. It's yours, now."

She handed it over and Esther took it. It was a faded gray book that was speckled with mildew, with pages that were warped and rippled. Esther was ashamed to discover she could not even sound out the words on the cover.

But now was not the time to ask her sister.

Sarah's eyes were fluttering shut, and Esther knew enough to let her sleep. She removed the glass of water from her hand and set it on the bedside table, next to the uneaten porridge.

She blew out the candle and was about to exit, taking care to leave the door ajar. But she was called back by a sound.

Her sister had pulled herself up to a sitting position. The effort cost her; when Sarah spoke, Esther was forced to bend her ear close to her lips to make out the words.

"People say that criminals and outcasts sometimes go to the fenced-in fields off the road leading to town," Sarah whispered. "You could try there for Caleb. But it's dangerous. If you go, be careful."

Esther squeezed her sister's shoulder in thanks.

FOURTEEN

ALONE IN THE NIGHT, CALEB PACED IN HIS CELL.

But it was not really a cell. He only felt he was a prisoner. He was in a wooden stall, one of dozens in a broken-down, one-story building several miles from the heart of Prin. The stall had a cement floor still covered with decayed straw. There was an oversize wooden door, the top half of which was made up of iron bars; it swung on heavy hinges onto a dusty passageway. Metal rods also formed a bin that was bolted against a wall, with wisps of ancient hay still clinging to it. A strange contraption made of strips of rotted leather and rusted rings hung from a hook on the wall.

Caleb gazed at a desolate view outside through a crack between two planks. The moon was full. By its light, he could just glimpse the large, circular track he crossed to get here three days ago. The dirt surface was rutted, cracked, and barren, baked to a hard pottery by the endless sun. It was one of three such fenced-in tracks, all surrounded by the remains of large structures open to the elements, with risers on different levels. These, too, had been mostly destroyed by weather, looters, and time, with few of the seats still intact.

If there was anything here that was once of value, it had long since been stolen. There was nothing, not even decent protection from the sun and rain. That was why few came, only a scattering of transients and outcasts, the violent and the mad, seeking shelter near town yet away from those who had Shunned them.

Caleb did not blame the citizens of Prin for what had happened. He understood the depth of their fear. He also knew what desperate and unrealistic hopes they held out for him from the start, what miracles they thought he could deliver.

When he recalled Levi, Caleb was filled with churning emotions, a strange mixture of both despair and rage. He had lost a sibling at the exact moment he had found him. Until Caleb was able to get his son back, his only family, really, was Esther.

At the thought of her, the touch of her lips, her stubbornness, her spirit, Caleb felt his heart contract painfully. If something were to happen to her as well, that would be unbearable.

When he first arrived at the shelter, Caleb was racked by

frustration, desperate to search for her yet unable to do so. Instead, he attempted to question the others who shared the building, lost souls who were fleeing their own pursuers or demons.

"Have you seen her anywhere?" he asked one boy, describing Esther as best he could.

The boy was scrawny and squirrely, someone who seemed to harbor unsavory secrets. He lay in a bed of dirty straw, not bothering to get up.

"For sure I seen her," he said. His voice was hoarse as if he didn't talk much and what few teeth he had were black with rot.

"Is that right?" Caleb said. "Where?"

The boy sighed. His rancid breath traveled across the stall and Caleb winced. "What are you gonna give me if I tell?"

Whatever he said, it was certain to be a lie. Caleb felt his face turn to stone. "How about I let you live?" he whispered.

The boy just shrugged, giggling. "I ain't seen her, anyhow." Then he turned away and feigned sleep.

That night, Caleb tried to search for Esther himself. By the light of a new moon, he made it as far as the outskirts of Prin, checking alleys, abandoned buildings, and other places an outcast might favor. But he saw no one, and the effort cost him; his wound reopened, began to bleed. He barely made it back to his stall, falling onto his makeshift bed before losing consciousness.

In the dark, he saw scenes that were more like visions than dreams.

Levi, holding a bow and arrow, walked alone down the streets, his eyes obscured by his mirrored sunglasses. A barren field, with a girl in red trying in vain to hide in the branches of a tree. A sky that grew dark overhead with the threat of poisoned rain.

Caleb awoke with a start.

It was still dark. With difficulty, he got to his knees, then his feet. He gazed through the crack yet again and was on guard. In the distance, he saw a flicker of movement.

Someone was approaching.

The intruder was covered in a white robe, its face concealed. Caleb flattened himself against the wall, steeling himself for an encounter. If anyone attempted to overpower him in order to steal his meager supplies, Caleb would lose; he didn't have the strength to fight back. Still, he could bluff and attempt to intimidate whoever it was by staring him down first.

The person entered the building and left his sight.

Caleb moved to the door and looked out through its bars. Whoever it was headed down the hall, pulling its hood.

Esther.

Caleb stepped out from his cell. She froze for a second. Then the tension in her face and body melted as she ran to him. Their embrace was awkward at first, because of the bulky shoulder bag Esther wore; she shoved it aside so she could go into his arms. The two headed back through his barred door, into the cool darkness.

There the moonlight streamed in through the cracks in the walls and a jagged hole in the ceiling, casting long shadows. Esther could not remove her despised robes quickly enough.

Caleb tugged the door closed behind them. It barely swung shut. Should anyone else pass, it was all the privacy they were going to have.

He glanced at her and cocked an eyebrow in a silent question. Esther realized that in the moonlight, he could see that her dirty face was streaked with tears.

"It's my sister . . ." she started to say, then fell silent.

She rubbed her sleeve across her eyes.

"Go ahead," he said. "You can tell me."

So Esther did. As she spoke, she felt that something long dammed up was breaking loose, sweeping away everything in its path. She talked not only of her sister's sickness; she talked about Sarah herself, about their long and painful relationship, full of recrimination on one side and resentment on the other. And she talked about the pain of beginning to understand who her sister was at the moment she was about to lose her.

When she finished speaking, Esther felt spent, drained of all emotion. Yet she also felt at peace, and forgiven somehow. She realized with a start that Caleb, too, had just lost a sibling. She knew that each was all the other had.

It was as if they were sharing the same thought.

"I love you," Caleb said.

Esther started. It was the first time she had heard the words from another human being. They changed things, these words, just as her first kiss had. There would be no returning to a world before the words were said.

"I love you, too," she replied.

There was a pause. Then Esther looked around, seeking

something. She shrugged. She gripped the bottom of her red sweatshirt and tore a long strip of fabric from its hem. Then she looked at Caleb.

He smiled and nodded once. Even as Esther took the ragged piece of cloth and tied it around her right wrist, he was reaching over to take the other end. He knotted it around his right wrist, as well.

"I promise to be true to you and always be your friend," he said.

"And I promise to comfort and support you in all things," said Esther.

It was the partnering ceremony. It went beyond law and ritual, custom and decree. It was perhaps the only thing in their shattered world that was holy.

Their palms grew moist, the cord around their wrists tight and hot. The moonlight poured down on them. Held in place, otherwise unmoving, they kissed again, this time more deeply.

Esther found she was trembling. Then Caleb reached down and stripped the cord off both of their wrists, and tossed it aside. Together, the two lowered themselves to the ancient straw that littered the floor. Soon his shirt landed on top of the cord, and so did the rest of their clothes.

The two explored each other, gently at first, with hands and lips and tongues. Esther found the arrow wound high on Caleb's shoulder and kissed it.

But their urgency grew, the straw sticking to them. When Caleb entered her, Esther felt pain, shocking and sharp, and she cried out; but it dissolved into a swirl of other, greater sensations and emotions. Soon, they were moving together, awkwardly, then expertly, bright with sweat.

At last, the two lay still, naked and curled, their bodies gleaming white in the darkness, nearly indistinguishable from each other.

Esther found Caleb's hand in the dark and he intertwined his fingers with hers.

"This is forever," she said.

"Yes," he replied. "Forever."

At dawn, Caleb awoke.

Esther was huddled against him, breathing through her open mouth. He disentangled himself from her and stood. The day was already getting hot; he reached down and draped his shirt over her small, sleeping form.

He was drinking from one of the plastic jugs of water she had brought when he noticed a book lying in her messenger bag. Esther had mentioned it last night, when she spoke of her sister. He picked it up and squinted to read the title.

Across the room, Esther stirred. Caleb realized he had been reading out loud, sounding out the syllables one by one. She sat up when she saw what he was doing.

"That's Sarah's book," said Esther, her voice fuzzy with sleep. "The one she found for Levi."

Hearing his brother's name, Caleb recalled the stacks of paper on Levi's desk and his easy ability with written words; he felt a pang at his own ignorance. Yet as he sat next to Esther and leafed with her through the book, he was puzzled to see that it featured more than mere text. The pages were filled with rows of numbers, dense and tiny like black ants, next to strange, abstract images: squiggling lines and shaded areas.

"Why'd he want this?" he asked, bewildered.

Esther shrugged. She had pulled on Caleb's shirt and now knelt behind him, draping her arms around his bare shoulders, touching and exploring his hairless chest, the chest of her partner. He kissed and teasingly bit her hand, which she yanked away, pretending he hurt her. Then he returned to the book.

"Why would Levi want this?" he repeated.

She leaned over his shoulder to look. "Well, it must have something to do with Prin," she said. "Right?"

"I guess." Caleb flipped to other pages now. Up until now he had only seen crudely drawn diagrams, like the ones on Levi's wall. "You think these are maps?"

Esther shrugged. "If they are . . . they might be of Prin." She pointed. "Look, that could be the old lake. And those could be the mountains."

"So he wants to find something here?"

Caleb recalled Levi's words when they first met, the thing he hinted at as they stood watching the townspeople toiling beneath them at the Excavation.

They're digging for something. Something important. Even precious.

Esther was furrowing her brow. "I always wondered about the jobs," she said. "Not the Harvesting. That makes sense, I guess, on account he needs gas for the Source. But that doesn't explain the other jobs. They say the Gleaning is to find stuff that's worth trading. But everyone knows that all the buildings and houses around here were emptied years ago. So maybe that's not what it's really for. Maybe it's so that people end up looking for something else. But what?"

"Like the Excavation," said Caleb. "Everybody is digging all across town. But nobody knows what they're looking for, either."

"Maybe this book tells him where it is, and that's why he wants it so bad."

The two continued flipping through the pages with greater urgency. Yet neither could read more than a few words, and the drawings had grown too confusing. They were so close and yet could go no further.

Frustrated, Caleb closed the cover. Then he placed the book back in Esther's bag.

The night before, both he and Esther had felt that the other was his or her missing piece. Together, they formed a whole that was invincible; nothing and no one else would ever be needed by either of them again. Now he realized that they were only two people, limited in both power and knowledge and ostracized from everyone else. And their opponent had never been more powerful.

But in the face of such hopelessness, Caleb realized there was also nothing to lose. There was still one thing he could try to do—the most important thing of all.

"I have to get my son," he said. "I got a feeling this is my last chance."

He started to stand, but Esther held him back.

"You can't," she said. "You're not strong enough."

It was true. Even the act of standing was exhausting and his left arm hung weak and immobile, useless in a battle. "Besides," Esther continued, "everybody in Prin thinks you're the enemy now. You'll never make it past the town, much less into the Source."

"I'll take the risk," he said.

"No," Esther said. "*I* will."

Caleb smiled despite himself; Esther was brave and impulsive in equal measure. "That's crazy. The town will be on the lookout for you, too. And you've never even been inside the Source."

"So? You can tell me where I should look."

"But I don't even know where they got him hidden."

"I can search for him, then. I'm good at that." When Caleb hesitated, Esther pressed her point. "Whoever goes has to be able to move fast, without being seen. And maybe I don't know the Source, but I know Prin. It should be me."

Still, Caleb hesitated. He thought about the labyrinthine layout of the Source and Levi's boys posted on every floor. They both knew how dangerous the guards could be. "But you're no good at fighting," he said.

She shook her head. "I know. But I'm just going to get in, find him, and get him out without being seen. There won't be any fighting."

Caleb touched her cheek and then gave a brief nod.

When he thought about it later, Caleb wondered why he agreed. Yet at that moment, he trusted her absolutely.

"The Source seems to have three levels," he said. With effort, he squatted down to push aside the straw by their feet; then he drew his own inexpert map in the dust with his finger. "The goods are mostly on the main level. Levi has a girl, Michal. That's where her room is, around the back. It's near the loading dock, the other entrance. Your best approach is probably through there, though there's a kind of eye that can watch your movements. In fact, they're all over the place. There's a basement, and guards are everywhere. The top floor is mostly empty, although Levi's office can move up and down between all of them."

Esther listened as she pulled on her own shirt and jeans, and laced her sneakers.

"I don't know where they're keeping Kai," he continued. "They may have moved him since they know I saw something. I think your best bet is either the ground floor, off to the side. Or else the basement."

Esther nodded. She had taken the food and most of the water out of the messenger bag for him. She kept the rest, looping the shoulder strap across her chest. Then, atop it all, she pulled back on the robes that obscured who she was.

The last thing she did was pick up the strip of fabric from the floor, the partnering cloth. She tore it in two, wound one side into a ribbon and tied it around her wrist.

Caleb did the same, on the opposite hand as hers. Then he kissed her once, hard. He didn't say, "Be careful"; he felt he didn't need to. Yet after Esther was gone, as he lay there, he wished he had. Closing his eyes, he thought it over and over, like a prayer.

* * *

Esther ditched Caleb's bike on a scrubby hill behind the Source. She lay as flat as possible on the ridge, just out of sight, as she considered the imposing building. She was facing the back entrance at the loading dock. In contrast to the massive electrified front door, this one was small and poorly patrolled with only one guard on watch.

She had assumed she would be able to scale the wall and get in from the roof somehow; but now she was here, she realized that her plan was unworkable. The structure was too enormous and utterly smooth, with no apparent footholds: no one, not even the most skilled variant, could possibly get in that way. While her impulsiveness had always served her in the past, Esther realized that now there was too much at stake to be hotheaded. Instead, she would have to slow down, think everything through, and exploit whatever opportunities she could find.

To strategize, as Skar would say.

It felt like years had passed since she and Skar had played Shelter amid these scorched fields, hiding from the work teams as her friend taught her variants' skills. Esther felt she carried the spirits of both Skar and Caleb inside of her and was being guided by their love.

As if he could hear her thoughts, the guard looked over in her direction. Esther froze. He noticed nothing and turned away again. Restless, he now sat down on the metal steps that led to the Source's entrance and reached under his black hood to wipe his brow.

Let nothing go to waste, Skar always told her. *Use what is available.*

She glanced around, frustrated. Scattered in the dead, bleached grass were pebbles and twigs, but they were too small to hurl. Nearby, she found a crushed soda can, a broken pair of glasses, a dusty bottle cap. It was all trash, the usual insignificant garbage that cluttered the fields and streets of Prin. How could she possibly find any use for objects that were so worthless?

Esther remembered another thing Skar used to say, and it made her smile: *Make a bad thing into a good thing.* Certainly, everything about her current situation was a bad thing: the fact that she was alone, outnumbered, unarmed. Moreover, it was unusually hot even though it was early morning, with waves of heat billowing over the dusty parking lot. Although she rubbed her sleeve across her face, sweat dripped down, stinging her eyes.

But that might be the kind of bad thing Skar was talking about.

Prin's blazing sun.

Esther's mind raced. She might be able to find something that could reflect its rays, something that could blind the guard. Yet even as she considered it, she was already discarding this plan; he wouldn't stay blinded long enough for her to sneak by.

But another idea was forming in her mind.

Making sure to keep her profile low, Esther began to collect the detritus around her, scraping it off the ground: dry leaves, dead grass, papery scraps of bark. This she cobbled together into a scraggly pile.

She didn't have matches or a firestarter on her; those were precious items that were only kept at home. But she did have the broken pair of glasses. Esther picked them up and used a piece of her sweatshirt to rub the dirt off the one lens that wasn't shattered. When she raised it to her eye, she was satisfied to see how well it magnified.

She hoped it was strong enough.

She held it above the pile of tinder, moving it up and down by minute degrees until she was able to focus a ray of sun into a tight and tiny beam of heat. Then she waited.

A feather of smoke began to curl up, and Esther's hope grew. But it was too early to celebrate. So she kept the speck of heat trained on the pile as she began to gently blow on it. Before long, a small flame flickered upward, which she fed with more dead leaves and dried grass. The dry bed beneath it ignited and fire began to spread. The flames were about a handspan high now, but it was only when they were strong enough to leap to a nearby patch of dead grass that Esther crawled away on her belly, putting as much distance between herself and the flames while staying as close to the Source as she could.

Then she stopped and peered over the ridge.

The guard was watching the ground by his feet, still paying no attention to his surroundings. But after a few moments, he lifted his head and seemed to sniff the air.

He was mostly faced away from her; Esther couldn't tell from his stance whether he was annoyed by the distraction or happy to have something to do. In any case, he lumbered to his feet. Then he started walking toward the fire.

Esther sprang to her feet and, keeping low, ran farther along the ridge, increasing the distance between herself and the fire. Then she breached the crest of the ridge and, still running low to the ground, made for the Source and the loading-dock door.

Above it, she saw a strange metal box attached to a strut. This had to be one of the "eyes" Caleb warned her about. Praying that she was coming in at too sharp an angle to be detected and moving too fast for anyone to notice even if she was, she bolted up the cement steps two at a time and disappeared into the entrance, without an interruption. The door banged behind her, and the huge, dark, and silent interior seemed to swallow her whole.

Inside, Esther avoided any open areas and stayed close to the heavily stocked shelves, hiding in their shadows. She paused to get her bearings, remembering the map that Caleb drew. After she checked the ground level, she would try to make her way downstairs.

Esther ran as she was taught, noiselessly and low to the ground, keeping both hands in front of and beside her. She slowed down as she passed a door to what had to be the room of Levi's girl; it was empty. Beyond it, there were more enclosed spaces, as well as the remains of an eating area. She saw that all of these places were empty as well; and so she veered off into the main room again, back into the dim jungle of tall shelves stacked with cartons, trying to stay out of the sight of the mechanical eyes, wherever they might have been.

She was not prepared for the barbed wire.

There was a loud ripping sound as Esther was yanked backward. She had run too close to the shelves and had been caught by one of the giant coils of barbed wire that surrounded them, the sharp metal slashing through and catching in her robe. Cursing to herself, she backed up, reaching out with one hand to try to untangle herself from the cruel razor edges. Far off, she could hear the sound of a guard saying something in a loud voice, then laughing. She didn't know if he was approaching but she needed to free herself at once.

Yet it was hard enough to do without having to hurry. Esther tried to jerk free of the wire, not realizing it was now snagged on her sleeve. As she pulled away, tearing the garment, the entire coiled length unexpectedly came with her, knocking over the huge cardboard crate perched on the edge of a shelf.

Esther winced, waiting for the crash.

But instead of thundering to the ground, the carton fell without a sound. Puzzled, Esther pushed it with her foot. Then she stooped to lift it. Although the crate was large enough to hold four of her, it was so light, she could pick it up with one hand. And it was unsealed, its tabs flapping open.

The box was empty.

Now Esther was confused. She slid out another carton on the shelf, one that was located behind the first, a giant crate marked GOYA: DRY ROMAN BEANS: 160 UNITS. This box was also light enough to be pulled out with ease and had been opened.

It was empty.

Esther pulled down another carton sitting on the shelf

above it, and another, and another. She turned and, taking care to avoid the barbed wire, pulled down the boxes behind her, along the entire row. The crates were weightless, bumping into each other like playthings for a giant baby.

Esther stood still in the dim aisle, the giant boxes piled up on the ground around her. Her mind was racing. She could not make sense of the fact that she was in the Source, surrounded by the cardboard crates that were filled with the food and water that kept Prin alive.

And yet they were all empty.

But she had no time to investigate further. Behind her, she heard the sounds of more guards talking, getting closer. Esther had made such a mess, it was only a matter of time before her presence was noticed. Making up her mind, she added to the pile, removing the ripped robes that could only slow her down. She had to get to the basement while she still had the opportunity. She took off again before she heard something that made her stop in her tracks.

A faint, high-pitched cry echoed in the darkness. Was she imagining it? No. Although she had only heard it a few times in her life, Esther knew what it was.

It was the sound of a baby crying.

It came from somewhere across the huge room and grew louder as Esther approached.

In a far corner of the main floor, she could make out two open doorways side by side in a recessed area behind a cement partition. Stopping in the shadows of a nearby shelf of boxed electronics, Esther squinted at the faded images painted on the wall beside the two doorways. The one to the right showed a crude image of a human wearing a short robe; the word WOMEN was painted below it. In the other, a similar figure was wearing pants; and below it was painted the word MEN.

The wails seemed to be coming from one of the two doors.

She assumed it was the entrance to the right; it was flanked by two hooded guards, weapons displayed in their belts. Again, Esther sorted through her options. The guards were bigger and heavier than she was, not to mention they were armed and she was not; yet with luck combined with the element of surprise, she might be able to waylay one and then get past the other. But once inside, what then? They would certainly come after her and there would be no escape. There was no way to tell if the room had another exit; she could easily be cornered.

Then her problem was solved for her.

A strange sound crackled through the air and one of the guards pulled out a black plastic device attached to his belt. "Security breach," it rasped. "Everyone, report to Section A-Seventeen. Aisle Five."

Esther ducked deeper into the shadows as the two guards, pulling out their weapons, lumbered past.

For the moment, the room was unguarded. Esther darted through the door. Inside, the child's cries were deafening, echoing off the hard interior. Everything in the room was white tile, gray metal, steel, glass. To one side was a series of stalls, each with a swinging door that opened on a built-in seat with a hollowed center. Old-fashioned and ridiculous, the seat was the ancient indoor waste removal contraption she had seen many times before, although rarely so many at once. Across from them was a bank of matching white sinks. Above that, Esther saw herself reflected in a long mirror that stretched down the wall.

And at the end of the room, standing in a wooden pen and sobbing, was a small boy.

Kai.

Esther started toward him.

Then she felt rough hands seize her from behind.

That night, the spill of electric lights revealed a short boy standing outside the massive front door of the Source. In days past, the building seemed to Rafe a sort of blind giant, a faceless god that watched over him and others.

All that, of course, had changed.

This was now his third visit, and so he was comfortable on its threshold, bathed in its welcoming shadows. That was not to say he was complacent about being there: No, it never ceased to give him a thrill to be near the impressive structure, and part of the elite allowed to enter.

Still, today, he was here on business, so he had to temper his excitement.

Levi had called him here so Rafe could give the results of the town meeting. And although Rafe knew this might be a *slightly* difficult report to present, he was confident he could do it without issue. He mumbled under his breath, practicing what he intended to say. He changed his words and intonation again and again; he even imitated the facial expressions and hand gestures he would use. Then he looked up.

A hooded guard stood before him at the giant door. Through mirrored sunglasses, he stared impassively ahead.

"Excuse me?" Rafe said. "I'm here for the meeting."

There was a long silence. "Who with?" the guard said.

"Well, with Levi."

The sunglasses and mask could not hide the look of disbelief on the guard's face. Rafe made a mental note to mention this rude lackey to Levi, who he was sure would have something to say about it.

"Yes," Rafe said condescendingly. "Levi asked me to come. Tell him Rafe is here."

At this, the guard's eyes narrowed. As if from a great distance, the name rang a dim bell. "Stay here," the guard said. He disappeared behind the massive door, which slammed shut.

Rafe told himself to be patient. Yet many minutes crept by. When the door reopened, Rafe was soaked with sweat.

"Okay," the guard said. Rafe patted some of the sweat from his face and adjusted his robes. The guard ushered him into the darkness, despite Rafe's repeated insistence that he knew the way. Annoyed, he comforted himself with the thought that the insubordinate fool would one day be working for *him*.

Soon they were standing in front of the small office, lit by an overhead bulb. It shone on the head and shoulders of one sitting alone at a large desk, the features in his pale face cast deep in shadow.

"Levi," Rafe said. Aware that some more formal salutation might be required of him, he bowed at the waist.

There was no response right away.

"Hello, Rafe," Levi replied at last. "Thank you for coming."

Rafe gave a sidelong smirk toward the guard, as if to say, *what did I tell you?* Then, with confidence, he turned back to Levi and plunged ahead with his prepared speech.

"I passed along your generous offer to the townspeople," Rafe said. "And naturally, it was way more than they were expecting. Frankly, Levi, between me and you, it was way more than they deserve. But surely, you must have taken that into account when you—"

"Get to it," whispered the guard.

"I'm happy to say," Rafe said, shifting quickly, "that there was widespread rejoicing. Just like you wanted, and just like I promised." He took a deep breath, aware that this next bit was the tricky part. "That being said, I think they were a little . . . well, let's just say they were overwhelmed by the offer. Don't get me wrong. They're with you all the way. Only they just need a little more time to make it official."

Rafe smiled, confident that this explanation would suffice. There was a seemingly endless pause, while he kept smiling. Soon the muscles on his face started to feel strained.

Levi murmured something, and Rafe leaned forward, cupping an ear. "Excuse me?"

Too late, Rafe realized that the words were addressed not to him but to the guard by his side. The hooded boy reached for something at his belt.

Then a lightning bolt hit Rafe's lower spine, rocketing through his body before it exploded out of his limbs and head at the same time. Rafe was facedown on the floor, convulsing in agony, before he passed out.

As the body was dragged from his sight, Levi paced, deep in thought. He was not surprised by the boy's incompetence, nor was he flattered by his cringing servility. As mildly entertaining as it was to see the expression on that idiot's face change, Levi was far more concerned about the threat to his plan.

Levi had given the people of Prin new reason to respect him. Then he had made them a fair offer to relinquish the town. Of course, he could never have paid them what he promised, but, most important, he had tried to make them part of the decision.

It hadn't worked. He could wait no longer for Sarah to deliver the book. The Excavation and Gleaning had both proven to be worthless expenditures. Shortages had grown so dire, he even heard there was a break-in at the Source earlier that day. Levi had no time to deal with the would-be thief, a girl from town, and only hoped the news didn't get out.

Levi was beset on every side by betrayal and ineptitude, while options faded and resources dwindled.

He had been counting down to this moment ever since he had taken over the Source, nearly six years ago; now, there was no more time to spare. Over time, he had devised a Plan B, a final solution that he hoped not to use. He feared it would be too unwieldy to execute, too cumbersome, and would strain the capacity of his team of guards to the breaking point. Now there was simply no choice.

Fleetingly, he hoped there wouldn't be too much bloodshed. Not that he cared about the people of Prin. But Levi knew that blood had a way of riling up even the most complacent of animals.

Still, if he had to, he was willing to risk chaos.

FIFTEEN

IT BEGAN EARLY THE NEXT MORNING, BEFORE THE SUN HAD EVEN RISEN.

At each dwelling, it was the same routine. There was a discreet knock at the door; two hooded guards from the Source stood outside. They carried no weapons on their belts, and they were courteous, even bland. One of them requested that the inhabitants leave their home and come with them. To the inevitable questions, the answers were always the same, vague yet reassuring at the same time:

It's Levi's idea. It's for your own good. Levi will explain everything shortly. There is no need to bring anything. You will be returning home soon.

A few had more pointed questions. One or two even

attempted to refuse and in private, they were more forcibly persuaded. Yet while they were confused and half asleep, most of the people of Prin felt that they could trust Levi. Docile and obedient, they came outside without a fuss, closing their doors behind them.

It was only when they were outside did some of the townspeople start to feel uneasy.

A long line of their neighbors snaked its way down the main street of Prin. As more and more people were roused from their sleep and brought outdoors, they were shepherded into the line by the hooded guards.

There were a handful of young children, some still asleep, carried by parent or guardian or trailing behind by the hand. One guard stood to the side and handed them toys from the Source: pinwheels, soap-bubble bottles with built-in wands, dolls still in their plastic wrapping. In the silence, there were delighted exclamations and sounds of laughter as the children opened their gifts and played with them.

"How long will this take?" asked a townsperson.

"Not long," replied a guard. "Get back in line."

In fact, the walk took longer than anyone expected, much longer, as they passed the town limits and continued west along a two-lane highway surrounded by the remains of a forest. Soon, the youngest started to cry, as the novelty of the toys wore off and the discomfort of the forced march began to mount. By now, the sun was well up in the sky. There was no water, no shade. Nearly everyone was still in their sleeping clothes and had no protection from the burning heat: no head coverings, no sunglasses. Many were barefoot. Any skin that was exposed had long since turned pink and then red. Soon blisters would form that would eventually blacken.

And still, they were forced to walk.

It was impossible to escape, even to stop for rest; guards were now positioned on both sides of the lines, and by now, they displayed bows and arrows, metal clubs, and the electrical weapons that had been hidden under their robes. Whenever those in line encountered a break in the road, a rupture of cement and underlying dirt, they were forced to scramble over it, sometimes on their hands and knees. When anyone faltered or stumbled, he or she was yanked to their feet and sent back to the line with an electrical shock or a resounding blow to the shoulders.

After four hours, the people of Prin reached their destination.

It was a large house, larger than even the grand old homes in the wealthy section of Prin, set off the road and hidden by a dense covering of overgrown trees and vines that surrounded it. On closer inspection, it seemed to have been spared not only by earthquakes, but by Gleanings, looting, and vandalism. It still retained much of its old-fashioned beauty, faded yet intact. Two large cars sat in the circular driveway, one silver and the other a dark blue. In fact, while both were dusty, they were untouched; they might never have even been Harvested. But that was not what the people of Prin were thinking about.

The entire house was surrounded by dense coils of barbed wire.

* * *

Back in Prin, a team of two dozen was assembled on the central street.

They were criminals, vagrants, and castoffs recruited early that morning by Levi's few remaining guards, a ragtag mob of the desperate picked up from the fenced-in fields on the outskirts of town. They were all desperate to work, frantic for the meager allotment of food and water that had been promised them as payment.

According to the rough map drawn up by Levi, the work would start at the center of town and progress block by block.

Working in teams of two, the day workers entered the homes that had been evacuated. Once inside, they gathered everything they could—furniture, clothing, housewares—and carried it outside, dumping it into the street. Soon, the air was full of the sound of smashing wood and glass and plastic. If any stores of food or water were found, they were carried to a separate pile, where two of Levi's remaining boys stood watchful guard, metal clubs drawn as they made certain that nothing was held back or hidden in pockets.

Within hours, the street was littered with detritus.

The workers were ordered to begin the next phase. Under close watch, they wielded construction tools, valuable objects found over the years at Gleanings and stored in the Source for just such an occasion: crowbars, axes, shovels, even several chainsaws and a jackhammer. Much of the cement flooring and underlying foundations in the homes of Prin were already badly cracked and irreparably damaged. With effort, it was not difficult to work the cracks open even farther, revealing ancient gravel, moldering two-by-fours, and the dirt underneath.

Unless great care was taken, an unexpected cave-in could happen in the blink of an eye, sending heavy beams, sections of floor and ceiling, and even entire buildings crashing to the ground. But there was no time for care. There were too few people to demolish too many homes and, for Levi, speed was of the essence; his last three guards, armed with Tasers and batons, made sure of that.

Wood and plaster chips rained down on crude living rooms and kitchens as clay, shattered bricks, and rubble began to pile up in what had been people's homes. When the walls got in the way, the workers destroyed them, smashing them with sledgehammers and sending clouds of plaster dust spilling into the street. When two townspeople were discovered hiding in their homes, the workers barely paused from their labors. In both cases, they surrounded the unfortunate resident with upraised axes and shovels; and while the screams were piercing, they were brief.

By the end of the day, the workers had broken through the basement floor in nineteen buildings along the central block.

But so far, it was useless. Despite their efforts, they had found nothing beneath, beside, or within what had once been the homes of Prin.

On the other side of town, Joseph was in his apartment, thinking about cat food.

Of everyone in Prin, he alone had no idea what was going

on. He would only find out much later that Levi's men had attempted to search his building for townspeople in order to evacuate them with the others. The precarious condition of his rotting stairwell, however, proved to be too daunting an obstacle and they gave up many floors beneath him.

Joseph was pondering his dwindling supplies. True, he was long accustomed to setting squirrel traps on his roof and down in the courtyard, but that was primarily for his own sustenance. His cats, however, were spoiled and preferred the food Esther brought them—dried rabbit, oat cakes, boiled rice. Yet he hadn't seen his friend since her unexpected visit during the last storm. Joseph missed her company. His cats, however, were not nearly as sentimental. He could only imagine their outrage when they saw what was on the menu today.

Armed with a mallet, Joseph walked down the many flights of stairs, accompanied by the best hunters of his brood, a tabby called Stumpy and a black cat, Malawi. Although the felines were not fond of eating squirrels, killing them was a different matter. In particular Stumpy could be counted on to deliver the final blow if he lost courage. They reached the ground floor, and Joseph was about to shepherd his feline companions across the lobby and toward the courtyard door, where the traps were.

Instead, he stopped in his tracks, as did Stumpy and Malawi. They all heard it: There was a repeated banging and hammering sound.

Someone was in the basement.

These were not the sounds of a Gleaning; these were

focused and purposeful in a way that made the boy uneasy. Joseph crossed the lobby and slipped inside the door that led downstairs; his cats followed. This stairway was not nearly as precarious, although it was quite dark and he had to feel his way along the wall, reaching out with his feet for each step.

By the time he reached the bottom, the noises had stopped.

Joseph headed down the long dark halls, where old corroded pipes lined the walls around them. Halfway through, he paused.

"Hold on," he whispered.

Joseph was convinced that his cats knew several words of English or at least the meaning of certain human inflections. The animals halted, their tails flared with interest.

The boy could make out the muffled sound of voices. It seemed that more than one person was down in the basement, several yards ahead.

As Joseph crept onward, the cats behind him, he became aware of dim shadows flickering against the basement wall. Whoever was down there had a lit lamp, or given the weakness of the light, perhaps a candle.

Even without looking, he knew where the voices were coming from. His visitors were in the boiler room. His boiler room.

"This is it," said a boy. He sounded excited.

"What do you think he's gonna give us?" said a second.

Joseph tiptoed closer, then flattened himself against the wall near the doorway. The cats started to curl around his feet, bored of this game and wanting a new one.

He peered through the gap, careful to keep out of view. In the light of a candle stuck onto a brick jutting out of the wall, he saw two boys, their faces red from exertion and gleaming with sweat. Later, he would find out that these were two of Levi's criminal recruits. Both were holding tools of some kind and were gazing down at the ground, staring with greed and wonder at what was revealed by a newly widened hole in a floor long damaged by earthquakes and decay.

It was a gently natural spring, caused in turn many years ago by a fissure in the earth. It had been there as long as Joseph had been in the building. In fact, it was where he got drinking water for him and his cats, collected in a plastic bucket he brought down to the basement.

Thoughtful, he pulled back from the sight, lightly kicking away the cats. It hadn't crossed his mind that anyone might be searching for his water and that strangers would come in with shovels and picks to help find it. Then he realized with a start that no one had ever known about the spring. He wondered why this was so and discovered that the answer was simple.

No one had ever asked.

SIXTEEN

CALEB WAS UNAWARE OF THE FIRST STRAY BEAMS OF SUNLIGHT THAT illuminated the ceiling of his cell. Unable to sleep, he had spent the night working by the light of a small fire, fixing his weapon. It still lay in pieces before him, but it was nearly finished.

It had been two days. And Esther hadn't returned.

He rebuked himself for the thousandth time for letting her go to the Source alone, even though he knew they had no other option. Caleb realized that he was far from whole. When he tried to move his left arm, a stabbing pain seized his chest, forcing the breath from his lungs and blood to seep through his bandage, now filthy and encrusted. Yet he had seen enough of

Levi and his guards to understand what they were capable of. He had to go to Esther's aid, no matter what the cost.

Caleb fit the final piece of his weapon into place. As he tested the wheel to make sure that it spun, he recalled with frustration that he had no ammunition left. He would have to collect some on his way, a time-consuming task because it entailed finding stones that were the right shape and size.

Still, there was no other choice. He hoisted his pack onto his shoulders, wincing at the effort. The sooner he was on his way, the better.

He heard the creak of a distant wooden floorboard and Caleb froze.

The day before, Levi's guards had come and rounded up everyone hiding in the other cells. Even though Caleb had no idea why this was being done, he knew enough to hide. He had managed to pull himself up to the rafters just as a guard peered into his stall. After a cursory glance, the boy had moved on.

Now Caleb heard the sound again, faint but distinct. Someone was creeping down the hall, someone who did not want to be heard. With a pang, Caleb glanced at the smoldering remains of his fire. The smell of smoke traveled far. He had been aware of the risk last night but decided to take the chance anyway. As a result, he had apparently brought his enemy back to his door.

Caleb lay his pack down on the floor. Without ammunition, he would have to depend on his bare hands; but in his weakened state, he was not sure how much fight was in him. He would have to strike first, and strike hard.

He moved to the wall next to the door and flattened himself against it. Out in the corridor, he heard another wooden door being swung open, then after a pause, closed. Then two more at once. Then another. More footsteps. The sounds moved down the corridor, coming closer to where he stood, waiting.

Caleb did a quick calculation based on sound. There were at least two people outside in the corridor, perhaps even three.

One of them stood outside Caleb's cell. The door swung outward and someone stepped inside.

It was not one of Levi's guards. It was a townsperson of medium build, wearing a hooded robe. But Caleb could take no chances. Before the stranger could turn, Caleb made his move.

He clamped his right hand over the person's mouth. At the same time, Caleb wrenched the other's left arm up by the wrist, yanking it up his back as he dragged him (for it was a male) into a shadowy corner.

The boy struggled but Caleb's crushing grip warned him not to continue.

"Don't move," he whispered.

An eternity of several seconds passed in which the two figures stayed frozen in the dark, locked in a tableau of adrenaline and mutual fear. Then the door swung open again and a second boy, short and slight of frame, entered.

"Eli?" he said. "Where'd you go?"

There was no reply. He turned to leave but at the last second, noticed the two boys standing in the shadows. He froze in the doorway and at that moment, an older girl joined him. Turning to see what he was staring at, she gasped in disbelief.

Caleb was confused. The two were not only unarmed; they seemed surprised to see him there. If he wasn't their intended prey, then who was?

"What are you doing here?" he asked.

"We're just looking for a place to hide," the boy said. "Away from Levi's guards."

Caleb's grip relaxed; and the person he was holding, the oldest of the three, broke free violently. He joined his friends, rubbing his shoulder as he glared at Caleb.

"What do you mean?" Caleb asked. "What's happened?"

The boy and girl, Bekkah and Till, explained all that had happened to Prin over the past twenty-four hours. How the entire town was rounded up. The forced march. The crowded barracks outside of town where everyone was compelled to stay, without food or water. And how the three had managed to escape, by climbing up to the roof and jumping past the barbed wire when the guards weren't watching.

Throughout, the oldest one, Eli, said nothing and stood glowering in the corner.

As he listened, Caleb realized that whatever Levi was planning, Esther was in greater danger than either of them had anticipated. If Levi had driven everyone out of Prin, this meant the situation had escalated. There was no way to tell what he was going to do next or how far he would go to make sure that nothing interfered with his plans.

"And so you came here, to hide?" asked Caleb.

The boy and girl traded a look, then shook their heads.

"We got to do something," Bekkah said. "What's going on ain't right."

"Only we don't know what to do," added Till in a smaller voice. He sounded plaintive.

Caleb realized that his position had improved. A few minutes ago, he had been an army of one. Now there were three more on his side.

And yet, when he looked them over, he could not help but feel dismayed. They weren't even among the townspeople he had trained; they were inexperienced, physically slight, and at least two of them were too excitable. Yet they were all he had to work with.

"I know something you could do," he said.

Bekkah and Till looked at him, willing to listen. The biggest one, Eli, still hadn't lost the angry and contemptuous expression he had worn since he wrestled his way free, and Caleb wondered what was causing it.

"I want to go to the Source," he said. "But I can't do it alone."

A quick glance passed among the three.

"But . . ." Bekkah hesitated to say the word, then plunged ahead. "You're a coward."

"Yeah," said Till, emboldened as well. "You run away from the last fight with the mutants. We all saw it."

Caleb knew he could not afford to get angry. "That's something you're going to have to judge for yourselves," he said.

Bekkah and Till both nodded. But it was Eli who spoke.

"Why," he said, "should we help you?"

His voice radiated a contempt that Caleb could not figure out. There was something beneath his response, something that cut deeper than the humiliation and shock of having been ambushed moments ago. Whatever it was felt personal, so Caleb looked at him and spoke without guile.

"This isn't about helping me," he said.

"No?" Eli was snide. "Then who?"

Caleb took a deep breath; he found he was shaking.

"Levi is holding two prisoners," he said. "One's my son. The other's Esther. My new partner." He swallowed hard; it was the first time he had said the word out loud. "I love them both," he continued. "Before I see either one of them hurt, I'll die. I swear I'll die in the Source if I have to. If you're not willing to do the same, then don't come with me."

To Eli, the word *partner* came as a blow to the stomach.

He hadn't realized how much he had been hoping all this time that Esther's infatuation with the stranger was just that: a fleeting whim, a momentary obsession. If he was patient enough to wait, he had reasoned to himself, she would surely change her mind someday and choose him instead.

To learn that the two were partnered altered all of that. Even now, his unwilling eyes took in a detail he might have noticed earlier, had he been looking for it: Caleb wore a strip of red cloth around his wrist. It was a partnering tie; and Eli did not have to look twice to recognize it as being torn from Esther's sweatshirt.

Eli grudgingly found himself impressed by Caleb's bravery. It was more than that: He was moved by his sincerity. Did he,

Eli, love Esther any more than Caleb did? Could anyone? If Eli refused to help him now, he knew it would only be from pettiness and jealousy. He was not certain he could live with that.

Eli looked Caleb in the eye.

"Just tell me what to do," he said. Behind him, the other two seemed ready to go wherever Caleb led them.

But Caleb was already thinking ahead.

"We need more people on our side," he said. "Those who can actually fight. And I think I know where to find them."

In the mansion across town, rumors were spreading like brushfire.

It began with the guards. Standing in the shade of a giant elm that dominated the front yard, they whispered among themselves of something that had been discovered in the basement of one of Prin's buildings, something precious. Inside, a boy eavesdropped through a shattered window and caught a handful of isolated phrases and words. He passed them on to another, then another. Word spread and as it did, the rumor transformed and distorted until it was accepted as fact.

Release is imminent. We are going home.

But the longer the townspeople waited, the more doubt grew. Soon, panic and despair began to take hold. It was now well into the second day. There were nearly a hundred people crammed together in the heat, in a building meant for a quarter as many as that. By now, the conditions were unspeakably filthy. What was worse, they had not been given anything to eat or drink since they were brought here.

On the first day, two boys and a girl had managed to escape by making their way to the roof and jumping past a stretch of barbed wire that was unguarded. No one had followed. It seemed much too much of a risk to take, especially when an explanation, not to mention supplies, were surely coming at any moment.

But now, hysteria whipped the flames of a new rumor.

We have been abandoned by Levi. There is no more food or water left at the Source. We have been brought here to die of thirst and starvation.

Shouting and pushing, townspeople fought their way into what had once been the opulent kitchen. They tore open the chestnut cabinets and the oversize refrigerator, smashed the glass windows of the ovens, ripped open drawers in the pantry, and dumped the silver cutlery onto the ground. There were rodents' nests and scurrying insects amidst the dusty china and crystal glasses, still intact after all these years, and cardboard boxes and metal food canisters with contents that had long since rotted to nothing.

In one cupboard, a girl found a forgotten can of tuna fish, bloated and stinking of decay. She and another girl fought over it, pulling each other's hair and slapping. The winner tore apart the corroded metal with her bare hands and ate the putrid mess inside. Not long after, she was curled in a corner, retching violently.

All day, the air had been thick and humid, and now, the sky darkened as wind began to whip the trees. When the rain came, the guards took shelter in a nearby building used to house cars.

Inside the mansion, flashes of lightning revealed that rainwater was dripping from the many holes in the ceiling and leaching down the stained plaster walls.

Most of the townspeople shrank back in terror. Others were too desperate to care. They stood, mouths open, trying to catch the drops on their tongues. Some even attempted to lick any stray moisture off the walls, oblivious to the death sentence they were bringing on themselves.

One girl watched with a special sadness.

Sarah sat huddled against a wall. She was one of the few who had had the foresight to bring a robe; now, she covered herself with it, intent on disguising any evidence of her illness.

But no one noticed. They were too busy fighting and rampaging, taking out their fear and helplessness and panic not only on each other but on their palatial surroundings. Stained glass windows were smashed, a chandelier pulled to the ground, and marble fireplaces defaced; satin bedding was shredded and sofas and armchairs gutted, their stuffing littering the stained Oriental carpets.

It was the only beauty the people of Prin had ever seen. And they were destroying it.

It was too painful to watch, and soon Sarah's eyes, already blinking with fatigue, closed.

Four riders were on the main road heading out of town.

Caleb pedaled in front, next to Eli. Bekkah and Till followed close behind. They were on their way to find reinforcements, riding bicycles that they had stolen from outside Prin's destroyed homes.

They stopped at an intersection. "I think we go that way," Bekkah said, pointing.

After a hesitation, Eli shook his head. His voice was gruff and barely audible. "No. We go *that* way."

From his bike, Caleb turned and nodded his thanks to Eli. The boy caught Caleb's eye, then glanced away.

After that, there was little time for talking. The road continued for a long time, past the parched lake, the forest, and beyond.

"This is it," said Eli at last.

The four, gasping and trembling with exertion, paused at the foot of a mountain. Overhead, the sun had passed its zenith. Faint tire tracks and footprints in the dust marked out the trail that disappeared among the trees in front of them.

Bekkah and Till traded one last look and the smaller child turned to Caleb.

"Are you sure?"

Caleb didn't answer and Bekkah took the opportunity to speak. "We could stay down here," she offered. "If you think that would help."

It was Eli who replied, scowling. "This is why we came," he said. "We all stick together."

And so they began the arduous climb, getting off their bicycles to push them alongside when the ascent became too steep. It was easy to lose the trail; if there were marks, they were so subtly done that they were invisible to the untrained eye. Caleb and the others were so intent on finding their way, it was only when they approached a clearing at the plateau that they realized they had reached their goal: the place that everyone in Prin had always heard about but few had seen.

The variants' camp.

Warily, they looked at the strange lean-tos and huts, the still smoldering communal fires, the racks of drying meat. Off to the side were empty crates from the Source, starting to deteriorate from the sun and rain: discarded testaments to a time of trade and prosperity, now over.

Caleb barely noticed.

Six or seven variants had turned to face them and more were spilling out of their homes or from the woods. Soon, the variants far outnumbered the four norms who stood before them, now shrinking back with unease. The variants murmured loudly to one another, all wearing expressions of open disbelief, suspicion, and hatred.

Their anger seemed directed at Caleb, who gazed back at them evenly. Beneath his cool appearance, however, his heart was beating wildly and his stomach felt like lead.

All noise ceased; someone was cutting through the crowd. As the others fell back, the largest male among them stepped forward, his eyes blazing with anger and disbelief.

Caleb recognized him at once: it was the warrior he had fought on his first day in Prin, so long ago. After his humiliating rout by Levi, the variant leader seemed more than ready for a confrontation, especially with his entire people present as witness.

"What is this?" Slayd asked.

Bekkah and Till recoiled, falling back a step. Eli, too, could not help quailing in front of such fury. Caleb, however, stood his ground, although he could not control the twitch that flickered across his cheek.

"We need your help," Caleb said.

At this, the crowd's agitation grew. "How dare you come here and ask us a favor?" Slayd said. "You above all, who fought us and took a special pleasure in it?"

"Kill him!" someone shouted, and the murmuring grew louder, more restless.

Slayd held up a hand for silence.

"We need your help to fight Levi," Caleb said.

The variant leader did not pretend to hide his surprise and gestured for explanation. With his voice shaking a little, Caleb proceeded to give him one.

Caleb told all assembled about the wrongs done to him by Levi: about the kidnapping of his son, the murder of his first partner, and the foiled attempt on his own life. He revealed that Levi was holding those he loved against their will.

"Many of you are raising young ones," Caleb said. "You can imagine how I feel having my son taken away. And many of you are partnered. So you too might understand how I feel to have lost my partner, Esther, as well."

In the silence that followed, Slayd stared at Caleb. Then his lavender eyes narrowed. Despite himself, he was moved by the norm's words and thought for the first time about the human cost of the crime he had so blithely hired others to do. Still, he showed nothing in his face.

With a sinking heart, Caleb read the silence as indifference.

"Don't you have a score to settle with Levi?" he asked, this time speaking to Slayd. "Didn't Levi break your deal and betray you after you trusted him? Why not join with us and pay him back?"

Caleb's barb found its target; Slayd winced, as if struck. It was clear that the memory was not only fresh, but still painful. Yet the variant pulled himself up and said in a haughty voice, "That is not your concern."

Too late, Caleb realized his tactical error. Reminding Slayd of Levi's betrayal had embarrassed the proud leader before his people by making him appear weak and foolish. Without intending to, he had caused Slayd to lose face. And he knew this was something the variants did not forgive.

Again, the crowd grew restive; the delicate trust had been broken. As Caleb glanced around, he now saw that most of the variants were beginning to slip rocks out from their pouches and pockets, loading up slings or wielding them in their hands.

Slayd stepped aside. When he raised his hand, all of the variants fell silent. They were cocking their weapons.

Desperate, Caleb gave a final look at the three behind him. They too were aware of the deadly shift in tone that had just occurred. Sensing impending disaster, unsure whether to fight or flee, they backed up on their bikes.

Then a voice broke through the silence.

"*Stop!*"

A lone female fought her way out from the crowd. A

boy, most likely her partner, tried to hold her back. She said something inaudible to him. When he did not relent, she broke free of his grip. With no fear whatsoever, she approached the variant leader and addressed him.

"Esther is my friend," she said. "She is also a friend to us all. If this boy is truly her partner and says she is in trouble, we must help."

Slayd looked down at the girl, his arm still raised and his face a mask of fury.

"You are certain, Skar?" he asked. And she nodded once, emphatically.

At that, the impossible happened. Slayd's features softened. His hand, about to signal mayhem, fell back to his side.

He turned away from the girl, back to Caleb.

"You're lucky that I believe her," he said in a gruff voice.

Skar smiled to herself. She clearly did not want to gloat, yet could not resist doing a little dance that Esther alone would recognize.

Slayd pointed at her with obvious pride mixed with respect and not a little exasperation.

"My little sister," he said, "has never led me wrong."

SEVENTEEN

IN THE HALLWAY, ESTHER COULD HEAR ONE OF THE GUARDS TALK ABOUT dinner.

How hungry he was. How long it had been since he had eaten a good meal. How desperate he was for a bite of something juicy.

"Yeah," said the other guard; "but we got orders. Besides, I like pigeons with a little more meat on them."

As the key turned in the lock and the door swung open, both laughed. Esther, lying on the cold, cement floor, squinted upward at the sudden light. They were talking about her, she realized. Her cheeks burned with shame and fury, but she said nothing.

One of the guards set a bowl of food on the floor and shoved it toward her. The first few times, they had stayed long enough to watch her eat, guffawing at her pathetic efforts. With her wrists and ankles bound behind her, Esther was forced to inch toward the bowl on her side, then attempt to eat out of it like a dog. But after two days, the routine was not as entertaining as it once was. She had barely made a move before they exited, slamming the door shut and throwing her back into total darkness.

Esther stayed still on the cement floor as she waited for the sound of their footsteps to fade away. Once she was certain they were gone, she worked her way to a kneeling position and shuffled on her knees across the floor.

When Esther was first imprisoned in one of the small rooms in the basement of the Source, she discovered a wooden bench near the wall, bolted to the floor. Exploring it with her bound hands, she located what she was looking for: a tiny rough edge on one of its metal legs. Since then, she had been spending hours every day rubbing her nylon wrist binds against it.

Today, she was able to cut through the final fibers. Then she untied her ankles.

Wincing at the pain, Esther attempted to rub blood back into her limbs as she got to her feet to take stock of her surroundings. The only illumination was the tiny strip of light below the door. She clapped her hands once, sharply, trying to get a sense of how big the room was by the faint echo that bounced back. This was something Skar tried to teach her to do for fun, on several occasions; but as before, she found her ear was too insensitive and untrained to detect anything at all.

So she walked ahead, sightless, reaching out. Starting with the door, Esther began to grope her way around the room. There was a smooth expanse of what felt like painted brick, with a small switch set in a metal plate. Esther clicked it and waited; nothing happened.

She reached the second and then the third wall; it was a medium-size room, rectangular in shape. Near the bench, her fingers encountered something metal, a shallow and boxlike structure that was taller than she was and built flush against the wall. It sounded hollow when tapped and by touch, she assumed it to be a series of narrow closets of some kind, side by side, with ventilation slats. There were a dozen or so per wall, each set with a small metal handle. Esther went down both rows, trying to jiggle each one open, but to no avail.

The fourth wall was smooth and bare; when she rounded its corner, she found herself back at the locked door.

Esther was trapped. Yet she recalled a variant phrase, the basis of everything Skar had taught or tried to teach her.

Look with new eyes.

In other words, there were always options to any situation, different paths, other choices. The secret was to discover what they were. As far as Esther knew, there was only one way in and out of the room. Yet she realized she only assumed this because that was what her fingers told her, here on the ground.

What about higher up?

Esther faced the bare fourth wall. She brushed her fingertips against its painted surface, exploring its bumps and cracks.

And then she began to climb.

Within seconds, her sneakered feet were scraping against the smooth wall, unable to find a purchase, and her fingers scrabbled in vain for the next handhold. Esther gave up and dropped back to the ground with a light thump.

Even Skar could not scale a wall in the dark; it was virtually impossible to climb anything without being able to see where next to grab. Esther decided: If she could not see, then she would have to learn the wall by trial and error and memorize her route.

Gritting her teeth, she tried again. And again.

She got higher her fifth time, and even higher her sixth. As she hoped, she was also getting a better feel for the wall, remembering where the best cracks and irregularities lay.

On her eleventh try, she was able to reach the ceiling, which she judged to be a little more than twice her height. As she released one hand to explore the area around her, she grazed the edge of something built into the wall before she lost her grip and dropped to the ground.

But Esther, who had explored countless old buildings with Skar and knew their odd construction well, had found what she was looking for.

Within moments, she took one step to her right and began again the laborious process of teaching herself to climb a new surface. After more than a dozen tries, she reached her goal.

It was a rectangular metal grid embedded high in the wall, just below the ceiling. The square openings were thick with dust and just big enough for the tips of her fingers to fit through. This allowed Esther to not only hang on, but to walk her feet up the wall so they were on either side of the metal plate.

She cautiously pulled backward, then with more force. As she did, the grating started to shift in her hands and the ancient mortar crumbled away, freeing rusty screws that pinged to the ground below. She steeled herself, then with one violent motion, yanked back as hard as she could while pushing off with her legs. The grid wrenched out of the wall and Esther went flying backward.

She managed to land standing up while still holding onto the grid, staggering back under its weight. Then she dropped it and clambered back up the wall, to the rectangular hole that now gaped open in the dark.

Esther found herself in a narrow chute made of flimsy metal. Wriggling forward on her belly, she found that even moving slowly made it contort. The joins were especially fragile; as she pulled herself over them, she noted that several of them were on the verge of giving way. Esther could only pray that the structure held up under her weight; she did not care to imagine what would happen if it didn't.

Since she could not see where she was going, Esther touched the walls around and in front of her to check if they branched out. The first time she found a new passageway, she noticed a dim light glowing at the end of it. When she pulled herself closer, she found herself peering through a filthy grating, looking out onto a small room lit by an overhead glass coil. Below her, one of Levi's guards was seated with his back to her. He was at a table crowded with strange glowing boxes, flickering screens with moving images.

Esther was moving as carefully as she could, but her meager weight caused the metal beneath her to buckle, making a loud noise. The guard swiveled around in his chair, his hand on the club at his waist, and she froze.

There was silence.

"Damn rats," he said. Then he returned to the bank of monitors.

Esther eased her way back to the central passageway. She thought of her promise to Caleb and was filled with despair. Precious time was slipping away and yet she could not go any faster, trapped as she was in the dark. All she could do was keep going. She was not even sure what she was looking for: an empty basement room, she supposed, with an unguarded door so she could again make her way to the main floor, where Kai was kept.

Another passageway branched off to the left and when Esther turned onto it, she saw that it too ended in a dimly lit grating. She assumed it would also be a room with a guard and was about to continue on, when something made her hesitate.

Look with new eyes. To assume anything is foolish.

She turned to the left, making certain to distribute her weight over the flimsy metal. When she was close enough, she glanced through the grating.

What she saw made her heart skip a beat.

Below her was the baby.

He was sleeping on a purple blanket surrounded by a small

wooden pen. There was a jumble of toys scattered around him, obviously new; their bright colors and childish designs clashed with the industrial setting, the gray cement floor and painted brick walls.

Kai had been moved here recently. If there was a guard, he was most likely posted outside the room.

Esther grabbed the metal grating with both hands and attempted to shove it. It didn't budge. She tried again, to no avail. She would need to work it loose, although it was a risky process; with each movement, she could feel the thin passageway sway and bend beneath her.

Esther began to rock the grid back and forth, again and again. At first, it was as if she was trying to tease a full-grown tree out of the earth with her bare hands. But soon she felt it starting to give way. Bits of ancient brick began to crumble from the constant friction of metal screws; she could hear them raining down on the ground below.

Esther was able to push out, as hard as she could. The grid gave way, just as part of the passageway collapsed beneath her legs.

When she landed on her feet, still clutching the grating, she saw that the child was now awake. He stood clinging to the side of his pen, two of his fingers in his mouth, staring at her.

Esther reached over the side of his pen and lifted him. She had only seen a few babies in her life and had never held one before; Kai was soft and warm and surprisingly heavy, so much so that she nearly dropped him. She tried to carry him face up, across her arms, but he didn't seem to like that; he began to fuss and struggled to sit upright. Finally, she found a position that suited them both, with him perched on her hip, his face close to hers.

"Garrrh," he said, reaching out to grab her chin.

Esther knew she must get him out of the Source, and yet she could not help herself. She closed her eyes for a moment to better feel the touch of his tiny, soft hands as they explored her filthy face. She found she was enchanted by this mysterious little being, this baby.

The boy looked like Caleb: He had the same dark hair and the same hazel eyes. And yet, there were subtle differences: his rounded chin. His forehead. *He probably took after his mother as well,* Esther thought with a pang. Yet instead of being jealous of her, she was surprised by the pity she felt for the dead girl, as well as a strange sense of connection.

In the meanwhile, Kai had seized the string to her hood and was attempting to suck on it.

"Don't do that," admonished Esther; "it's dirty."

Then it occurred to her that he might be hungry. It would be too risky trying to escape with a fretful child, she reasoned; his cries would alert the guards. Looking around, she noticed an untouched bowl of rice in his pen. As she stooped to pick it up, he was already reaching for it, grabbing at the cereal with both fists and pasting it onto his face.

"Slow down," Esther whispered. Then she made a decision.

Feeding him would only take a minute or two. Once they were on their way, she would give him more food from the meager supplies she had remembered to pack in her bag.

She had thought of all things, except one.

The security camera in the corner of the room.

There was a loud bang, and Michal screamed.

But it was only the sound of a bottle being opened, a bottle of rare and special wine that fizzed and bubbled when exposed to the air. Levi had read once that champagne was traditionally used by kings and generals for centuries to celebrate important victories; and he had long saved several bottles unearthed during a Gleaning for a moment such as this. For he had never felt more like a king than he did today.

Levi had won everything he wanted.

He had conquered his despised brother while visiting revenge on the ghosts of their parents. He had found an heir, a healthy boy tied to him by blood, whom he would raise to succeed him as ruler of all he had created. The townspeople were out of the way, for good. Levi was only seventeen; he had at least two good years left. Maybe he could live even longer now that he had found clean, drinkable water in Prin, where none had existed for decades. Who knew what he would be able to accomplish in that time?

And it was all due to his singular vision, his perseverance, his strength; you might say it was because of his *genius*. Such an occasion called for a momentous celebration, one he had thought hard about and planned accordingly.

There was only one detail left to attend to.

As Michal carried the champagne away from his office to pour it into special glasses, Levi watched her go. Earlier, he had ordered her to apply her makeup with extra care and selected which clothing she should wear: tight, colorful clothing that accentuated her figure. *She had never looked better*, he thought to himself.

It was almost a pity.

When she returned with the drinks on a silver tray (Danish sterling, from a Gleaning), she looked flushed and expectant. She offered him a heavy glass goblet that sparkled with rainbow facets (Austrian lead crystal), then set the tray down on his desk.

"To the future," he said, raising his goblet.

"To the future," she replied, her eyes lowered.

They clinked glasses, and he knocked back his drink in one swallow. He had never tasted champagne before; the bubbles gave the wine a remarkable airiness, a tingling sweetness, that made him shiver.

"I could get a taste for this," he remarked.

Michal giggled. She was about to raise her own glass when Levi stared at her.

"And don't think I've forgotten about you," he said. "I have a little present I'd like to give you."

He reached into a drawer. Without taking his eyes off her, he pulled out something that he tossed onto the desk between them.

It was a filthy piece of cloth. Michal leaned forward, smiling if puzzled, to examine it. Levi was amused to watch her jerk back in terror when she realized what it was.

It was Caleb's shirt—stiff and blackened with his blood,

and torn in two places where the arrow had broken his skin.

"I can explain," she stammered. All of the color had drained from her face. But Levi ignored her.

"I searched your room," he said. "You weren't there, of course." He was watching her, studying with almost clinical interest the open expressions of terror, denial, and helpless defiance that played across her pretty features. "This was stuffed under a corner of your mattress."

"I . . . I don't know how it got there," she mumbled.

Levi smiled. "I suppose you were waiting for an opportune moment to dispose of it," he suggested. "Unless you were keeping it as a souvenir of your good deed?"

Two dots of red appeared in Michal's pale cheeks, and she flashed a look at him that was strangely confrontational.

"What are you going to do?" she asked in a low voice.

Levi rocked back in his chair. "I've given that quite a bit of thought," he said, as he drew on first one, then a second leather glove. He sounded as if he was talking about the weather or what to order for dinner. "I could, of course, have you banished, or killed. But those are too general, too common. No, I wanted a punishment that would really suit *you*."

He bent down to pick something up from the ground beside him. It was a square metal canister with an open spout. Before Michal had a moment to react, he hurled its contents into her face.

She let out a high-pitched shriek and jumped to her feet as clear liquid dripped down her front and splattered her clothing. Wherever it landed, the bright colors instantly dissolved and started to run in long streaks.

Levi made a gesture and two guards materialized on either side of Michal. She was clawing at her face, screaming in a voice that seemed more animal than human.

"Industrial-strength lye," Levi remarked. "The label says it dissolves fatty acids, which makes it wonderfully effective for cleaning a place as big as the Source. But it's a little hard on human skin."

He followed as Michal was dragged, shrieking, through the halls of the Source. He watched as one of the guards activated the machinery that raised the giant metal door. The girl was shoved outside into the glaring heat of the day. She fell to the dusty ground and crouched there, still clutching her face, rocking back and forth in agony.

With a nod, Levi dismissed his guards. Even he had the desire to keep some things private.

"Don't worry," he said. "It may burn for a while, but you'll almost certainly survive. As for your pretty face . . . well, I'm afraid that's another matter. I'm not sure who's going to want to look at you very closely again."

He turned to go but was unexpectedly stopped.

"At least I'll be in better shape than you," Michal said.

Her voice sounded hoarse and ravaged, either from the lye or her screams; it was hard to tell. Levi looked back down at her.

"How's that?"

"Your drink," she said. "I put rainwater in it."

Levi froze. Then he attempted to laugh it off.

"Did you hear me?" she said, raising her voice. "I been saving it up. I put it in when I poured the drinks. That's why I didn't have any. I put rainwater in your wine, Levi. You're a dead man."

Levi was walking away from her, walking fast, before breaking into a run. Behind him, her voice rose to an unholy shriek.

"You're dead!"

But he was already inside the Source, stumbling to get to the controls to lower the door, to shut out her voice. He could not accept what she had said. After all he had accomplished and what he looked forward to doing in the next few years, it could not be true.

It must not.

And in fact, it wasn't.

Driven by shock and pain and on the spur of the moment, Michal had blurted out the one thing that she knew would hurt him the most. More than anyone, she was aware of Levi's terror of both water and the sun. Now she could only hope that her lie would spread unchecked throughout his body and mind, weakening both almost as effectively as the poison he so feared.

It was not much, but it was her last and only way to retaliate.

Michal got to her feet and stood, swaying, her hands still pressed to her face. Every movement was sheer torture. She realized she had nothing left in the world: no home or shelter, not one possession or a single friend. She had no idea where to go, but one thing was certain.

It would be far from the town of Prin.

Inside, as the door of the Source rumbled to the ground, a guard ran up to Levi. "There's been another security violation," he said. "The camera caught the thief with the baby."

Levi felt as if the wind had been knocked out of him.

"Are they still on the premises?" he asked. For the second time in his life, he found himself trembling violently.

The guard nodded. "They're still down there," he said.

Levi nodded. Without a word, he took off at a run.

He had received a death sentence. That he understood abstractly, as if it were happening to someone else. Yet even while the full truth had yet to sink in, he felt more alive than ever, his nerve endings and his mind surging as they responded to this latest threat.

All he knew was that there was only one thing left in the world with any value, and it was about to be taken away from him.

Levi could not trust the others to do his work for him. He could not depend on anyone who was not his equal; they were full of envy and would only look for ways to cheat and betray him. He was foolish to have taken in Michal, he understood that now, to have shown her any sort of kindness or generosity; for she repaid him like the animal she was. And now, he had to take matters into his own hands if he was to protect his new son and heir and only legacy.

He must save the child.

When Esther heard the door burst open behind her, she whirled around with Kai still in her arms. Levi stood in the open doorway, staring at the two of them.

For a fleeting moment, she could see the resemblance to his younger brother. But unlike Caleb, Levi had hair that was swept back from his paper-white forehead, and his eyes glittered like black stars. Right now, he was cooing, saying strange things as he approached.

"Don't be frightened," he said. "Everything is going to be all right."

Esther realized with a sickening lurch that he was talking to Kai and she tightened her hold on him. She tried to dart past Levi to the open door, but he slashed out at her. She had not noticed the knife he carried and the blade barely missed her arm.

"Esther," he said, recognizing her.

He sounded pleased, as if he had just run into a familiar face at a boring gathering, and his smile seemed genuine. "It's been such a long time. You were just a little girl when I knew your sister, Sarah. You've grown up very nicely. But you'll have to hand him over to me. You know that, don't you?"

Esther shook her head and backed up. She needed to stay free of his reach without allowing herself to get cornered. But Kai was restless and growing heavy in her arms. As Levi drew closer to them, she stumbled on a toy, nearly falling.

"I had some good news today," continued Levi, in a strange, absent tone. "Exceptional news, in fact. I discovered water. Fresh, drinkable water, bubbling up from the ground. But I need my son." He sounded so plaintive, so reasonable. "I need him to help me celebrate. What good is it when you have good news and no one to celebrate with?"

With a start, Esther realized that she must do more than merely react to Levi, backing away from his advances. At the moment, he was behaving in an odd and distracted fashion, but it would be foolish to underestimate him. The open door lay at an equal distance between the two of them. If she could engage with him, she could perhaps distract him enough so she could escape with Kai.

"Don't you have friends?" she managed to say.

Levi chuckled. "You mean my employees?"

Despite his mocking voice, he seemed to be considering her question. Esther realized with a shock that her hunch was right: in some crazy way, Levi wanted to have someone to talk to. She took advantage of the moment to take an unobtrusive step toward the exit.

"You've seen them," Levi said. "They're hardly the stuff of companionship, wouldn't you say?"

"But you must have other friends," she continued.

His expression darkened and he lowered his eyes. This allowed her to sidle closer toward the door.

"Friendship," Levi mused. "That's just business mixed with sentiment. Two people at the same level . . . if they're of service to each other, they call each other 'friend.' But if they aren't equals, the whole idea is impossible. It can't exist."

Esther decided to take a chance. "You were friends with my sister," she said.

Levi seemed to be listening, nodding his head. "It's true. Sarah provided a valuable service when she taught me how to read. But even back then, I was aware of her limits. I didn't think she was going to amount to anything. And I was right. Your sister was going to stay where she was. I wasn't."

Esther bristled, but forced herself to bite her tongue. She was almost at the door.

"But there must be *someone*," she said.

"Like my . . . companion?"

His eyes flashed with understanding. With one move, he was on her like a cat, twisting her free arm behind her back and holding the knife against her jaw. She held still, feeling its point digging into her flesh.

"What do you know about Caleb?" he breathed into her ear. "You aren't by any chance a friend of his, are you?"

Esther would only have had a chance of escaping if she dropped Kai; and she was not about to do that. Instead, she stood silent, as Levi wrenched her arm harder and pressed the knife even deeper into her skin.

But then he stopped. He had noticed the red strip tied around her wrist.

"I see," he said. Then he smiled.

So his younger brother had not been destroyed. If Caleb

sent this girl as his emissary, he was still in Prin and bent on revenge. For a moment, Levi almost felt pride in his sibling's persistence.

But he had the advantage.

The life of Caleb's partner had to be worth a great deal. He was quite certain it could be used to barter for something valuable.

And if that turned out not to be the case, at least ending it would bring him the very real pleasure of creating more agony for his enemy.

Downstairs in his windowless basement office, a guard scanned the flickering monitors arranged in front of him with renewed vigor.

The guard was relieved he happened to be paying attention earlier, when the girl broke into the baby's room. He shuddered to imagine what Levi would have done to him if he had been napping or looking elsewhere or daydreaming like he usually did and the baby was kidnapped during his supposed watch. He and the others still carried the painful marks of Levi's earlier displeasure.

Now Levi had asked him to be especially alert for the return of the stranger, the boy they had left for dead. Doing so was the only way to avoid more pain.

Then he did a double take.

Someone was looking up at one of the cameras and waving. It was the guard stationed outside the front door. He and another one of Levi's men were propping someone up between them, a boy who seemed barely alive. One of them lifted him up by his hair so the camera could better see who it was.

It was Caleb.

Excited, the guard jumped to his feet, knocking over his chair. He was halfway down the hall, heading for the stairs, and pulling out his walkie-talkie so he could communicate with the others.

"Meet at the front gate. We got him."

Outside the Source, the two guards in their black hooded uniforms waited outside the giant metal door. Their mirrored sunglasses reflected not only the broiling sun, but the prisoner they held up between them.

"Do you think they're coming?" one of them whispered. It was Eli, disguised.

"If they were watching," replied Caleb. He kept his head down, and half-stood, half-leaned against Eli and the other guard, Bekkah.

Pressed against the building on either side of the metal gate, well out of the sight of the cameras, crouched Slayd, Skar, and more than thirty variants, all with their weapons drawn. Farther off in the underbrush, Till had just finished gagging the two actual guards, who had been stripped of their hoods and robes and bound. Then he joined the others as they all watched in silence.

They did not have long to wait. After no more than a minute, there was a grinding sound.

The giant metal door was opening.

* * *

Esther thought she must have been imagining things. But then she heard it again, faint but unmistakable.

It was the sound of Skar's whistle.

Levi heard it, too. He cocked his head and pushed the knife in deeper.

"What's that?" he asked. When she didn't answer, he jabbed her with its point.

"It means you're surrounded," she replied.

Levi chuckled, then yanked Esther by her arm. "We'll see about that," he said. "Take the boy."

He wrapped his arm around her throat, the knife held to her side, and pushed her out into the hallway. He seemed rattled when he saw that there were no guards on duty. Then he shook it off. With Esther held tightly in front of him, he advanced down the hallway and up the dim staircase.

The main floor of the Source was as dark as ever, and eerily silent. The only sound was the click of Levi's boots on the concrete floor as he advanced into the open.

"Caleb?" he shouted.

His voice echoed in the cavernous space. There was silence. And then someone stepped out from the deep shadows. It was his brother, followed at a distance by three others with their hoods down, two boys and a girl.

Caleb looked drawn and exhausted; and his companions were so thin and scrawny, they looked as if they would not outweigh one of his boys even if put together. Furthermore, the four were clearly unarmed, their hands empty.

Levi burst out laughing.

"Are these the warriors who have me surrounded?" he asked Esther. "Am I supposed to be frightened?"

Then something caught his eye. By the side of the open door, he saw that all of his men were tied up, wrists to ankles. There was a sound from above; and Levi, puzzled, glanced up.

Perched on the highest shelves, standing on crates and cartons, were dozens of variants. Some held loaded slings; others carried spears; at least one had a bow and arrow. All were aimed at Levi, whose smile died.

Skar, for one, had her arm cocked back, a throwing stick loaded with a spear balanced on her shoulder. Across the room, she glanced at Esther, and the two locked eyes. Then the variant girl flashed her a quick smile and a wink, before resuming her stern expression and warrior stance.

"Caleb!" shouted one. It was Slayd, who stood with his sister. "Should we kill him? Give the word and it is done."

But Caleb held up his hand, stopping them.

"No," he said. "Leave him to me."

On Slayd's instructions, the variants dropped to the ground and fanned out across the Source, searching for any remaining guards.

As one kept a watchful eye on Levi, Caleb ran to Esther and his child and embraced them. Esther shifted the baby into his arms, and he buried his face in Kai's soft neck. Then he glanced up. Amid all the activity, one person was standing still.

Eli was staring at Esther with a look filled with longing, sorrow, and loss. It was impossible to miss. As for Esther, it was equally apparent that she was avoiding his gaze. Caleb now understood what had fueled the boy's lingering hostility. But instead of becoming angry, he had a sense of understanding, as well as sympathy.

Caleb handed the baby back to Esther. Then he approached Eli.

"You know where the others are being held?" he asked him in a low voice. "The place where you escaped from?"

It took a moment for Eli to turn his attention to Caleb.

"What about it?" he asked.

"Will you take the others there?" Caleb asked. "I need you to be in charge."

When the words sank in, Eli's face flushed with pride. Caleb reached out and the two boys shook hands.

Then Caleb went into his pack and withdrew something.

"Here," he said. "You might need this."

It was his weapon. He demonstrated how to load and fire it and Eli took it, gratefully.

"Thanks," he said. Then Eli waved at the variants and the others. "All right," he called. "Let's go."

Slayd glanced at Caleb, to confirm the hierarchy. He was, after all, not accustomed to following the orders of strangers. Caleb's nod was enough for him. With a slight shrug, Slayd lifted his hand and directed his people to follow Eli.

Esther, still holding Kai, ran to Skar, and for several seconds, the two girls hugged without a word. Then Esther pulled back to look her friend in the face.

"Thank you," was all she could say. But Skar smiled, shaking her head.

"When you came to us, we should have given you refuge," she said. "This was the least we could do to make up for it."

And with that, Skar turned her attention to the baby. She took Kai into her arms, cooing and nuzzling. "Here," she said. She pulled a length of cloth from her pack and showed Esther how to make a sling, bundling the child close to her body. Then she hugged her friend once more and wished her luck. As Skar returned to her brother and the other variants, Esther approached Caleb.

"I'll take Kai somewhere safe," she said. "I have a friend who lives high in a building on the edge of town. It's secure there."

Caleb nodded. Then he kissed Esther and his son. Soon she was gone, slipping out even before the others had left. He watched the rest exit the Source, taking the light with them.

Then Caleb turned. There was still the question of Levi.

EIGHTEEN

ELI BICYCLED ALONGSIDE SLAYD ON THE ROUTE LEADING BACK TO THE
mansion where the townspeople were being held. Behind
them, Skar, Bekkah, Till, and the rest of the variants spread out
in a loose V formation.

As they rode, the variant leader questioned the norm about
the place they were going to try to liberate. *What were the best
approaches to the building? Were they open or hidden? How many guards were
there, and where were they posted? Were there townspeople strong enough to
assist? Were there any breaks in the barbed wire?*

Eli answered as best as he could. He was both relieved and
proud that he could provide enough details to satisfy Slayd.

As for the variant, he was impressed that the boy was able to mount a successful escape with his two companions. Despite their initial and mutual distrust, the two leaders now discussed a possible attack plan, one that capitalized on the fighting prowess of the variants as well as the norms' knowledge of the layout and the people involved.

At the mansion, Levi's guards had no idea what was bearing down on them. They stood at attention at newly assigned posts, just beyond the strands of razor wire that coiled around the house exterior. On the first day, the boys were left to their own devices. As a result, they spent the day clustered in a group, making bets on flipped coins, wrestling, and gossiping. But after three of the prisoners escaped, word came from Levi that all guards were to be stationed around the perimeter.

Despite their grumbling, the boys were too intimidated not to comply. As a result, they were openly indifferent to the sounds of rioting from within: screaming, the smashing of glass, and the splintering of wood. Whether the townspeople lived or died was of no consequence to them. The guards only thought about their own welfare.

But staying at attention was too hard for most. One guard rested at his station by the front of the house. A hulking boy with shaggy hair that stuck out around the edges of his hood, he used a stick to scratch a game of solitary tic-tac-toe in the dust by his feet. He no longer even heard the ragged voices on the other side of the barbed wire, pleading for water or news. But after a while, he did hear something else, and he glanced up.

There was a scrabbling coming from the roof above his head.

Pebbles rolled across shingles and rained down on him, as if dislodged by someone above. He smiled as he got into position to catch the escaping prisoner who was so obviously climbing down. It was almost too easy. He was one of the few who had been assigned a Taser, which he now took from his belt and tapped against his palm with anticipation.

But the threat did not come from above; with the guard facing the house, his back to the yard, it instead came from behind. An object winged through the air, followed by a loud crack. The boy's knees buckled as he sank to the ground, blood from his temple staining the damp grass.

The prisoners watching from inside fell silent as Bekkah and a variant boy emerged from their hiding places. As the variant bent down to grab the weapon from the guard's still-twitching fingers, Bekkah was pulling something out from her jeans pocket. It was a cutting device taken from the Source for just this purpose, with sharp edges and rubber handles.

She got to work on the razor wire. There were at least four coiling strands blocking the front door and the metal they were made of was sturdy. By squeezing as hard as she could, Bekkah was able to snip through one piece. The wire, however, sprang back abruptly and one of the razor edges slashed her across the bare arm. Wincing, she kept working.

Eli was watching from a car abandoned in the overgrown driveway, a silver Lexus. "It's taking too long," muttered Eli to Slayd, who knelt next to him.

"That is why we must attack now," Slayd replied under his breath. "Before it is too late." Out of courtesy, he made a point of glancing at the norm for confirmation. Eli hesitated before nodding, and Slayd put his fingers in his mouth, giving a piercing whistle.

Eli took out Caleb's weapon.

And seconds later, the attack began.

A barrage of rocks was unleashed from all angles: from behind trees, abandoned cars, the roof of a gardening shed. Taken by surprise, Levi's men had no time to defend themselves. Two of them managed to duck the flying projectiles, batting them aside. One even succeeded in breaking loose. He took off down the circular driveway at a sprint. But he was no match for two variants, one on his bicycle and the other perched on his rear wheel pegs and taking aim as he whirled his loaded sling overhead. Within seconds, there was a final loud crack. All of the guards had been felled, and the grass was littered with their bodies. Slayd and the others started searching them and removing their weapons.

At first, the townspeople shrank back from the windows, in fear of the flying missiles. Now they crushed together at the front door, where Bekkah was still struggling to cut the last few strands of razor wire.

Blinking in the light of the sun, the exhausted residents emerged, some barely able to stand. One by one, they glanced down at the unconscious guards, anonymous in their bloody hoods and cracked sunglasses. Just moments before, they had seemed omnipotent. Now, a small boy kicked one as he passed, and another spat on the unmoving forms.

"Animals," he hissed.

Eli pushed his way past the released residents, back to the place where he too had so recently been imprisoned. Once inside, he did a quick search of the home, going from room to room to make sure no one was left behind. As he did, he winced not only at the filth and stench, but the senseless damage. Everything he saw spoke of impotent fury: the floors were littered with glass, the furniture was smashed, and the walls kicked in.

He saw that the mansion was almost empty; only the final stragglers were left. But in one corner of the house, a motionless form swathed in a white robe despite the unbearable heat huddled against the wall.

Eli bent and, with surprising ease, picked her up; she seemed weightless. Then, walking through the now vacated prison, he carried Sarah to safety.

It was hard work running with a small child tied to one's back.

It was not so much Kai's weight; he was just a baby, and Esther had carried far heavier burdens before. But no matter how carefully she ran, the jostling made him wail and struggle in his harness. He even managed to kick a leg free and Esther, terrified that he might fall out, was forced to slow to a walk. So it took her twice as long as she expected to reach the Gideon Putnam Hotel.

When she did, she was alarmed by what she saw.

The apartment complex, Joseph's beloved but decaying

home, was guarded by Levi's men. Two of them, armed with bows and arrows, flanked the shattered glass entrance.

Esther realized this would be no safe haven for her and the child. Yet she also knew she had to get inside somehow and see what had happened to her old friend. Esther debated for a moment whether or not to hide the child someplace nearby. Then she made up her mind. Lacing her fingers behind her back to give the sleeping boy extra support, she slipped her way with him through the undergrowth brush to the back of the complex.

It was as she hoped: no one had been stationed to protect the gaping hole that had once been the picture window overlooking the courtyard and playing grounds. The familiar lobby was deserted. She was about to slip across to the far side when she heard footsteps descending the staircase.

Esther had barely enough time to duck behind a cracked pillar when two guards entered the lobby. She listened until she could no longer hear them.

Esther sensed Kai stirring in his sling. Now was the moment to get moving. She ran to the staircase, glancing around in case there was anyone else. Then she began to climb.

Even if she had not seen the guards, Esther would have known that strangers had been here. Several sections of the staircase, already fragile, had collapsed and she had to navigate the metal railing instead, praying it held up under her weight.

Joseph saw her anxious face moments later in his doorway.

"You're safe," she said, relieved.

His eyes lit up with surprise when he noticed what she was carrying on her back.

"Is that a baby?" he said, as he drew close. Joseph had only seen infants a few times in his life, and that was many years ago. This one was awake, staring at him with a comically quizzical expression.

One cat, Ginger, pawed at Esther's leg, expecting food. Annoyed, she shooed the animal away.

"We have to get out of here," Esther said. "Levi's men are downstairs."

"Oh, I know," Joseph said. All the time watching the child with fascination, he explained the situation, why the hotel was guarded, how they had discovered his private supply of water.

Esther blinked. "So that's what Levi meant? There really is clean water? And it's here? And you knew all along?"

Joseph glanced up at Esther, taking note of new details. He was impressed by her new gravity, her mature attitude, not to mention the band around her wrist and the baby. This kept him from responding right away.

"Are you even listening?" she asked. "Why didn't you ever *say* anything?"

The one answer Joseph could give seemed likely to inspire more criticism. So he just shrugged.

"You always offered me a cup of it when I visited," she said. "I guess that was your way of saying."

Esther shook her head, marveling at Joseph's cluelessness, though with obvious affection.

"Here's what I think," he offered. "There's water deep underground. And it pushed up through layers of rock and sand somehow. I think that's what cleaned it. That's all I know."

In Esther's face, he saw a new, more surprising emotion. He'd never seen it in the eyes of another person. It was respect.

"So what's all *that*?" she said, stepping inside.

She gestured at the calendars that lay scattered around the apartment. Before, at best, she had indulged him about them.

Joseph was rather proud of the simplicity of one particular creation, a circular wooden board. Now, he explained that so many hours formed a day, then a week, then a month, and so on. But instead of needing to create new lines, his calendar circled back on itself every seven days. Months and years were indicated by advances in either green or blue pegs.

Esther listened, nodding here and there, asking the occasional question. She didn't whistle with impatience or smile politely, as she used to do. She pointed to the single red peg set in the center of the board.

"And what's *that*?" she asked.

"The day I was born."

Esther gasped at this, which perplexed Joseph. Everyone in Prin had some idea of when and where they were born, if only in crude approximations counted on fingers or scrawled on walls. It was the relative surety of his calculations, as well as the elegance of his presentation, that impressed Esther, he assumed.

"I'm—" he started to give my age.

"Don't tell me," she said. "*I'll* figure it out."

She used his calendar, competently, her fingers moving, her eyes darting. Joseph watched, feeling a new emotion himself: pride that he could only describe as paternal.

Esther gasped again, recoiling from the calendar. Then she turned and stared at him.

"Twenty-six," she said. "You're twenty-six years old!"

Joseph squirmed a bit, embarrassed. To hear it said like that made him feel so old. But then, he supposed he was.

Levi walked with painful slowness back to his office, followed by Caleb. The two were now the only ones left in the Source.

The older brother seemed dazed, unsteady on his feet. But that was all the weakness he was willing to reveal. Even beaten and powerless, Levi still held his ground, now worth nothing.

When Caleb thought about what his brother had done, of all of the pain and misery he had caused, hatred instinctively surged in his breast. He deserved no mercy; why should he, when he had never shown any to anyone else? The world would be a better place if he were to throttle Levi now, to squeeze the slender white throat until he extinguished his life forever.

And yet, he hesitated.

Levi had accomplished everything on his own, using only willpower and intelligence. What might he have achieved had he not been so tortured a soul? How would their lives have been different if their parents had kept him instead of casting him out? *It was such a waste,* thought Caleb, with a sense of profound sadness.

Despite his anger, Caleb could not deny the blood that still linked them.

"So," Levi said, his back still to his brother. "I see you've saved me for yourself." With his hand balanced on the edge of his desk, he seemed calm, as if resigned to his fate.

"What?"

Levi turned. "You could have let those animals kill me," he said. "And yet you didn't. I don't blame you . . . I'd do the same thing. Though of course, I'd enjoy it. I suppose you're going to have misgivings."

From the taunting way he spoke, Caleb realized that even now, Levi was jockeying for position, trying to anger him in order to throw him off balance. Yet Caleb wouldn't take the bait. Now that he had Esther and Kai, Caleb no longer felt any bloodlust. The urge for revenge had been purged from him. What would one more casualty achieve? All along, Caleb had only been trying to right his world after it had been wrenched askew.

Rage and revenge would not be his constant, lifelong companions. He would make certain of that.

"Not everyone's the same," he said.

"That's what you think," replied his brother.

But Caleb refused to be drawn into an argument. "I can't deny I never want to see you again," he said. "But I'm not going to kill you."

This surprised Levi, who raised one eyebrow. From his expression, however, it was clear he was not so much relieved as amused and more than a little contemptuous.

"So what do you propose instead?" he mocked. "That I promise to reform? To do good works for the people of Prin?"

Again, Caleb refused to be drawn into a fight. "I don't care what you do," he said, "as long as you leave and don't come back. Ever. Take whatever you need or can carry. Though I'd advise you not to look back."

Levi was toying with one of the silver rings on his fingers. Then he shook his head.

"Thank you for your generous offer," he said. "But I'm not going anywhere. You see, there'd be no point. Because I'm as good as dead, anyway. Courtesy of my beloved."

Caleb gave him a sharp look and the older boy smiled. "Michal slipped rainwater into my wine," he continued. "Who would have thought she was capable of thinking that one up, much less carrying it off?"

"You mean you're—" Caleb started, but his brother cut him off.

"Dying," he said. He was incapable of hiding the self-pity in his voice. "That's another way you've gotten the better deal, you see. Girls fall in love with you. They poison me."

Then, suddenly, unbelievably, Levi's face crumpled. He started to cry.

He held open his arms and, for a moment, Caleb didn't understand. Then Levi took him by the shoulders. As Caleb, confused, moved into his brother's arms, Levi pulled him close.

To his shock, Caleb realized that Levi, too, yearned for connection, the kind you have with blood, with family. Caleb returned the embrace, astonished by the warmth he felt.

All at once, there was the rumble of machinery. Caleb tried to turn but Levi's arms had turned into a vice. By the time he wrenched himself free, the doors had shut, sealing the two inside.

Levi was behind his desk, pulling something out from beneath it. He now hoisted it up, balancing it on the arm of his chair.

It was a large metal can of Able Accelerant.

He shrugged, as if to apologize for the obviousness of his choice. Caleb lunged across the wooden surface in vain. Levi managed to keep the desk between them as he ripped off the plastic cap. Then he began splashing the can's contents in every direction, across his desk and among his papers, filling the air with its dizzying fumes. Even as his brother was on him, trying to wrestle it away, Levi managed to hold on to it, upending it onto any surface he could find, dousing both of them with fuel.

Caleb lost his footing on the slippery floor, and his brother fell from his grasp. Levi stood across from him, panting a little, his eyes glittering. He had fished something from his pocket, which he held aloft. It was a plastic firestarter.

"It'll be nice," he said, "for us to finally be together."

Caleb felt a weird stillness overtake him, as if time had slowed to nothingness. He could see his life laid out in hundreds of strands; everything in his past was happening again at once. He saw the face of his mother. The sight of his newborn son, slick with blood and afterbirth. Esther's eyes. And he saw his brother and himself as if from a great distance and he realized that he was not afraid.

"The world doesn't need any more orphans," he said. "You above all should know that."

His brother stared at him, then recoiled, as if punched in the stomach. *What did he see?* Caleb wondered. *Did Levi picture Kai and his own infant self merging, as injustice was handed down to another generation? Did he know that, this time, it would be his fault?*

Caleb would never know.

Levi reached under his desk. With a grinding sound, the door began to open, then stopped, leaving just enough room for someone to fit underneath.

"Go," he said.

Caleb looked at him one last time, then was gone.

Alone, Levi stood near his desk, immobile. He considered Caleb's offer, the prospect of being Shunned himself. But where would he go? The Source was his home, the only true home he had ever had. And he knew the poison was working its way through his body, invisible and unstoppable, like rot taking over a carcass.

If he closed his eyes, he could practically feel it.

He gazed at the partly open door, then pressed the unseen button, raising it.

As if in a trance, Levi walked alone through the massive store. Unseeing, he passed aisle after aisle stacked high with crates made of cardboard and wood, all labeled. POLAND SPRING WATER. GOLDEN BLOSSOM HONEY. DOMINO SUGAR. GOLD MEDAL FLOUR. Every single one was empty. All they were good for, really, was tinder.

He reached his destination. It was the room in which the gasoline was kept, the untold gallons and buckets and bottles of fuel that the people Prin had been collecting for years, keeping

Levi and his people in light and comfort. He was holding the nearly empty can of fuel. He fingered the firestarter, idly.

The explosion would be heard for miles.

Just then, Esther and Joseph felt a tremor. They rushed to the window and saw the rising smoke coming from the Source.

Shock and anxiety passed over Esther's face.

"Caleb," she said quietly.

But there was another reason for worry. Joseph's home, previously weakened by earthquakes and other disasters, now began to shift. Both Esther and Joseph stood stock-still, hoping for it to end. But the rattling did not; it grew greater. The blast had been strong enough to threaten the hotel's very stability.

"Joseph," Esther said, "we have to get out of here. Now."

Joseph knew that she was right. Yet it was more difficult than even he expected to round up ten cats. He trusted several of them (Stumpy, Malawi, and a few of the others) to follow on foot. But the others he had to hunt down and stuff into their nylon carrying bags, a process that involved much yowling, wriggling, and scratching. He also grabbed a few belongings: a folder of newspaper clippings, some books, a calendar.

Meanwhile, Esther kept a grim watch by the door, her face drawn with impatience and concern. When Joseph was ready, she took three of his cat carriers without a word and hoisted them onto her shoulders, where they competed for space with the baby. She handed him her messenger bag. Then they set off, a strange caravan of people and animals.

They were no more than several steps down when the

staircase started to falter.

At the same moment, plaster and rubble began to rain down on them. They froze for a moment, then quickened their pace. Through choking white dust, Joseph could see cracks widening in the walls. In some places, the stairs themselves looked as if they were about to shear off completely. Entire sections of the staircase started to vanish. The cats could leap over these gaps with ease, but the humans were not so gifted. Esther helped Joseph as they clung to the central railing and worked their way across.

They were only two flights down when more fissures became apparent.

This whole time, the child had not cried, even as the staircase shook so much that the very bones in Joseph's body seemed to rattle. In front of him, he saw that Esther's dark hair and red sweatshirt were whitened with plaster dust, as were the baby's head and what had once been dark green cat carriers. When she abruptly turned to face him, Esther's eyes were like black stones in a field of snow.

Above, they heard the sound of a massive metal beam breaking loose. It came crashing down a few feet away from where they stood, shearing off another section of the staircase and narrowly missing one of the cats.

Esther shot Joseph a look that was half plea, half command.

"I have to go fast now," she said. "You're going to have to keep up."

Joseph nodded.

Without being asked, she took his two cat carriers and

added them to her overburdened shoulders. Then she seemed to coil up like a spring before she took off. Joseph watched with open-mouthed amazement as she leaped off a shard of ground, made brief contact with the wall, pushed off with her foot and grabbed the handrail, swung sideways and landed on a ledge one flight below.

There Esther stood, looking up as she waited for him.

Joseph had to shake himself out of his astonishment. Even his cats seemed surprised by what they had seen. Then he did his best to follow.

He could not keep up with his friend; it was impossible. Yet they did manage to go much faster. Joseph, however, was not used to such exertion or excitement. His heart pounded and his legs shook. He suggested more than once that she would go faster without him. But Esther stayed with him, always finding a secure spot or foothold where they could both rest.

They were close to the lobby by the time the ceiling began to break up more. A cascade of white dust crashed down on them from above like a waterfall. Joseph could not see, his eyes and nose and mouth filled with plaster, and he choked and coughed.

"Come," Esther called over the roar of collapsing bricks. Joseph felt the pressure of her hand in his. Blindly, he stumbled after her, down a few more steps. He landed on some rubble and stumbled, twisting his ankle and giving out a cry. But Esther refused to let him stop. She pulled him into a clear area, which he only vaguely recognized as his lobby. Still rubbing his eyes, he let her guide him across the ruined space for what he realized would be the last time, until he sensed she was leading him up and across the empty frame of what was once the picture window.

"Now run," she said.

And they did. Ignoring the pain in his ankle, Joseph ran as fast as he could across the courtyard, the cats close on his heels. Esther sprinted in front of him, still wearing cats and baby in a way that might have seemed funny if it wasn't so impressive. They ran past the asphalt court with its lone basketball hoop, past the lot filled with abandoned cars, and still they kept going.

"Don't look back," Esther said.

So Joseph didn't. Behind him, he could hear a rumbling that grew to a roar that seemed to suck the sound out of the world.

Without looking, he knew what had happened. His home had been destroyed.

Joseph's heart was still pounding wildly, especially when he realized how closely they had come to being destroyed with it. He thought about all that he had lost: nearly all of his library, calendars, and timepieces. These were precious, beloved items he had spent a lifetime collecting, repairing, constructing. All he had left was what he had with him at the moment.

But he was brought back to himself by the feel of something at his ankles.

It was Stumpy, winding herself about his legs and complaining in her tiny voice. Joseph did a quick headcount and marveled. All of his cats were accounted for and, by all appearances, eager for a snack. He shook off his regrets and turned to Esther.

"Oh well," he said. He tried to sound philosophical. "It was only a matter of time."

They turned. Before them was a collection of boys dressed in black hoods, Levi's boys who had been guarding the building. They, too, had escaped and now stood, staring at the wreckage, too astonished to be dangerous any more.

"Look!" Esther said.

All around them, water was seeping up from the ground and forming puddles amidst the rubble of bricks, mortar, and steel. Soon great geysers of water began erupting from the base of the spring, freed from the ground by the disruption.

Esther stared at the sight for a long moment. Then she glanced up at Joseph, who nodded. She took a deep breath, then in one quick gesture, she knelt and dipped a cupped hand into the spray, brought it to her lips, and drank. Then she sat back on her heels in the mud, blinking, as if stunned by her own audacity.

Suddenly, she was not alone. The guards were kneeling, as well. They pulled their hoods off and tossed them to the side. Cold water rained down on their upturned faces, their open mouths, drenching them and leaving streaks on their gritty skin and filthy hair. The air rang with their shouts of pleasure.

Then Joseph turned. Before what used to be the front of his building, a boy was dismounting from a battered bicycle. Esther gave a cry and rose to her feet. She handed the baby to Joseph, much to his dismay. The child kicked his feet with displeasure, as the older boy cooed incompetently at him.

Esther flew to the stranger and kissed him, which made Joseph blush. Then she pulled him over. He looked like he had been through a hell no one could imagine, and yet he had survived.

"Joseph," she said. "This is Caleb. That's his son, Kai."

She told Caleb all that had happened, even while she peppered him with questions. Then she showed him where water bubbled up from the ground.

"Look," she said. "This is what Levi was searching for all these years."

She had a new thought. Joseph had set her messenger bag on the ground. From it, she snatched Sarah's book, which she handed to him.

"Tell us what this means," she said. "I know that you'll know."

Joseph opened the book, marveling at the information and illustrations inside. And after looking them over, he *did* know.

Stumbling a bit, he explained that the maps were not just of roads above ground, but of underground waterbeds and formations, as well. He explained some of the words that they couldn't decipher. Finally, he flipped through the book to show them the most important map of all.

"Saratoga Springs," he said, pointing. "It must be where we are. It was a town built on a mineral spring, a long time ago. Look—here's where my home might have been."

Esther and Caleb shared a puzzled glance. "But how come it's called Prin?" he asked.

Joseph paused, then brightened, pointing at the letters. "There was a town sign, with the whole name. But 'Prin' is all that's left. See?" He covered the other letters to demonstrate.

Saratoga Springs. Prin.

Joseph glanced at Esther. He could tell she was about to ask why he had never figured this out before, but then she stopped. She knew she wouldn't have listened, just months ago.

She was so much younger then.

They all were.

Beneath its bleached surface, the soil was surprisingly dark and rich.

When the hole was deep enough, Caleb hoisted himself out. Knocking the clay off his shovel, he joined Skar and Joseph. The variant girl was tending Kai, holding him on her hip and bouncing him up and down to keep him quiet. Having become more comfortable around babies, Joseph made funny faces in order to amuse him. But then he remembered that this was a solemn occasion and he stopped.

Off to the side, Esther stood in silence with the body of her sister held in her arms.

Wrapped in a white sheet, Sarah was curled on her side like a sleeping cat. She was oddly heavy for one so frail, her limbs stiff and unyielding. It was how Esther had found her that morning. In death, the terrible fever had broken for good; the unexpected iciness of her skin was a shock. With the lines in her face relaxed, Sarah had seemed at peace and almost pretty again, as if the illness had never happened.

And it was a good death, if such things existed.

Sarah had died at home; against the decree of the town, Esther refused to allow her to be Shunned. Over the weeks, she kept her in the shattered remains of their home and tended to her, feeding and changing her like a baby even as the lesions spread and the dementia grew.

For most of the time, Sarah slept. This was a blessing; the pain and the fever were almost too much for anyone to bear.

But early in the mornings, before the heat of her body would spike and she would lose sense of where she was, Sarah would have a few moments of lucidity. Esther would sit next to her, feeding her water from a spoon, and the sisters would talk. Without acknowledging it, both girls understood that an entire lifetime of unspoken thoughts, confidences, and memories had to be shared in a few precious weeks. From outside the bedroom door, Caleb could hear only a few whispered words, even an occasional peal of laughter.

And now that Esther had finally grown to know her sister, it was time for her to take her leave.

She handed the body to Caleb; then she jumped down into the freshly dug grave. Reaching up her arms, she took Sarah. She held her sister for a moment. It was maybe the third or fourth time she had done so in her life; it would be the last, as well. Then she placed the curled-up body on its side, on the exposed red clay.

"Good-bye," she said softly.

Filling the grave did not take long; she, Skar, Caleb, and Joseph took turns with the two shovels they had brought. The one not digging took care of Kai; Joseph was eager for his turn.

Bright-eyed, the child seemed enchanted with everything he saw. He marveled at the brown and brittle leaves that littered the dark soil. He put dead grass and bits of twig in his mouth and spat them out, laughing and babbling.

Now he heard a sound and looked overhead so abruptly, he fell backward and sat down. Joseph assumed he was frightened and wondered if one of them should pick him up and tend to him, comfort his fears.

But Kai didn't mind. Above him, he saw birds flying in a V, their honking cries echoing, as they journeyed to a better place.

And he clapped his hands with pure delight.

EPILOGUE

With Levi gone, everything had changed. His old laws no longer applied: Overnight, the jobs were meaningless, Esther's presence in town was unquestioned, and drinkable water was in endless supply. With the crisis over, people had turned their attentions to rebuilding the town and pooling the remaining resources so everyone would be fed.

After helping defeat Levi, the variants had mostly retreated to their camp. Still, it was apparent they were aware of the town's need. Gifts appeared on the main street, early in the morning before anyone was awake: two full sacks of cornmeal and one of rice, remains of Levi's payments. A newly slaughtered deer.

Three fat partridges. There was a spirit of holiday in the air, so much so that it was hard not to feel optimistic.

Yet Esther for one was uncertain. It was not just the fact that the people of Prin were reduced to living in shanties and lean-tos or amid the rubble of what had been their homes. The wreckage of the Source still stank of fire and smoke and burning plastic. Despite Prin's current bounty, its supplies of food would soon be exhausted.

Esther did not doubt the strength or the will of the people. More important, she saw hope in Caleb's righteousness and in the wisdom the two of them had gained at such a painful price. She saw hope in their love, a bond that seemed to grow stronger with each day. And she saw it in the eyes of the child, Kai.

There was certainly a future for them; that much she knew. Only she was not so certain it would be in Prin.

For now, however, Esther put her doubts aside. Tonight the entire town was celebrating, and although the afternoon sun was already low in the sky she still had to fetch Joseph.

With his home destroyed, her old friend was living with her and Caleb. Yet he seemed frightened to even venture outdoors and had to be escorted everywhere, coaxed like a small child.

Upstairs, Joseph was waiting for her with a tense expression.

"Are you ready?" she asked. "Caleb and Kai are already there, with everyone else."

Joseph nodded. Esther noticed that he had smoothed down his hair and put on a relatively clean T-shirt.

"Come," she said, patiently holding out her hand. But still he hesitated.

"You know," he said suddenly, "it actually *is* a holiday today."

Off her puzzled look, he continued in a rush. "According to my old calendars, today is a day when people used to celebrate abundance, while preparing for the hard months ahead. It is a day they called 'Thanksgiving.'"

Esther paused.

"Thanksgiving," she repeated, as if to herself. Her expression was thoughtful.

"And it is also," Joseph added, blushing, "the first party I have ever attended. And as the new town elder, too."

"Imagine that," Esther said. Then she met his eyes and smiled.

Wordlessly, the two headed downstairs and onto the street. The sun had set and for a moment, Joseph held back, frightened by the blackness that seemed to engulf them. Yet Esther saw that there was already a sliver of moon overhead, casting a pale yet steady light. And if you lifted your head and sniffed, you could make out the faint but inviting smell of roasting venison and the far-off, happy sounds of festivities.

Esther confidently led the way through the darkness.

READ AN EXCERPT FROM BOOK TWO OF
THE WASTELAND TRILOGY!

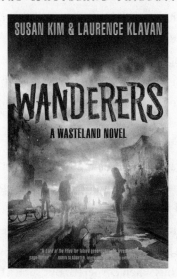

A RAVAGED STREET RAN THROUGH WHAT WAS ONCE A BUSTLING SUBURB.
There were no signs of life; even the treetops were motionless,
etched in black ink against a dirty-yellow winter sky.

A flicker of movement broke the stillness.

It came from a hedge by the side of the road, overgrown
and dying, its tangled branches spilling onto the sidewalk. The
foliage trembled again, and a moment later a girl in battered
sunglasses and a torn red hoodie emerged from its depths. She
wore a leather quiver across her thin chest and a fiberglass bow
dangled from her hand.

It was a January morning and so the air was relatively cool.

Even so, Esther's throat was parched and she could feel sweat trickling down her back. She had been tracking her prey for nearly two hours, and it was painstaking work. This kind of patience, careful and focused, had never been her strength. She preferred action, and as unskilled as she was at killing, she was tempted to rush forward now and attempt an attack. Yet there was too much at stake to fail, so she forced herself to remain still.

Her target was across the street. It was a large animal, shaggy with gray, bristled hair, a feral pig that was making its way past the abandoned houses that lined the street, grunting as it rummaged for food.

This was a rash choice, the girl knew. Even to an experienced hunter, a pig was formidable prey, surprisingly fast for its size and dangerous when cornered. But such a beast could feed her family and friends well for weeks. And what Esther lacked in hunting skill, she could make up for in stealth.

Or at least she hoped.

Moving noiselessly in her shredded sneakers and staying upwind so the animal wouldn't catch her scent, Esther managed to keep distant pace as the pig continued to root its way through the trash that spilled from open doorways and abandoned cars. She only moved when the animal was distracted, when it paused to nose through the sections of broken pavement that exposed tree roots and red clay. At such moments, she tried to imitate one of the many cats owned by her friend Joseph: moving in tiny yet swift increments, freezing after each time.

Even so, it seemed impossible to get close enough to draw an accurate bead on her target, much less get off a good shot. Esther had only three precious arrows with her, spindly feathered shafts that were so weightless, she had to keep checking her quiver to make certain they were still there. She would likely need all three to finish the job, and that was only if she was lucky enough to immobilize the animal with her first shot. And arrows were growing rarer by the day.

As if it could hear her thoughts, the pig now raised its head and Esther again froze. She could see its tufted ears twitching as it gazed around. Its obsidian eyes seemed to slide over her, unseeing. Then, with a grunt, the creature turned and ambled past the overgrown yard and into the woods that lay behind the house.

Across the street, Esther swore under her breath.

But there was perhaps still hope. The pig was trotting, not galloping. That meant it wasn't frightened; clearly, it hadn't seen her. Gritting her teeth, Esther took off across the street in pursuit.

The small forest was carpeted with dead leaves and household trash, piles of moldering clothes, and filthy and broken bits of furniture and plastic. It was as if the garbage had leaked out of the house it surrounded, like putrescence oozing from a dead thing. In addition, the woods were choked with vines and fallen branches, making it difficult to navigate.

Still, it wasn't hard to guess where the pig was headed. Esther could hear the steady sounds of its progress in the distance: twigs snapping, leaves swishing. Feeling reckless, she put on speed; and it was a pleasure to move swiftly, to hurdle dead trees and push past branches that whipped her face. Then she stopped short.

To her surprise, she found she was much closer to the animal than she had thought; it was no more than a few body lengths in front of her, partly hidden by a mound of leaves. It had its head down and appeared to be rooting, too immersed in whatever it had found to notice her, to even look up.

Inwardly rejoicing, Esther forced herself to slow down as she approached the leaf pile from behind a tree. To lose this advantage due to overeagerness would be terrible indeed. Barely daring to breathe, she drew even closer, and the pig had still not moved away.

She was almost upon it.

Esther took an arrow from her quiver and fit it to the bow. Then, in one swift movement, she raised the weapon to her shoulder as she pulled the bowstring back past her cheek and stepped around the tree, aiming downward.

The pig but did not see her. Its head was turned away, butting something with its snout as it made a soft sound that was half grunt, half chuckle. Beneath it, nuzzling its underbelly, was a smaller version of itself, faint stripes visible on its still-soft fur.

The pig was a female, a mother nursing her child. And even as Esther took aim at the animal's heart, so close she swore she could see it beating beneath the shaggy pelt, she was shocked to find herself trembling, her aim wavering.

She hesitated, confused. Then she steeled herself, trying to shake off the feeling. But it was no good.

Esther had no false sentimentality about the wild animals that roamed the streets of Prin. And she needed no reminder of the urgency of her situation. Until recently, it had been disease that everyone feared. The illness, carried in water, was both invisible and inevitable; it meant no one lived past the age of nineteen.

But in the past few weeks, it was hunger that threatened to kill them all. And it would strike, regardless of age.

Even now, Esther knew her loved ones awaited her at home, starving a slow yet certain death—as was she, as was everyone else in the town of Prin. Yet for reasons she could not explain, Esther felt her grip on her weapon weaken. Then she lowered the bow.

Trembling, Esther stepped behind the tree, out of sight. She was about to stumble away when she sensed someone watching her.

Several yards away, a figure stepped into a shaft of sunlight. Androgynous and small of stature, the person had sun-darkened skin and a bald head that were covered with an ornate pattern of scars and primitive tattoos that acted as a kind of camouflage. The bulging lavender eyes placed far apart crinkled as the creature smiled, revealing a mouthful of tiny teeth.

It was Skar.

Esther was about to exclaim, surprised as she was to encounter her oldest friend, whom she had not seen in many weeks. But the other one silenced her with a finger to the lips, first gesturing toward the nursing sow, then indicating that they should leave the woods. Esther understood and fell into step behind her.

As they walked, Esther's joy at seeing Skar was tempered by the shame she felt knowing that her friend had most likely witnessed her inexplicable cowardice. The variants, after all, were skilled trackers and hunters, and while Skar was never cruel, she would surely tease her friend about her odd behavior. Esther tried to explain her jumbled feelings once they had made their way to the street, but the other girl cut her off.

"You were wise to leave that one alone," Skar said. Her voice was unusually somber. "There is nothing more dangerous than a mother. If you attempt to kill one, you must do it in a single stroke, without hesitation. Otherwise, she will take advantage of your doubt and kill you instead."

There was a pause. Then, her lecture over, Skar smiled. "It's so good to see you, Esther."

Yet when Esther tried to hug her, Skar flinched and drew back. At first, Esther was puzzled, then hurt, as a familiar wave of sadness washed over her.

The two girls had been best friends since early childhood, their relationship flourishing in spite of the tension between their two communities. It was a tremendous relief to both when the variants and the "norms" had reached a sort of truce in the past few months. Real distance between them had only come about recently, seemingly overnight, and for reasons more personal than either could have anticipated.

It happened when both girls became partnered.

It was to be expected, Esther now thought with a pang. *After all, they weren't children anymore; she and Skar were both well into their middle years, fifteen, and so they had both chosen mates. Life wasn't meant to be the same after you were partnered.*

Or was it?

After partnering with Caleb, Esther felt the same as ever, only stronger and happier. The love she felt for Caleb was still new and remarkable, constantly astonishing her with its depth and power. Beyond that, nothing had changed; she was still the person she had always been.

It was Skar who seemed different, who had become remote and formal after partnering with Tarq. It was she who had broken off the relationship with Esther, without warning, and who until now had avoided her oldest friend.

Esther shook off her misgivings. Skar was here and there was no telling when the two would see each other again. It seemed foolish to waste any of their precious time together on hurt feelings. Instead, she clasped Skar by the hands.

"It's good to see you, too."

Although Skar squeezed her hands back, Esther again sensed a slight awkwardness, something unspoken that confused Esther. While the variant girl seemed happy to see her, there was an odd restraint to her manner, a formality that seemed strange compared to her usual affectionate behavior. But as they walked through the familiar and desolate streets, Skar began to relax and soon seemed more like her old self.

The two talked of family and friends, and of the terrible famine that was gripping the area. The shortage was starting to affect even the variants, who had never before needed to rely solely on hunting for food. The situation had grown so dire that Skar's partner, Tarq, had allowed her to leave the variant camp that morning in search of game. On an impulse, she had decided instead to visit Prin.

As Skar talked, Esther noticed something odd. Skar, like all variants, wore nothing but a short, sleeveless tunic. Other than a few bangles, wristwatches, and a necklace made of braided leather, her ornamentation consisted of the elaborate scars and designs etched on her skin with pigments pounded from rocks and rubbed into fresh cuts. But now, there was something different about her throat and upper arms. They were heavily daubed with what looked like dried and cracking patches of red clay.

"What's that?" Esther interrupted, reaching out.

But again Skar flinched, ducking away before Esther could touch her.

"It's nothing." Then she changed the subject. "Here," she said, nodding at the weapon Esther still held in her hand, "you need help with that. If you like, I can teach you how to shoot better."

The girls spent the afternoon practicing how to aim, draw, and release the bow. For a target, they used a sodden and stained mattress they found in the gutter. It was soft enough not to blunt the tips of Esther's precious arrows, which they retrieved and wiped off after each use. Then Skar took her into the woods and taught her how to identify rabbit warrens and squirrel nests and opossum scat.

"If you're hunting something," she explained, "it's usually better to lie in wait than to try chasing it down."

By the time the sun was low in the winter sky, Skar had managed to shoot three quail and a rabbit. She took her time aiming the shiny black bow that was half as tall as she was, never wasting any of her arrows. After many failed attempts, Esther also managed to kill one squirrel, something that felt at the moment like an enormous achievement. Yet now, as she weighed the small body in her hands and imagined attempting to feed four people with it, she was filled with a feeling of utter hopelessness.

Skar must have thought the same thing, for without speaking, she handed over the two fattest birds. And while Esther normally would have refused such charity, she now bit her tongue and accepted them, nodding her thanks.

As the two girls said good-bye, Skar promised she would try to visit again soon. Yet despite her generous gift and warm words, the variant girl once more kept her distance, avoiding Esther's embrace. This made Esther wonder whether Skar, who she once thought incapable of lying, was telling the truth. Such conflicting thoughts filled Esther's mind as she watched Skar mount her bike and take off, pedaling powerfully until she disappeared from sight.

Esther was brooding about Skar when she sensed rather than heard someone approaching her from behind. Before she could whirl around, she felt a quick tug on the back of her hair, where it was the shortest and spikiest; and she broke into her first real laugh of the day.

"Hey!"

Caleb had pulled up next to her on his bicycle, smiling. He

stopped so he could gather Esther into his arms for a kiss. Then she pulled away to look at him.

Even though they had been partnered for several months, it was astonishing how he still looked new to her, like she was seeing him for the first time: the hazel eyes, the dark, tousled hair. It was, she decided, a little like falling in love again each time she saw him, although she would never say so out loud. Even so, she could not help but notice with a fresh pang his terrible gauntness, the shadows that hollowed his face and made the underlying bones protrude so painfully.

But he had already seen the game hanging from her belt and gave a low, admiring whistle. "You catch all those yourself?"

"Only the one," Esther admitted, indicating the squirrel. "Skar came to visit and helped me with my shooting. Then she gave me these."

Caleb nodded as he handled the birds. "She's a good friend. I just hope it don't get her into trouble at home."

Esther didn't ask how Caleb's day of Gleaning had gone; she didn't need to. His backpack seemed almost as flat as it had been that morning. Still, he had had some luck; he had Gleaned a dusty box that read DOMINO SUGAR on its faded label.

Gleaning was what they used to do, what everyone did in Prin, in the old days. It entailed breaking into abandoned buildings and searching them for anything even remotely of value. You would bring whatever you found—old tools and clothing, as well as books, weapons, and strange objects of plastic and metal whose purpose no one even pretended to know any-more—to the Source in exchange for clean water and food. It was the only way they knew how to feed themselves and the only sustenance they ever had: packets and jars of dried beans, flour, coffee, honey, salt. But the Source had burned to the ground two months ago. Since then, the people of Prin had been forced to Glean to feed themselves.

Of course, it was pointless. There was little to be found anywhere and most of that—the rare can of vegetables, soup, or fish—had long since rotted to poison. Everything in Prin, every house and office building and store, had been picked clean months, even years ago. But the habit of Gleaning proved hard for people to break. *It gave them the feeling*, Esther thought, *of doing something besides waiting for death.*

When they reached home, the shattered building at the end of the main street called STARBUCKS COFFEE, Esther held the bicycle and waited. Caleb scaled the fire escape and then the gnarled tree in front, checking the squirrel traps he had set that morning. It was more ritual than anything; the traps were useless because there was never any food with which to bait them.

But at least for now, there would be fresh meat for dinner. If they were sparing in their portions, they might even save one of the quail, which would keep for another day. For there was no telling when and where their next meal would come from.

Caleb dropped back to the ground as Esther pushed open the front door, hanging crookedly on broken hinges. Upstairs, she could hear Caleb's son, Kai, crying; as always, the sound made her insides clench with anxiety. She could also hear the murmuring of their friend, Joseph, who was trying to soothe him. Joseph was an awkward soul with more good intentions than talent for nurturing. She could picture him holding Kai in his arms, rocking him while trying to get him to suck on his favorite toy, the ring made of clear rubber with tiny plastic fish bobbing inside. It was the only way any of them knew to distract the child from his hunger, even for a short while.

By the time they made it upstairs, Kai's cries had subsided to hiccups. Joseph, flustered, was pacing, the baby held close to his shoulder.

"Please," Esther said. "Let me take him."

Relieved, Joseph relinquished the child, and Esther took him in her arms. Kai was soft, warm, and surprisingly heavy.

"There," she whispered into the baby's neck. "That's a good boy."

But it was a mistake. The boy's eyelashes, long and dark and dappled with tears, fluttered open. He opened his mouth and despite Esther's best efforts, he began to wail once more, his face turning red.

How could anyone calm a hungry baby? she wondered, stricken.

It seemed impossible.

It was so hot.

Esther was bound, her arms and legs crushed close to her body, struggling to break free. Around her, the walls of her prison pulsated in a powerful rhythm. She could not breathe and was filled with panic, fighting for breath; she would suffocate from the heat.

She tried calling for help, but it was no good. When she shouted, her voice

*was inaudible, like the mewing of a kitten, and her words were sucked away
from her.*

*The redness behind her eyes seemed to bloom into an obliterating brightness
as Esther sensed the walls around her start to give. Her lungs exploding, she
fought her way through the shimmering wall in front of her as she broke free.*

*And then she was safe. As she took in shuddering gasps of air, she was
enveloped in arms that were warm and gentle. Far above her, she sensed a face
gazing down at her own, a face that was both kind and strong.*

*Esther wanted to see who it was. She needed to see for herself, once and for
all, the face of her rescuer.*

Her mother.

But she could not make out her features.

Esther jolted upright. In the moonlight, Caleb lay next to
her in bed, awake. He was propped up on one elbow, watching
her.

"What were you dreaming about?" he said.

Already, the images of her dream were rushing away. "I
think it was my mother," Esther said. "I never knew her. But I
guess nobody does."

Caleb nodded and Esther realized too late that he might be
thinking of his first partner, Miri. She had been murdered the
year before when her son, Kai, was only an infant. But Caleb
gestured for her to keep talking and, after a moment, she did.

"I wonder who she was." Moonlight streamed in the cur-
tainless window, casting shadows on the bed. "Just a girl, I
reckon. Nobody special. I bet she wanted to take care of me.
Protect me from bad stuff. Keep me fed. The only one who did
that for me was my sister."

At the mention of Sarah, Caleb spoke up. "You were lucky."

Silence filled the darkness between them. Esther knew he was thinking about his older brother, Levi: ruler of the Source, provider of Prin, and his enemy. She had never learned what happened between the two boys on the day of the fire that destroyed the Source and killed Levi; Caleb never spoke of it. But it was clear it still haunted him.

She touched his cheek, cradling it in the warmth of her hand. It had been forever since they had last spoken like this, just the two of them. The apartment had become so crowded, it seemed, with so many things and people to look after.

"We'll take care of each other now," Esther said.

He seemed to have the same thought, for they turned to each other at the same time. Caleb kissed her cheek, then her lips. She responded, her hand moving beneath the sheets, caressing him.

"I love you," he whispered.

It had been so long, too long, since they had last touched each other; they both missed it too much to say. Esther clung to his shoulders, shifting to be beneath him. Caleb yanked the sheet from her, pulling her oversize T-shirt above her knees, and higher.

Then he stopped.

"What is it?" she whispered, her arms around his neck. But he was alert to something she did not understand.

Then Esther became aware of it, too.

It was smoke.

* * *